THE RETURN

A Novel

BOB MADDUX

BOB MADDUX
For information, contact:
Ezekiel 12 Publications
San Deigo, California
bob.maddux@gmail.com

Printed Worldwide
First Printing 2025
First Edition 2025

10 9 8 7 6 5 4 3 2 1

Interior Book Design by Walt's Book Design
www.waltsbookdesign.com

To Claudia

My beloved wife of fifty-six years, who has been the constant vintage in my life, deep, steady, and full of quiet strength. Your faithful editing hand and your loving heart helped refine this book as surely as time refines wine.

AUTHORS NOTE

A Note on Craft and Collaboration

What follows is the result of a conversation between human imagination and a digital writing partner. I bring fifty-five years of caring for people, sitting with the dying, watching families fracture and sometimes heal. This tool contributes pattern recognition and linguistic precision, and together we've created something neither of us could have made alone. I name this plainly because transparency matters more than pride. The story is mine, the characters are mine, the plot is mine, the writing style and the worldview is mine. The pain is mine and the hope is mine: I was a prodigal. The polish comes from partnership. In an age where such tools exist, the question isn't whether to use them, but how to use them honestly.

I invite you to read what follows and decide if the partnership serves the story.

Bob Maddux

San Diego, CA – December 2025

CHAPTER ONE

SILICON VALLEY

CLUB NEURAL LINK

"Wine makes all things possible,
good friends truer, false friends clearer."
Italian proverb

Ethan Weinhardt was hardwired to Neural Link. The hip club's atmosphere alone gave him a high. The biometric entry, the retinal scan to get into the VIP Core, where he was stretched out on a lounge, haptic wristbands that pulsed with the bass, micro-dosed aromatherapy drifting from the vents, and then the crowd. Crypto whales, biotech entrepreneurs, holographic performers spun by a DJ with cult-level status, and some of the most beautiful women in the Valley.

All of it made up the Neural, but insiders called it simply the Core, the place where money, power, and excess mixed in a single heady cocktail.

Ethan let the bluish haze roll across him, but even though his head was buzzing, the high was already fading. These days it always does. Each fix weaker than the last.

He looked around. The lounge had the usual cast: hangers-on angling for selfies, rich kids who never had to earn anything, leggy girls scanning the room for the next whale to hang on to, and the Valley insiders who wore notoriety like a silk coat. They sprawled across the couches in curated clothes, showing off wealth in the understated way the truly rich did in this part of the world. It was the same every night, a carousel of power and vanity.

But Ethan was not tapping in anymore. His brain used to light up the way it had the first time he hit powder. Pure, uncut, like plugging into a kaleidoscope of sensation and possibility. That was gone. Now it felt stretched thin, diluted, cut with something cheap. There was a virus running through his consciousness, and he knew exactly where it came from. His phone.

Kat was beside him, gorgeous as ever. Even in this light, even in this setting, she knew how to pull attention. The raven hair, the long legs, the confident smirk. But he knew another Kat, too. A Kat who had layers, who let him see something real when her hunger for attention quieted. She had told him once about her family, a mother who clung so tightly that her demands drove Kat away, and a father whose absence left her chasing approval in every man she met.

He remembered one night more than any other. They had walked along the bay, fog curling off the water, salt air wrapping around them. Maybe it was the fog that loosened her, or perhaps the pull of nostalgia for her home on the Maine coast. Her voice had gone soft, but carried that edge, that bittersweet tone you never forgot.

"When I was in school, Ethan," she had said, holding his arm against the chill, "I made a big point of being the funny one. Life of the party. I didn't want to coast on my looks."

"So, you knew you were beautiful," he jabbed, smiling.

She nudged him, half a smile fading. "Come on, Ethan, I'm trying to share my heart."

"You're right." He squeezed her hand. "I'm just kidding. You're one in a million."

Her eyes turned soft, then insistent. "It was like I had to earn their respect. I wasn't the smartest in my class, but I knew one thing. Girls who coast on beauty die a little each year as it fades. I wanted something that would last longer."

He had smiled at her then, admiration mixing with the tease. "Well, Kat, when you're high, you've got it in spades."

She had laughed and leaned into him. They walked deeper into the fog, and for a moment, he saw the real Kat. Not the glamour, not the mask, but the woman beneath.

Now, here under the blue haze of Neural, she looked like a doll. Plastic. A raven-haired Barbie soaking in every pulse of sensory overload. The sculpted curves, the tight, feminine muscle, the perfected features. It had always drawn him in. Not tonight. Tonight, he was crashing.

The phone buzzed in his hand, a message from Lex. Curt, sharp, no sugarcoating.

Lex: *Someone's stolen the code and flipped it to a Shenzhen fund. Servers wiped, backups gone, even the secret one you set up. It's all gone. We're history, man.*

Ethan typed fast: *How, who?*

Lex: *Chen. I told you I had doubts about him. He always had the correct answers, but his eyes were dead. Like looking into a burned-out volcano. Just smoke. He knew our burn rate was alarming. He smelled collapse.*

Ethan's gut clenched. Chen had stolen *Athena*, the crown jewel. Their self-writing AI platform, which generated its own code and solved problems faster than any human engineer. Other companies were chasing the idea, but CortexAI had been in the lead until now. With Athena gone, the IPO was dead. As dead as Theranos.

Lex: *He took it all. Trained model weights, API keys, cloud creds. Everything. You know what this means.*

Ethan knew. It meant ruin.

The phone buzzed again. Goldberg, Apex Ventures.

Goldberg: *What's this I hear about Athena? Lex just told me. Has Chen gone rogue? My board was ready to bring a 2.3 billion valuation based on this. I took your word, Ethan. Why would you let this happen? You're toast. My lawyers will be in touch.*

The glow of the screen felt brittle, like broken glass.

That was it. Suddenly, he was swimming with sharks. He had poured in his money, his sweat, endless hours, bringing in the best talent. But the Valley had its temperament. Merciless. Predatory. They circled when you faltered, ancient and hungry. He thought he was riding them to riches. Now he saw the truth. He was bleeding in the water.

He remembered a kinder place. Coastal Sonoma. The rolling hills are damp with fog, the soil is dark beneath his boots, and the scent of the sea is carried inland. And above it all, the faint sweetness of vineyards in bloom. Winemakers called it the smell of promise. Out here, in the Valley, there was no promise, only threats, sharp as contracts and sterile as the salt flats crusting the bay.

Another memory pressed in. The day he pruned five vines too close; he cut off the buds. Those vines lost their grapes that year; for them, the whole season was wasted. He could smell it even now, the green shoots crushed under his blade, the earth still damp from the fog, his father's sweat in the air. His father's voice had carried patience, not anger. *It will grow back, son, nothing now for another year. But you'll remember this.* Then the hug, and silence. His father never mentioned it again.

His brother, though, merciless. A hired hand had told him, and Ethan had not heard the end of it for a week. That was family. Grace and cruelty in equal measure. This was the Valley. Here, there was no grace.

The vineyard memory pulled another dream with it; one he'd buried under term sheets and pitch decks. After the IPO, after the exit, he'd open a restaurant. Not in wine country, but right here, in the heart of Silicon Valley. Something like French Laundry dropped into the glass and steel. He'd bring the soil and soul of Sonoma to this place that had forgotten what earth smelled like. These people ate molecular gastronomy and drank biodynamic wines without ever touching dirt. He'd change that. Farm-to-table, but real, not the sanitized version they served in Palo Alto. Servers who knew which field the lettuce came from. A sommelier who'd actually pruned vines. He'd even found the spot, a forgotten lot in Los Altos, where he could build gardens between the office parks.

But planting season was a dream away, and his seeds had already been stolen. The voice from his left brought him back to the harvest of his failures and it was smooth as good tequila. "You look like someone just gutted your company."

Ethan turned. Marcus Valdez was settling into the lounge like morning fog settling into the valley, silent, inevitable, filling every hollow before you realized it was there. Some called him The Architect. Not for building anything. For knowing exactly where to place the charges when it was time to bring something down. He'd been in three of Ethan's funding rounds, always on both sides somehow. Introducing the money, then whispering in their ears. Making himself essential.

"Marcus." Ethan kept his voice flat.

Kat's whole body tensed beside him. "No, not him." She shifted closer to Ethan, a reflexive movement. "That guy gives me the creeps."

Marcus noticed her reaction, seemed to feed on it. "Katherine. Still dating beneath your potential? You know, the Hindawi brothers were asking about you. Their fund just closed at two billion."

"Still pretending you matter, Marcus?"

"I don't pretend anything. I connect. Speaking of which," he turned back to Ethan, "Chen's in Shenzhen already. Met with three funds yesterday. Your Athena code is the belle of the ball."

How did he always know? Marcus had introduced Chen to them eighteen months ago. Of course he'd know where Chen landed.

"That face tells a story." Marcus studied him with eyes the color of old ice. "Two-point-three billion valuation. Goldberg's already lawyering up. But here's the thing, Ethan. The Koreans are looking for exactly what Athena does. I could make some calls. Get you in a room."

"With what? Chen took everything."

"Not everything. You still have the vision. The knowledge. Sometimes a phoenix story plays better than a unicorn." Marcus caught Antoine's eye, made a small gesture. The host hurried over, nervous energy crackling around him. "Something special for my friend. He's had a death in the family."

"I'm not your friend."

"No? Introduced you to Goldberg, to the Saudis, to that biotech exit that promised to fund your Series B. If that's not friendship in the Valley, what is?"

He produced a silver case from his jacket, slim as a cigarette pack. Inside, crystalline capsules caught the club's blue light and threw it back in fractals. They looked expensive. They looked like escape.

"This helps with clarity. I know at least three unicorn CEOs who won't take a board meeting without it. Makes the impossible feel inevitable. Makes hard choices feel like destiny." He selected one capsule, held it up. "First taste is free. Professional courtesy."

Kat grabbed Ethan's wrist. "Don't. Whatever he's selling, it's poison."

Marcus laughed, a sound like ice cracking. "Everything's poison, Katherine. Every term sheet, every partnership, every line of code. The only question is whether the high is worth the hangover."

"I don't need your charity," Ethan said.

"Charity? This is what I do. I showcased your company, now I'm investing in your recovery. The Koreans will want to meet next week. You'll need to be sharp. Sharper than you've ever been."

He set the capsule on the table between them, then stood, straightening his jacket. "Chen wasn't the only one watching your burn rate, Ethan. But unlike Chen, I bet on the aftermath. Some of us profit from creation. Some of us profit from the cleanup. Both have their place in the ecosystem."

Marcus moved back into the crowd, but Ethan felt him there, circling like everything else in this place. Waiting. The capsule sat on the table, catching light, making promises.

Near the VIP bar, out of Ethan's sight, Marcus pulled out his phone. The conversation was quick, practiced. "Yes, it's done. He has no idea." A pause. "Of course, Ms. Morrison. The timeline is holding. Chen delivered as promised." Another pause, listening. "I understand your boss has specific requirements about the... family situation. The Weinhardt boy is crashing exactly as predicted." He glanced back toward where Ethan sat, oblivious. "No, there's no risk he'll trace it back to me or you for that matter. He's too focused on Chen to see the bigger picture."

Back at the lounge, Ethan knew none of this. His world had shrunk to the immediate catastrophe.

"He set you up," Kat said quietly. "He probably told Chen exactly when to run."

But his eyes stayed on the capsule. Such a small thing. Like everything that mattered in the Valley. A chip. A line of code. A connection. A betrayal.

Kat's hand brushed his arm. "Ethan, what's up?"

He barely heard her. The hole in his gut stretched wider. He waved Antoine, the VIP host, over. "I need something strong."

Minutes later, it was in his hand, disguised in a champagne flute. K-Dream. Everyone knew what the K stood for. He had tried it once, for fun. Tonight, he needed it.

"Sharing?" Kat asked, her tone more intimate than playful.

"Sure." He took a deep mouthful and passed her the glass.

The lights overhead turned harsh and unforgiving, each bulb a small sun boring into his skull. The bass from the speakers became something physical, each beat landing like a punch to his chest. Every scent in the room merged into something sharp that clawed at his sinuses. Cologne, wine, sweat, all of it burning.

Chen's betrayal kept replaying in his head, each loop bringing fresh nausea. The room was too hot, too loud, too full of bodies pressing close. He needed air. Needed space. Needed to think.

Someone's wine glass hit the floor with a bright crash. Kat's voice cut through the music, high and frightened. The smell of spilled Pinot mixed with copper. Blood from someone's cut hand. Ethan pushed himself up from the table or tried to. The floor seemed to shift beneath him like a boat deck in rough seas, and then it simply wasn't there anymore.

"Mike," he rasped. Big Mike, head of security caught him before he hit the ground.

"I need an Uber," Ethan muttered.

"Forget it, Ethan," Mike said. "Ride this out. Sit down."

The couch swallowed him whole. The sharks were gone. Darkness was easier than answers.

Somewhere in the club, Marcus Valdez watched the security team help Ethan to a quieter corner. He typed a final message: "Package delivered. The son begins his fall."

The response was immediate: "Good. Mr. Vega will be pleased.

Marcus deleted the thread, as he always did. Some names were too dangerous to leave traces of, even in the Valley where everyone had secrets, especially when those names belonged to those who collected on old debts through the next generation.

CHAPTER TWO

VALLE DE CASABLANCA, CHILE

Something of vengeance I had tasted for the first time
as aromatic wine it seemed...
Charlotte Bronte

T he Pacific fog pushed inland that morning, same as it had for centuries. You could taste the salt in it if you stood still long enough. The marine layer funneled through the valley, trapped between the hills, keeping everything damp and cool.

The vines liked it that way. Slow ripening meant better fruit. Any winemaker worth his salt knew that.

From his terrace, he could see the whole operation. Eight hundred hectares of vines marching in perfect rows toward the mountains. The new gravity flow winery gleaming like a statement of intent. Everything modern, efficient, profitable.

"You're brooding again." Valentina emerged from the bedroom, moving with that dancer's grace she'd perfected in São Paulo nightclubs before she'd decided wine money was better than music money. She stretched in the doorway, silk robe falling open just enough. "We sold fifty thousand cases to Hong Kong last week. The Syrah got 94 points. But you stand here like someone stole your harvest."

He didn't turn from the view. "The Syrah should have scored 96."

"Lucien." She moved closer, ran her fingers along his shoulder. She smelled like jasmine and last night's wine. "Most men would be happy. You have three vineyards. An empire. But you spend your nights staring at maps of California."

"You've been in my office."

"Of course I have." No apology. Valentina apologized for nothing. It was part of her charm. "I know wine, querido. My father owned vineyards in Mendoza before the bankruptcy. I can read a profit statement as well as I can taste tannins." She poured herself a glass from the decanter. His 2019 Reserve. "This is beautiful, by the way. Dark fruit, tobacco, a little green pepper. Very Carménère influence for a Bordeaux blend."

"You have a good palate."

"I have good everything." She smiled, but her eyes stayed serious. "So, tell me. What happened in California and why do you keep staring at that map. It seems like you grind your teeth every time the wind comes from the north?"

The memories were always there, fermenting like wine in a barrel, getting stronger with age. The smell of Sonoma earth. The fog different from here, colder, grayer. The way the old German families ran their fiefdoms like Europe never ended.

"I was twenty-five," he said. "Working for one of those old Sonoma families. Germans. Five generations on the same land. The owner saw something in me. His sons were young; he saw me as a son too. Paid for my training in Bordeaux. Sent me to conferences, tastings. He thought I'd be the future of his operation."

"But?"

"But he wanted evolution. I wanted revolution." Lucien turned from the window. "I saw inefficiencies everywhere. Ancient equipment. Primitive techniques. Workers doing things the way their fathers did because that's how it was done. I had ideas. Precision viticulture. New fermentation protocols. Modern logistics."

Valentina curled into the leather chair, watching him over her wine glass. "They didn't like change."

"The Patriarch thought he was guardian of some sacred tradition. We fought constantly. So, I went around him. Talked directly to the workers. Showed them how much more money they could make with better yields, better systems." His voice hardened with the memory. "Got thirty of them ready to strike unless my methods were implemented."

"Dangerous move."

"It would have worked. Should have worked. But the old man..." Lucien poured bourbon. "He called me into his office. Said I'd betrayed his trust. Said my arrogance would destroy what his family had built over the years. Threatened to remove me from my position. That's when I rallied the workers, got a third of them to go on strike."

"So, you forced him to a compromise?"

"No, somehow, he brought in the harvest without them. It was almost miraculous."

"What happened then?"

"He threw me out. I was blackballed in the entire county."

"So, you found other opportunities."

"My brother opened doors. The cartels needed someone who understood shipping, distribution, quality control. Same principles, different product." He gestured at the valley beyond. "Don Sombra, the head of the cartel, gave me seed money for this. Three vineyards now. Soon to be four."

"All to prove them wrong?"

"To destroy them." The words came quiet, certain. "See, I've been patient, Valentina. Built my reputation. Made connections. Even helped one of their own sons destroy himself."

Her eyebrows rose. "How?"

"The younger son had ambitions. Tech startup, all that AI stuff the Valley loves. I had some of my agents set him with some Chinese associate. The perfect COO for his startup, he thought. He played him perfectly. Stole his code, destroyed his company, just got confirmation," Lucien smiled. "He's picking up the pieces of his life, what's left of it."

"That's... elaborate."

"That's just the beginning." He moved to his desk, pulled out a folder. "There's another German family near them. New money but they want a name for themselves. Perfect for what I need."

"Which is?"

"Don Sombra needs new ways to clean his money. I need leverage in Sonoma. We approached this family with an investment opportunity a year ago. Overseas partnership, expansion capital. They were grateful. Pride can be manipulated."

Valentina set down her wine. "You want to launder cartel money through a Sonoma vineyard?"

"Through their vineyard to get to my real target. Once we're partners with the neighbors, we suggest a merger. Consolidation. Economy of scale."

His voice stayed calm, reasonable, like he was discussing weather. "Two old German families joining forces. Who could object?"

"And once they're merged?"

"We move in through intimidation, muscle, force, whatever it takes. Push out the old guard. Bring in our people. Soon we're not just making wine, we're moving product through one of California's most respected names." He picked up his phone. "The politicians up there are cheaper than you'd think. A few donations, some friendly judges, and La Serpiente Dorada has a legitimate foothold in American wine country."

"While you get your revenge."

"While I take everything they denied me." He found Don Sombra's number. "Their land, their name, their legacy. All of it."

Valentina stood, moved to him. She was beautiful in that practiced way, every gesture designed to distract. But her eyes were sharp, taking in angles, calculating survival. "You know this might take years."

"I've waited fifteen years. I'm not waiting any longer. Now is the time to strike?" He dialed.

"Besides, the groundwork is laid. One son destroyed. Now for the rest. I'm on a mission. Once they have taken the money, I'm putting them on a countdown."

The phone rang twice. That gravelly voice answered. "Lucien. To what do I owe the pleasure?"

"Don Sombra. I'm calling about our Sonoma investment."

"Ah yes. The wine country expansion." A pause. Lucien could hear a lighter, the pull of smoke. "How are things developing?"

"Our German family. Like I suggested, I've let them sit on our investment for a year so they could plan. They've promised me, now it's time."

"They're ready to move against your... other interests?"

"Yes, and once they've forced them to the table a merger will work and that's when we move in."

Don Sombra laughed. "You always did think bigger than wine bottles, my friend. Fine. But Lucien, I want more than clean money. I want routes. Distribution. Political protection."

"You'll have it all. Give me three years, and we'll own half of Sonoma. The legitimate half."

"Make it two years."

"Done."

"Remind me, who is watching over our interest there in California while you're in Chile."

"Alejandro Vega, his brother is a long-time associate. I trust him."

"I assume he's got the means to recover our investment should your plan fail."

"They have the means, lots of them from Bario 18. They've been taught by the best."

He ended the call with that assurance. Valentina hadn't moved, still watching him with those dark eyes that missed nothing.

"Satisfied?" she asked.

"Getting there." Outside, workers moved through his vines, checking sugar levels, testing for readiness. Everything precise, ordered, his. But his mind was already in Sonoma, walking those old fields, taking what should have been his from the beginning. "The harvest is coming."

"Here?"

"Everywhere." He pulled her close, felt her warmth against the perpetual cold that lived in his chest. "Some harvests just take longer to ripen."

She kissed him, and for a moment he almost forgot the bitter taste that never left his mouth. Almost. But the wind was shifting, bringing fog from the Pacific, and with it came memories of another coast, another life, another man's dreams he'd make his own.

The game was finally coming full circle.

CHAPTER THREE

MOUNTAIN VIEW, CALIFORNIA

"In victory, you deserve Champagne; in defeat, you need it."
Napoleon Bonaparte

At 9 a.m., Ethan stood at the entrance of Building 7 in the Prometheus Technology Park, seven weeks after Chen's departure. He faced the skeletal remains of Cortex AI corporate offices, the bones of what had been his dream. The human flesh and brains that ran the place were gone; designers, coders, engineers, and marketers all gone. All that remained were the tech tools, lifeless without the bodies that made them work. Gone were the pioneers, those who had been forging his AI kingdom.

The open floor told the whole story: abandoned desks littered with personal items and Post-its bearing useless passwords. These lifeless monitors had last displayed desperate Slack messages about Chen and missing code. Half-empty La Croix cans and molding kombucha bottles sat exactly where they'd been left during the hasty exodus. The workspace looked like everyone had vanished mid-sip. The silence felt heavy and wrong.

How fitting, now that Athena was stolen, that this temple to the modern god of technology appeared as devastated as her uninhabited sanctuaries in Greece. Those temples were a testimony to empires built on brilliance and brought down by the betrayal of priests who stole the gold. CTOs steal the "gold" now.

Walking through the reception area was painful, with its succulent garden, unkept but still alive; those plants needed so little water, yet they were the one sign of life in the place, placid, stoic, seemingly unconcerned with his plight. He needed moisture. Anything. His mouth was dry, but it wasn't water he wanted. It was all of it: the lines of coke that made meetings bearable, the drinks that made him feel powerful, and the girls who made him forget. All gone. His whole body felt like a dying phone battery, which makes you panic when you're at 2% and nowhere near a charger."

He walked onto the floor, which was empty except for its workstations. It had only been a month and a half since everything had crashed, and the staff had picked up their belongings and walked out, some angry, others dejected, and others empty-eyed, as if they'd experienced it all before. Startups failing in the valley were as common as Teslas in a Whole Foods parking lot.

Dusk, cobwebs, wads of paper scattered amid rows of empty workstations, once alive with the masters of the tech universe, the ones who were creating entire worlds through the mystery of AI, out in the plains of cyber space, now gone." Athena could have been the Manhattan Project of AI," he said to himself, "except this "bomb" required fresh capital and it would no longer be available. The VC generals didn't believe in it anymore."

Voices from the executive suite near the back caught his attention. He could see Operations Manager Lex Stokes and Maria Santos, his Executive

Assistant, no doubt handling equipment returns and coordinating with the liquidators.

Lex forced a smile as he approached.

Maria looked up from a box of hoodies. "TechCrunch won't stop calling. Third time today." She held up a stack of mail. "And vendors keep sending crap like we're still in business."

"Five hundred a day." Derek Washington, their IT Admin, leaned against the doorframe, arms crossed. "That's what the AWS is burning just to keep the security footage from when Chen screwed us over. You want me to pull the plug or what?"

"Yes," Ethan said, "just make sure we get all of that part on a hard drive." He'd been keeping the shutdown squad paid from his personal reserves. Now, they were down to what his attorney called 'coffee money', enough to keep the lights on but not much else.

Lex didn't look up from his laptop. "I agree, pull it. Cancel everything, the cards, servers, all of it. I need these chairs counted before the vultures show up tomorrow."

"Wait, Mr. Weinhardt," Tyler Kim, their unpaid engineering intern, pushed past Derek, laptop clutched against his chest. "We could still pivot, right? My dad says that's what startups are supposed to do. Maybe if we refocus, Athena could have daughters."

Sam Medina from building maintenance wheeled his mop bucket past the kid. "Crypto bros upstairs said that too. One day they're pivoting, next day the lights are on but nobody's home." He caught Ethan's eye. "Wow, boss. You look like crap."

Maria grabbed some papers off her desk. "Sign these. Termination docs." She paused. "Oh, and Ethan? Those ferns in the lunchroom, the ones you loved. They're almost dead."

"I'd expected that," he said. The contract they'd had with Peninsula Plantscapes had been canceled on day one. They'd come every Wednesday at $350 a week to maintain what they called the 'biophilic workspace.' Just another testament to the foolishness and hubris that had dominated his mindset just weeks ago.

"Speaking of dead," Derek added, not looking up from his phone, "guess there goes everything, even that restaurant you were always sketching on napkins during board meetings. What did you call it?"

"Terra/Tech," Ethan said quietly. A farm-to-table place where venture capitalists could taste actual soil-grown tomatoes between term sheets. Where code could meet terroir.

"Yeah, well," Derek shrugged, "that dream's gone like a CompuServe email address."

Maria almost smiled at that. Almost.

His schedule had been like this for the last seven weeks, sorting through what was left of his dream and, at the same time, wondering where he could go next. He'd hit up every "friend" he met in the last two years in the valley. Many of them were sympathetic, expressed concern, and offered personal loans, which he couldn't accept with a clear conscience. Some were just pathetic, avoiding him as if he were malware in human form.

Then there were the sleepless nights, brain-spinning scenarios where he'd be drowning in debt until he died. But his attorney, Jonathan Patel at Sequoia Law Group, had talked him off the ledge. "Goldberg's just pissed about the optics," Patel had explained. "This was supposed to be his fifth IPO, he already told half of Sand Hill Road about his 'AI unicorn.' Now he's got egg on his face at the Rosewood bar."

The other investors, the early ones who'd come in before Goldberg, they'd barely flinched. Signed all the risk disclosures, knew the game.

"Goldberg would have lost what, half a million?" Patel had actually laughed. "That's pocket change for him. He would have brought in enough to lead the IPO. You lost three million of your own money. You're the biggest victim here, which makes you legally untouchable. Can't sue someone for losing their own fortune."

It was perverse comfort, too poor to sue, Silicon Valley's version of diplomatic immunity.

That memory reminded him he had to be at Patel's place by noon. They had a closing meeting over lunch in his attorney's backyard.

"I've got a lunch meeting. Thanks again, everyone," he said as he turned to leave. "I can only pay you till the end of the week. Plus, the landlord says, we're history after that. Lex, Maria, Tyler, Sam, and Derek, you've all been an enormous help. Sorry, I couldn't do more. See you tomorrow."

As he left, he picked up one of the succulents in the lobby.

CHAPTER FOUR

SANTA CLARA

"Friendship's the wine of life."
Edward Young

Jonathan Patel lived on Moraga Avenue. It ran straight as a ruler from El Camino to Lawrence, liquid amber trees dropping their spiky balls on the sidewalk. The trees had long since dropped their leaves, their bare branches reaching upward like arthritic fingers against the gray sky. RVs and work trucks filled the driveways.

His house was one of those tract homes built in '64 with the same floor plan as every third house on the block, three bedrooms, two baths, beige stucco over white. A former owner had converted half the garage into a studio apartment and created a casita out of a converted shed in the backyard, which was crowded up against an aging swimming pool.

As crazy as it seemed, he was renting out both units. Jonathan considered himself blessed to have been able to purchase it at all. Moving from Austin to California wasn't just a wake-up call, it was a housing nightmare you couldn't wake up from. In the valley's warped economy, engineers making $200,000 a year, with a family to feed and put through private schools, struggled to afford houses that blue-collar workers bought on single incomes when they were new.

They sat on a patio set next to the pool, where Jonathan had set out sandwiches and iced tea. It was a typical day for the valley, the last of the marine layer burning off. May gray.

The ice cubes clinked against the sweating glass as Ethan set down his drink, the condensation pooling on the weathered redwood picnic table. Above them, the faded green awning flapped in the mild Silicon Valley breeze, casting shifting shadows across the remains of their turkey sandwiches and two bottles of Topo Chico.

"So, I see you've picked up a new habit," Ethan said, gesturing at Jonathan's glass with a wry smile. "This Mexican Perrier, or whatever it is you're serving us today."

Jonathan chuckled, wiping mustard from the corner of his mouth. "Yeah, they drink it like people smoke here in California." He took another sip, grimacing slightly. "I can see it's an acquired taste."

"You weren't drinking this when we were at Stanford," Ethan observed, picking at a splinter in the table's surface. The wood was soft due to age, likely originating from when the house was built.

"Back then, it was brewskies and tequila shots." Jonathan's eyes crinkled with nostalgia as he glanced around his backyard. "Those were some great days," Jonathan continued, watching the fog retreat. "California culture was a total shock for this Virginia farm boy. Man, I'm glad you had my back when we rushed A-K-Psi that first year". You took me under your wing; I'll never forget it."

"Well, it looks like the saturation's reversed now, but I need more than a wing."

"So, how are you going to keep the wolf from the door. I know your bank account as well as you do.

"I put my name in a half a dozen career platforms; TechPath, NexHire, CodeBase, DevForge. Did it the day after Goldberg threatened me. Ghosts?

"Headhunters."

"Vertex Talent Group, Pinnacle Tech Recruiting. Hit up all three. Then there's Jameson at Catalyst Search. He's a friend from school, said he'll get back soon, but nothing yet." Now, fifteen years later, that faith felt misplaced. Ethan pushed the memories away as Jonathan leaned forward, his attorney instincts kicking in despite their friendship.

"So, what's your plan now, Ethan?" Jonathan asked, his tone careful. "You and Kat still together, now that everything's crashed?"

Ethan traced a water ring on the table with his finger. "She's still there, but..." He paused, searching for the right words. "To be honest, it seems like she's fading."

"What about the others?" Jonathan's eyebrows rose. "You had a whole bevy of those women around you. What about Sienna?"

"Ghosted me a week ago." Ethan's laugh was bitter. He picked up his sandwich, then set it down again without taking a bite. "So did Tessa and Lila. Now that they're not getting their weekly Coke infusion, they're history."

A mockingbird landed on the fence, its song cutting through the afternoon heat. Jonathan watched his friend pick up his sandwich, study it as if it were a term sheet, then set it back down untouched. The golden boy of Stanford's computer science program, the one everyone bet would be running the next unicorn, now sat across from him in this aging backyard, startup dead, the hangers-on already moved on to the next free ride.

Jonathan took a long pull on his Topo Chico and said, "Well, now that you've burned through most of your savings, what's happening with your housing situation?"

Ethan took a bite of his sandwich, and after a few chews and a lot of reflection. "I don't have a lot of options." He thought of his palatial place in Atherton. One of many owned by a VC guy who rented it out after he moved to New York City and depended on the additional income. "I have till the end of the month, and the owner is eager to get me out."

"Well, if you need a place to crash for a while, you can always stay here." Jonathan pointed to the casitas on the other side of the pool. "You'd just have to room with Sidney."

The thought made Ethan feel a little gnarly. "That would be difficult, Sidney's a code goblin." He couldn't imagine living in a cluttered cave of glowing monitors and half-empty energy drink cans, and stacks of cold pizza boxes with congealed cheese. "Thanks, Jonathan, for the offer. It may come to that. I'll know in a week."

"I won't charge you, just don't tell Sidney. I'm giving him a break on the price, but he won't like that you're there for free. His last roommate only lasted a month. Had to pay half the price and decided it wasn't worth it. Having to put up with Sydney's coding binges was too much for him to handle. Those 48-hour death marches finally got to him."

"Yes, those would be hard to sleep through," Ethan could imagine one of those death marches, the kind where a coder went unshowered and hunched, reeking of sweat and coffee, ripping farts without apology, burping between slurps of warm soda, and muttering at the screen like it might finally answer back.

"Well, if it's your only option, it's open," Jonathan said. "Think of it like the old college vibe, cheap meals, shared space, but I don't want you stuck in your car."

The mention of the car brought Ethan's focus back to the present. "That reminds me, I've got to get back to my place, they're coming to collect the Porsche. The lease has run out. Thankfully, the Tesla's paid off."

It was quiet for a moment, a long moment as the two friends drank in the reality of where things were really at.

"You know," Jonathan said finally, "this whole thing is like a system reboot. But it has its parallel. I know you hated your dad's simple platitudes, but I remember Karl was right about one thing. Cultivation takes faith. Sometimes you've got to know when to let a field lie fallow for a season."

"Well, Jonathan, the fields are scorched and salted. It's akin to trying to grow a harvest out of ashes. That's how I feel."

"Well, I'm here. I'll take care of the final steps on the bankruptcy, no charge. Keep me posted."

"I will," said Ethan as they hugged. "Thanks for the sandwiches and the Texas holy water."

Later, as Ethan drove to his place, the mention of his father earlier took him back to a discussion years earlier in his family's palatial but ranch-styled home, nestled among the redwoods. The house, a 10,000-square-foot understated elegance, had been built generations ago using redwood from the property, before such trees became scarce and sacred. It fit naturally into the rugged surroundings, tasteful rather than ostentatious.

They had gathered in the kitchen to discuss sending Ethan to Stanford and the sacrifice it would create for the family. Ethan had been there with his mother, Eden, his father, Karl Henry Weinhardt and Tawi, the native American who was the family's cook. Karl, a four-generation German immigrant, had married the daughter of a British family that had settled in the area in the 60's.

"You know, Ethan," Karl had said, his weathered hands wrapped around a coffee mug, "this is a big sacrifice for the whole family. Your brother, Ryan, isn't happy about it. But I can see you've got genius in you, and you've also got drive that's frustrated here."

Eden had nodded, her British accent still faint after decades in California. "Ryan's always been like that, Karl. He's the older brother, tied to this land. He doesn't understand Ethan's drive. It'll probably bother him, but what do we do?"

Ethan had been frustrated then, eighteen years old and bristling with ambition. He'd spent every summer working, sweating, pouring himself into tending cattle and harvesting grapes. Now, he was heading off to Stanford, he family covering tuition, housing, all of it. Still, he felt like he was owed something more.

Tawi had spoken up then, his voice calm and measured. "Do you remember the year, Karl, when it looked like the harvest would be the worst we'd had in years? However, we brought in an outside expert. There was a lot of work and patience, but the next year was abundant. It was a risk, outside our normal pattern of operation."

The cook had looked at Ethan meaningfully. "Ethan's different, but who knows what potential resources and knowledge he can bring to this operation someday? Even though he's going off to study computers. It's a mystery in some ways, but good things can happen."

Eden had looked over at Tawi and smiled, remembering the many times he'd rescued her in the kitchen. Even though he cooked most of the meals, he often gave her advice around the breakfast table, making her attempts at soufflés even more successful. She'd looked at Sterling. "I think he has a good point. I'll deal with Ryan."

Karl had looked at them both and smiled, then paused for that moment Ethan knew so well. "Let's just take a moment and listen. It was quite for a long stretch, then Karl smiled. That was all.

Ethan had been frustrated; his family often did this. Tawi had whispered a few words in his native tongue, and somehow, peace had settled over the entire gathering.

The truth was, Karl and Eden had never asked about the name Tawi. They'd unofficially adopted him with that name when his mother worked for Eden's parents, and it had never occurred to them it might not be his real one. Even the ranch hands, some who'd known him forty years, called him nothing else. Only Tawi, dove in the old Pomo tongue. His grandmother had whispered it to him when he was born, said it was a name for peace after war, for what comes after the fighting ends. Chief Marin had been the warrior. His descendant would be the healer. But that was his secret to keep, maybe forever. Some truths waited for their time, like wine in the cellar, gaining complexity in darkness.

Finally, Karl had looked up. "I have peace. It's going to be expensive, Ethan, but we're going to send you off."

That decision hadn't sat well with everyone. Ethan remembered another conversation, one he'd heard secondhand years earlier from Miguel, a ranch hand at his family's place. It was during one of his visits home from Stanford that Miguel had pulled him aside after dinner.

"Your brother, he wasn't happy when your father sent you off to school," Miguel had said, rolling a cigarette between his weathered fingers. They'd been standing by the cattle fence, watching the sun set over the Sonoma hills.

Miguel told him how it had gone down. Ryan had confronted their father in the equipment barn, arguing his case while Karl worked on the grape harvester.

"Dad, we need him on the ranch," Ryan had said, his voice tight with frustration. The smell of diesel and hay thick in the air. "How are we going to bring in the harvest? I mean, we've got plenty of hired hands, but we need his brains working with us."

Karl had kept checking the hydraulics, his weathered hands steady despite his age. "Listen, Ryan. Your brother's got great potential. I know he loves this place, but I don't want to hold him back."

"You're paying for his entire education," Ryan had shot back, kicking at a clump of dried mud.

"Well, it's just like the investment we make here in the vineyard." Karl had straightened up, wiping his hands on an oil-stained rag. "We never know what kind of crop we'll have next year, but we cultivate in faith. Same way with your brother."

Miguel had paused then, taking a long drag of his cigarette. "Your brother, he swore under his breath, gritted his teeth, and went back to work. But your father, he just kept working on that harvester, calm as anything. He knew what he was doing."

It was too much for Ryan. Stanford had been hard enough. But the startup was a stretch for everyone. Now they had lost the three million his father had fronted for the dream, and it was gone, like water through sand.

He remembered clearly. It had been ten years ago. He had just finished at Stanford when he had approached the family about fronting the money for his startup. That's when Ryan finally exploded. "Dad, you're putting the ranch in jeopardy and taking out a loan like that. What if the harvest fails? What if we can't cover the note? We'll be forced to sell off some of the land. Maybe lose the place."

But his father stood firm, jaw tight. He said, 'We'll never lose this place. Not while I draw breath. Ethan and I believe. We have faith.'"

Ryan hadn't let it go. "Faith may hold for you. But when it comes to Ethan, I don't think it's wisdom."

Ethan had felt the heat rise in him. "Thanks for the support, brother. All you care about is your inheritance."

Ryan's eyes narrowed to knives. "I don't trust you, Ethan. You're a dreamer."

"Dreams or no dreams, it's my shot. And if I have any inheritance, I'm glad Dad's willing to risk it on me."

Ryan had turned on his heel and left the room. The slam of the door had been going on for weeks.

Now the memory faded into the grind of traffic. El Camino was jammed. The freeway worse. Home would be a long crawl. And when he got there, it would be worse still.

The private room at Gary Danko overlooked the bay where fog was already creeping under the Golden Gate, swallowing Alcatraz first, then the ferries, working its way toward the city like it did most evenings. Alejandro Vega sat with his back to the view, watching the Kruegers work through their seared foie gras.

Hans, the father, cut his with surgical precision. Otto the youngest son, copied his father. Eric the oldest, just pushed his around the plate, nervous energy making his hands unsteady. The sommelier had already been dismissed after pouring the Chassagne-Montrachet. What needed discussing didn't need witnesses.

"Gentlemen," Vega said, voice smooth as the wine, "my associates are curious about your progress. Our investment buys many things, but patience has limits." He touched his napkin to his lips, a gesture that somehow carried weight. "You've had six months. The approach to the Weinhardts should be imminent."

Hans set down his fork, met Vega's gaze straight on. "Six months at the most. Our approach will put enough pressure on them. They'll have no choice but to come to the table."

Otto nodded, finding his voice. "The Weinhardts are already recovering from the younger son's tech failure. It cost them three million, and the stench of that disaster clings to the whole family. But we have something better. Ryan, the older son, has some extracurricular activities which we fully plan to exploit."

Vega smiled, but it didn't travel past his mouth. Outside, the fog had reached the Embarcadero, turning the city lights into watercolors. "Good. My associates have plans for that whole valley, and delays make them... creative." He raised his glass, the golden wine catching the candlelight. "To desperate families and the opportunities they provide. May the Weinhardts never see us coming."

The brothers raised their glasses, the crystal ringing sharp in the quiet room. Hans drank deep. Eric barely wet his lips. Vega noticed both, filed it away. Everything was data. Everything was leverage. Everything was moving toward the moment when the Weinhardts would have no choice but to accept the hand that seemed to save them.

CHAPTER FIVE

SONOMA COUNTY

SIX MONTHS LATER

"The wine sleeps in the bottle, but still, it is changing...evolving"
Ann Mah, The Lost Vintage

The marine layer was lifting, the morning sun burning through to reveal the coastal mountains on Sonoma's western edge. They tumbled toward the Pacific like weary travelers at journey's end. Green giants that had staggered west from the inland valleys and collapsed at the shore, their massive flanks now washed by salt spray and fog, their ridgelines sharpening as the mist pulled back like a curtain. They'd been here since the earth cracked open and pushed them up, unlike the Weinhardts, who'd only been working this land for a little over a century, their roots shallow compared to these ancient hills.

Ethan's family had carved out their piece here, on the coastal ridges, east of the sea and in the valleys below. They'd started with Riesling and other German whites, even Zinfandel, but ultimately built their reputation on Pinot Noir and Chardonnay, the grapes that proved best suited to the windswept coast. Their Heimkehr Pinot Noir, pronounced Heimcare, named when Johann and Elisabeth first saw these fog-shrouded hills and whispered "homecoming" in their native tongue, had become the stuff of legend.

Five generations of meticulous vine selection had earned it unprecedented recognition: multiple 100-point scores from Wine Spectator and Parker's Wine Advocate, gold medals from Paris to San Francisco, even the distinction of being the only California Pinot served at a White House state dinner. At $400 a bottle, it stood alongside Caymus and Scarecrow as one of California's most coveted wines. But to Ethan, it was simply the wine they opened on special occasions, when family returned or harvests exceeded dreams. Grass-fed cattle had grazed the eastern slopes at lower elevations for generations, just as they did to this day.

The dirt road kicked up dust behind the battered Camry as it wound through the property. The car rattled and wheezed, sounding like it might give up at any moment. Ethan pressed his face to the window, his breath fogging the glass.

He loved this land more now than when he'd left it for Stanford fourteen years ago. Each summer he'd wanted to come home. Each harvest season called to him. But there was always a new venture, always a new woman, and always the memory of Ryan's angry face that kept him away.

The last six months had been a ceaseless descent into depression. The job boards were graveyards; the headhunters came up empty. No one wanted the CEO of a failed startup. He'd ended up taking Jonathan's housing offer and scratched out a living as hired gun coder, but being a code monkey had driven him half insane.

He'd sold the Tesla to pay Jonathan back at least part of what he owed. Jonathan had offered his help for nothing, but living on a friend's charity gnawed at him. Sydney had been worse than imagined, like trying to live inside a digital dumpster, surrounded by empty energy drink cans and the constant clatter of keyboards through sleepless nights.

The break with Kat cut deep. He'd caught her with another man at the Pulse, a place he never went. He thought he loved her; thought she loved him. But she was done with his fall, and his dark moods only pushed her further away. She tried to lift him up, but inside he knew he wanted her gone. She reminded him too much of the life he'd already lost.

So, he'd made the choice that humiliated him most, going back to the ranch and facing everyone. Maybe he could sleep with the hired hands in the bunkhouse; it would be better than rooming with Sydney. The coastal air and working the land would be good for his state of mind.

Rounding the last bend, the Camry sputtered and died. He coasted to the gate as the vehicle took what seemed like its final breath.

Standing at the gate, Ethan's knees went weak. Not from withdrawal, that hell was months behind him but from something deeper. He dropped to the ground, grabbed fistfuls of earth. The smell hit him, loam and decomposing oak leaves, trace minerals from ancient seabeds, that particular sweetness of soil worked by the same family for generations. It filled his nostrils, flooded his brain with something better than any high he'd chased in the city.

Up on the ridge, movement. His father on the old Kawasaki ATV, bouncing down through the vines. Karl had been watching, hopeful and persistent, the way only fathers of prodigal sons could be.

Karl Henry Weinhardt, Karl to everyone but the bank, pulled up in a cloud of dust and grape leaves. Sixty-eight years old, sun-damaged skin like leather, hands that could still wrestle a fence post into submission. He killed the engine and just stood there, looking at his youngest son kneeling in the dirt.

The embrace came fast, fierce, as he knelt to reach his son. Karl's face crumpled, tears cutting tracks through the dust on his cheeks. In the early morning light, they glistened like dew on weathered bark after a long dry spell. He smelled like sweat and machine oil, coffee and earth. Like father. Like home.

"I don't know where to start, Dad." The words broke out of Ethan raw and ragged.

Karl raised a finger to his lips briefly, then dropped it, nodding for his son to continue.

"I can't find the words to say how sorry I am for leaving the way I did. But now... I want to come home. If you'll take me."

Karl's lips curled into the slightest smile, eyes crinkling with tenderness. "Yes, son, it's been a difficult season for our family. Truth be told, there've been many of those since you left."

Ethan nodded, his gaze dropping to the ground. "I know. I lost more than I can count, investments, friendships... my focus. And Chen, he stole it all. The software, everything. It's all gone. I chased the wrong things. Too much noise, too many parties, not enough purpose. I forgot what mattered."

Karl drew him close again, holding him in a lingering embrace before pushing him back to arm's length. The two stood, father lifting son up. His face filled with a tear-free smile now, gentler but steady. "Well," he said quietly, "you remember now. That's what counts."

Ethan nodded, his voice low. "Yes, Dad... I think I'm finally starting to see that. And this place..." he glanced toward the fields, the light on the vines, "I believe it'll help me remember who I am again. Like I said... if you'll take me, can this be home again?"

Karl's hand tightened on his shoulder, his smile both weary and proud. "It's always been your home, son. You just had to find your way back to it. You're more than welcome here again."

Karl pulled out his red and blue handkerchief, wiping his face and neck, never breaking his gaze from Ethan. That affirming smile unleashed fresh contrition in his son.

"I know I don't deserve to come back, Dad, but I was hoping you'd hire me on. I'm willing to take any job." Ethan pointed toward the closest row of vines. "I'd be glad to work alongside Jake and the field hands. I'm not expecting my old position back."

"Don't worry about that, son. There's plenty of room here for you. Lots of work to be done between now and harvest, so extra hands will be much appreciated." Karl motioned toward the ATV. "Let's get up to the main house. Your mother will be glad to see you've come home."

They rode doubled up, Ethan on the rear storage rack, watching the familiar landscape roll by. The Pinot blocks on the western slope, the same blocks where his great-great-grandfather Johann had first planted those smuggled Burgundian cuttings in 1891. The old Zinfandel vines, gnarled and arthritic, that his grandfather had planted during Prohibition, hiding them among the oaks. The equipment shed where he'd made his teenage mistakes, thinking himself clever.

Karl suddenly cut the engine, pulling to a stop beside a block of younger vines. The fog still lingered early that morning, leaving these particular hills washed in filtered gold. He climbed off, motioning for Ethan to follow.

"Want to show you something," Karl said, walking into the rows.

The vines shimmered in the light breeze, their clusters showing the first deep blush of veraison. Karl moved slowly, the dust kicking up behind his boots, the smell of earth and sun-baked grass rising around them.

The fruit hung lighter here. Ethan could see it in every row. Looser clusters, gaps between the berries, smaller bunches tucked under the canopy.

Karl reached for a cluster, rolling it gently in his calloused hand. "See that?" he said quietly. "That's what the wind does. Came hard back in May, shook the blooms just as they opened. Some of the vines never recovered."

Ethan nodded, running his fingers across a leaf still damp from morning dew. "So... less wine?"

"Maybe half a tank less," Karl said. "But the kind that wins medals. Fewer berries, but thicker skins. Every one of these'll hold more flavor than a fat crop ever could. Nature cut back for us, saved us the trouble of thinning."

They stood together, looking across the rows that rolled toward the ridge, sunlight flickering through the canopy. The vineyard was quiet, almost reverent. Karl seemed to study the vines with particular satisfaction.

"Sometimes," Karl said, his eyes on a particularly stressed vine, "the hard years make the best vintages. The vines that struggle produce the wine worth remembering. Your great-grandfather Heinrich never irrigated the old Heimkehr block, even during the drought of '47. Said the stress made them reach deeper, find what they needed. That vintage still holds up today."

Ethan remembered tasting that '47 at his twenty-first birthday, deep and haunting, like drinking history itself. That bottle would fetch twelve thousand at auction now, if anyone were foolish enough to sell.

They continued up the hill in silence.

"The Zin block looks good," Ethan managed, needing to fill the silence.

"Best year in a decade," Karl said over his shoulder. "Ryan's been working a new trellising system. Increased yield by twenty percent. He's got a good eye for the vines, like your grandpa William did."

Ryan. The name sat heavy between them. His older brother, the one who stayed, who'd warned against giving Ethan the money. The one who'd been right. And Willaim, their grandfather, who'd revolutionized their winemaking in the '70s, bringing back whole-cluster fermentation from Burgundy, insisting on indigenous yeasts when everyone else was buying commercial strains.

He was overjoyed to be home, beginning to restore his broken relationships. But if he was being honest, Ethan had nowhere else to turn. He was hungry, hadn't eaten in days. He'd lost close to thirty pounds. His drug habit had ended not by choice but by poverty. He'd considered worse options, but too much of his upbringing's moral fiber remained.

As they crested the ridge, the vastness of the family estate sprawled into view. Rows of vines blanketed the hillsides as far as the eye could see. To the west, through ravines, glimpses of the sun-bathed Pacific peeked through. The marine layer already crouched landward, foretelling its evening incursion. This daily cycle, fog, sea breeze, summer heat, allowed their grapes to fully ripen with fresh, complex flavors and lively acidity.

The onshore breeze carried up through the canyons, bringing the intoxicating scent of spring vines, fresh earth, and salt air, a trio of assurances that he was indeed home. Something else seemed to ride that breeze too, something deeper than memory or nostalgia.

"Remember when you were twelve," Karl said suddenly, "and you wanted to know why we grew grapes here instead of the valley floor?"

Ethan remembered. A hot July day, hiking the property line, his father explaining terroir like scripture. The word had sounded strange to him then, heavy and foreign on his tongue. His father had smiled and said it meant that every hill, every patch of soil, every shift of wind gives a wine its voice. "The land tells its story through the fruit," he'd said. "You just have to learn how to listen."

"You said the struggle made them stronger," Ethan replied. "That easy soil made boring wine."

"Still true." Karl's voice carried weight. "Works for people too. Every generation of Weinhardts learned that. Your great-great-grandmother Elisabeth used to say the vines teach patience, you can't rush greatness, only prepare the ground for it."

They walked in companionable silence toward the main house, where warm light spilled from windows and the sounds of celebration drifted down to meet them. Karl's stride was unhurried, the walk of a man whose family had traced these paths for generations.

"Your great-grandfather used to say this land would prove itself in its own time," Karl said, his eyes on the ridge ahead. "Not our time, its time. Hundred and twenty-three years we've been here now. Five generations of perfecting these vines, selecting from the best, propagating only from those that showed the deepest color, the most complex flavors." He paused, and Ethan caught something in his father's expression, a quiet anticipation that had nothing to do with what was ahead that day. "The petitioners come by every few months now. Asking about soil samples, climate data, our boundaries. They say we might finally get our name on the map. Official recognition. An AVA of our own."

The way he said it, our name on the map, carried layers of meaning Ethan was only beginning to understand. Recognition earned through generations of quiet work, not clever marketing or shortcuts. The kind of validation that comes to those who wait for it without grasping. Like the Heimkehr itself, patient, complex, worth the wait. An official AVA would only confirm what Wine Spectator and the hundred-point scores already knew: this land produced something extraordinary.

"Been hoping for two things this year," Karl added quietly, not quite looking at his son. "Seems I might get them both."

The main house materialized through the oaks, his grandfather's Depression-era masterpiece. Built when everyone said he was crazy, using redwood beams from trees on the property before it became sacred. Stone foundation quarried from the hill behind where the winery now stood. Every nail hammered when a day's work bought bread and hope was harder to find than money. The house had survived the 1906 quake's aftershocks, the fires of '64, the flood of '86. It would survive this too.

Tawi's, pickup was parked outside, a good indication dinner would be worth eating. The old Pomo appeared and disappeared according to his own mysterious schedule, but always there when needed most. His main duties involved cooking for the ranch crew from his kitchen near the bunkhouses, but he delighted in preparing family dinners too, much to Eden's relief.

His mother must have been watching from the window. The screen door banged open before Karl killed the engine. Eden Weinhardt stood on the porch in her gardening clothes, soil under her nails, one hand pressed to her mouth. "Ethan!" The word carried ten years of 2 a.m. worries, unanswered calls, prayers to a God she wasn't sure was listening. Eden's face transformed, smiles and tears in equal measure. She rushed forward, enveloping him in a mother's fierce embrace that lasted long seconds before pulling back, her expression shifting to alarm. "You're skin and bones, Ethan. You look like you haven't eaten in weeks!"

"You're almost right about that, Mom."

Ever quick to the heart of matters, she pressed, "So how did this happen?"

Ethan's composure broke. "It's a long story, Mom, but basically... I've hit rock bottom."

She embraced him again, and mother and son wept together for several long minutes. When they pulled apart, Eden wiped her eyes. "Your sister's at U.C. doing an internship. She'll be heartbroken she missed your homecoming, but she'll be back soon. I'll call her tonight."

"Esther's okay?"

"More than okay. Dating a nice boy, one she met there last year. Nothing serious yet." Eden's smile wobbled. "She asks about you. All the time."

When they collected themselves, they all gathered, including Tawi, around the great oak table in the kitchen's westward-facing alcove. High windows graced this room, with a covered porch beyond French doors where windows met the outside.

The kitchen hadn't changed. Same scarred table that seated twelve, built from a tree felled year ago in a local quake. Same view across vineyards to where sun painted fog gold and pink. Same smell of sourdough starter, the culture supposedly 150 years old, passed down from Gold Rush days and coffee, Tawi's herbs hanging from beams. Sage, bay laurel, yerba Buena.

Ethan sat in his old chair, muscle memory placing him third from the end, facing west. His hands trembled as he searched for words. Around him, the faces he'd fled watched and waited. His mother, beautiful still at sixty-five despite new lines around her eyes, worry lines he'd carved there. His father, dirt under his nails, love and wariness warring in his expression.

"Like I told Dad, I'm not sure where to start..." Fresh emotion halted him. His mother's face had always held a special place in his heart.

Memories of her constant care during childhood rushed back. Perhaps these next moments would prove most difficult because he was honestly confronting, for the first time, the selfishness that had wounded her.

"So first of all, I know now how much I must have hurt each of you," Ethan managed.

His mother reached across, covering his hands with hers. "Son, it's true." She paused before speaking again. Then this, slow but honest. "And I'm not sure how long it will take us to get over that hurt. But know this; you're forgiven. It will take time to work it all out, but we're glad you're home. And we hope that's for good this time."

"I am, Mom. I'm done running."

Eden's voice stayed steady, though tears threatened. "That's good news. But other things are running here, not your failed dreams, but wounds running when bandages fall away. Those wounds that should be healing, seep and won't stay covered. And yes, there are some deep ones, still raw. Healing those will take time. I won't lie about that. Ten years, Ethan. Ten years since we funded your dream. Ten years of hearing so little from you. Maybe a Christmas card. A random phone call here and there. But less each year. You were just …. gone."

"I know. The dream, the vision just took over my life. I'm sorry. I'm so…."

"Stop." She squeezed his hand. "Sorry is a start, not a solution. We'll need more than words."

Tawi appeared from the pantry, moving silent despite his size. The old man studied Ethan with eyes that had seen too much to be surprised by anything. His flannel shirt was the same style he'd worn for forty years, gray braid hanging past his shoulder blades. "You look terrible," Tawi observed.

"Feel worse."

"Good. Means you're still alive enough to feel." He set a glass of something green in front of Ethan. "Drink."

It smelled like grass clippings and tasted like punishment. Ethan downed it anyway, gagging.

"What was that?"

"Medicine. Old recipe." Tawi turned back to the stove. "Milk thistle, dandelion, other things. Your liver's probably screaming. This'll help it whisper."

"Since when do you make medicine?"

"Since before you were born. You forgot that too?" The old man's voice carried no judgment, just fact. Lunch in an hour. You're staying."

Outside, later, the fog had begun its assault, rolling through gaps in the hills like a slow-motion avalanche. The temperature dropped ten degrees in as many minutes. Through the window, Ethan watched vines disappearing row by row, swallowed by gray. The fog would be good for the grapes. Cool nights after warm days concentrated flavors, extended hang time. Even broken and empty, some part of him remembered the rhythms.

The kitchen fell quiet except for Tawi's cooking. The sizzle of onions in cast iron. The bubble of stock. Real sounds, honest sounds. Not the synthetic beats of Neural or the white noise of server farms. Just food and family and fog pressing against windows.

"So." Karl settled into his chair, old wood creaking. "Tell me about this Chen. And the company. All of it."

Ethan told them. The whole story through the lunch hour and as the day drifted into late afternoon. Athena, the AI that wrote its own code. The burn rate that ate money like fire ate wood. Chen's dead eyes and perfect answers. The theft, the Shenzhen fund, Goldberg's threats. The parties, sanitized in the telling. The rest left unspoken but understood.

"Three million," Karl said when he finished. "That's what we're out?"

"Plus whatever the lawyers cost. Goldberg's threatening to sue."

"Let him." Karl's voice stayed steady. "Your friend, Jon Patel still practicing?

"Yes, for free."

"Good. He'll handle it."

"Dad, you don't understand. This could get ugly. The whole Valley knows."

"The Valley." Karl snorted. "Sixty miles south and might as well be Mars. What they know doesn't matter here."

"Your father's right," Eden added. "This is Sonoma. We measure time in seasons, not quarters. What matters is what happens next."

"I don't know what happens next." Ethan's voice cracked. "I don't know how to do anything except chase the next deal."

"The next high?" Tawi's voice cut from the stove. "Yeah, we can smell it on you. That particular stink takes months to fade."

Ethan's face burned. His mother's hand tightened on his.

"But you're here," Tawi continued, not turning. "That's something. Seen plenty who never make it this far. They end up in city morgues or the bay. You made it home. Now we see if you can stay."

"I want to stay." The words came out desperate. "I just don't know how."

"Same way vines grow back after frost," Karl said. "Slowly. With help. One day at a time."

"Ryan's going to...." Ethan caught himself.

"Ryan's in Healdsburg at the equipment auction. Won't be back till later today." Karl's tone made it clear the delay didn't change what was coming. "We'll deal with that soon enough."

"I brought nothing back," Ethan said finally. "Ten years, and I'm coming home with less than I left with."

"You're wrong." His mother's voice carried certainty. "You're bringing yourself back. That's all we wanted. All we hoped for."

"Broken and broke."

"But here." She stood, moved behind his chair, wrapped her arms around him like when he was small. "My broken, broke, beloved boy. Home."

Ethan broke then. Really broke. Ten years of running after a dream, ten years of pretending he was building something that mattered. The weight of his failure all crashed down in his mother's kitchen, in her arms, with his father's hand on his shoulder and Tawi muttering something in Pomo that Ethan hoped was a blessing.

The fog had swallowed everything now. The world beyond the windows had vanished. There was only this kitchen, these people, this moment of return. Tomorrow would bring Ryan's anger, Goldberg's lawyers, the brutal reality of starting over at thirty-five with nothing but debt and damaged pride.

But Karl suddenly straightened in his chair, a light coming into his eyes. "You know what? This calls for something more than a quiet dinner. My son's come home." He looked at Tawi. "What do you say we fire up the pit? Do it right?"

Tawi's face cracked into the first real smile Ethan had seen from him. "Been a while we had a proper barbecue. Still got that side of beef hanging?"

"We do." Karl was already reaching for his phone. "I'll call Jake, tell him to spread the word. All the hands and their families. Time we celebrated something around here."

Eden's eyes widened. "Karl, that's, we can't just…"

"We can and we will." Karl's voice carried the authority of a man who'd made up his mind. "Our boy's home, Eden. That's worth more than any harvest."

He punched numbers on his phone. "Jake? Yeah, it's Karl. Listen, we're having a barbeque tonight. That's right, tonight. Ethan's home… Yeah, you heard right. My boy's back. Tell Miguel, Carlos, Tommy, and Luis. Bring the families. Kids too. Tawi's handling the beef… What? Of course, there'll be beer and wine. Just get everyone here by evening."

Tawi was already moving, energy filling his frame. "I'll need help with the pit. That beef's been aging perfect, it'll take some time but…" He glanced at Ethan. "Your boy looks like he could use a proper meal anyway."

"I don't…" Ethan started, overwhelmed. "You don't need to…"

"Yes, your dad's decided," said Eden. "These men, their families, they're part of this place. They need to see you're back. And you need to see that you still belong here."

Within minutes, the quiet homecoming transformed. Karl headed out to help Jake prepare the fire pit behind the main house. Tawi commandeered the kitchen, pulling marinades and rubs from the pantry, muttering happily about smoke rings and bark formation. Eden began gathering plates and glasses, her movements quick and sure.

"Mom, let me help," Ethan said, standing unsteadily.

She paused, studying him. "You remember where we keep the folding tables?"

"Barn storage, back left corner."

"Good. You're not so far gone you forgot everything." She smiled. "Get Jake to help you. Those tables are heavy, and you look like a strong wind could knock you over."

As Ethan headed for the door, he could already hear trucks pulling up, voices calling across the yard. The fog pressed close but couldn't dampen the sudden energy crackling through the ranch. His father's voice boomed instructions about firewood. Tawi emerged from the kitchen carrying the beef, a beautiful, marbled side that must have weighed sixty pounds.

"Haven't done this in too long," Jake said when Ethan found him by the barn. The older man's weathered face split into a grin. "Good to see you back, Ethan. Real good." He gripped Ethan's shoulder briefly, then gestured at the tables. "Come on, let's get these set up. Maria's already asking where her kids are supposed to sit."

The next hour blurred past. Tables appeared under the oak trees. Lights were strung from branches. The fire pit roared to life, sending smoke and sparks into the fog. Families arrived in beaten pickups, kids tumbling out and racing across the yard. The women gravitated toward Eden, arms full of side dishes, tamales, rice, beans, salads that hadn't been planned but appeared anyway.

Ethan found himself swept into the preparation, his body remembering the rhythms even if his mind struggled to keep up. He helped Jake Fisher arrange benches, listened to Miguel's story about the new calf born that morning, watched Carlos's kids chase chickens around the yard.

The smell of beef beginning to cook drew everyone toward the pit. Tawi presided over the fire like an ancient priest, turning the meat with practiced efficiency, basting it with a mop made from old towels tied to a stick. The smoke mixed with fog, creating a haze that smelled like home.

"This," Karl said, appearing at Ethan's elbow with two beers, "this is what you forgot about, isn't it? Not the land or the vines. This."

Ethan accepted the beer, looking around at the gathering, these people who worked his family's land, who had kept things running while he chased ghosts in the city. Their easy acceptance of his return humbled him more than any lecture could have.

"Yeah," he admitted. "I forgot all of it."

"Well," Karl clinked his bottle against Ethan's, "now you remember. That's what matters."

The months ahead would still be difficult. He could feel them waiting. But for now, in the smoky twilight with the ranch hands' children playing tag between the tables and Tawi calling out that the beef would be ready soon, he was home.

The rest would come. But first, this celebration. First, this gift of welcome he didn't deserve but was being given anyway. First, the slow work of becoming whole again in the only place that had never stopped believing he could.

CHAPTER SIX

WESTERN COASTAL RANGE

SONOMA

"Wine intoxicates for a time, but the end is bitterness."
Rachel Renée Russell

The fog clung to the vine rows like accusations. Ryan Weinhardt's boots left dark prints in the dew-slicked grass as he climbed toward the crown of the hill at three in the morning, needing air, needing distance from the conversation that had driven him from bed. The world at this hour was colorless, caught between night and the first false promise of dawn. This spot usually brought him peace but not now. Not the morning after Ethan returned.

His chest still burned from last night. The betrayal. The party. The sound of guitars and laughter while he stood outside, listening to his father celebrate his brother's return. Yesterday morning had been simple. Hot branding new livestock, the smell of singed hide and sweat, honest work that meant something. Then the drive to Healdsburg for the equipment auction, trying to stretch every dollar, making the ranch work while his brother burned through millions. He'd returned late, expecting quiet.

Instead, singing. Celebration. Jake meeting him at the barn, telling him about the barbecue, the spontaneous party for Ethan's homecoming.

"Your brother showed up this morning," Jake had said. "Looking rough. Your folks welcomed him back like a hero. Tawi's but beef on the grill. Miguel and Carlos brought their guitars."

The words had hit like a branding iron. They'd never seen Ethan these past years, only heard stories. Friends visiting from the city, whispering about his lifestyle. The drugs. The women. The clubs where he'd throw around money like confetti. Bragging about deals, about changing the world with AI while the ranch scraped by on tight margins.

Later, Karl had found him by the trucks, still in his work clothes, dust from the morning's cattle work mixing with road grime from Healdsburg. "Ryan, come in and join us. Ethan's home. I'm so thrilled. Tawi's cooking barbecue, your mother's making her apple crisp."

That smile on his father's face. Like nothing had happened. Like the last ten years hadn't happened.

The fight that followed still echoed in his head. His father's tears, that hand on his shoulder, the talk of forgiveness and rejoicing. Three million dollars gone. Their safety net. Their future. And Karl wanted to celebrate.

His house sat among the oaks, close enough to hear the celebration but far enough to pretend otherwise. Briana met him at the door, already fuming. "Ethan's home and they've thrown a party?" She didn't hide her anger, but something else flickered beneath it. "You've held this place together. He runs off, burns through millions, comes crawling back, and gets a barbecue?"

They'd talked through dinner, voices low so Sophia and Ryan Jr. wouldn't hear details. But now, in the darkness of their bedroom, the real conversation began.

"Still awake?" Briana's whisper.

"Can't stop thinking about it."

"I don't understand how your father can overlook everything."

"He's always been quick to forgive. But this is different."

Ryan shifted, the mattress creaking. "You know what makes it worse? I've been trying for months to get Dad to listen about the Vidoc Noir. The new French variety I've been cultivating. Three years I've nursed those vines, and he barely acknowledges it exists."

"The experimental block near the eastern ridge?"

"Block 12." His voice carried bitter satisfaction. "Dad seems doubtful. But that's the point, we need to take risks, try new directions. The climate's changing, Bri. What worked for my grandfather might not work for Sophia and Ryan Jr."

"When will you know if it's successful?"

"A month or two. I'm planning a barrel opening, right after our families traditional one." Ryan stared at the ceiling in the darkness, Bri warm beside him. "I drove the harvest crew pretty hard last season. Pushed for perfection in every cluster. Dad just watched from the edge of the vineyard with this look, like he was proud and worried at the same time."

He shifted, turning toward her silhouette in the dark. "Sometimes it feels like even though I'm the one here, working the land, planning for the future, he only sees the son who left. And now that son gets a feast. "When Dad tasted the grapes that morning, his face went completely still. He rolled the juice around his mouth, spit, then tasted again. No nod of approval, no hand on my shoulder. Just this long silence before he muttered something about sugar levels and walked away." His voice dropped lower, barely above a whisper. "I know that look. It's not disappointment, it's worry."

He found Bri's hand under the covers. "*Driven, not guided.* That's what he told me once, late at night over whiskey. The words stuck like thorns.

Briana turned toward him, and in the dim light from the window, he saw something shift in her face. "Remember the day Ethan left?"

Ryan's stomach tightened. Of course he remembered.

"I was there," she continued, voice strange. "At the gate. Watching him load that ridiculous car he'd bought. He looked right at me."

The memory hung between them like fog. What she didn't say, what they never said, was how it had been before. Before she'd chosen. Before Ryan had won by staying while Ethan chased dreams. The three of them, tangled in feelings none of them had words for. Until Ethan made the choice easy by leaving.

"He never fought for anything real," Briana said, but her voice caught. "Never fought for ..." She stopped.

"For you." Ryan finished it. The old wound scarred over but never healed.

"I chose you," she said quickly. "I married you. We have children, a life."

"I know." But did he? In the darkness, with Ethan back, the old fears crept in. His brother, brilliant, charming when he wanted to be, the one who'd made leaving look like winning.

"I love you," Briana said, fierce now. "But I can't forgive him. For leaving. For coming back. For any of it."

Ryan pulled her close but felt the tremor in her body. Anger or something else. After ten years, Ethan still stood between them, even in their own bed. Suddenly the mood changed, she could sense it coming.

"I need air," Ryan said. He got out of bed, quickly slipping on his clothes, murmuring something about needing to process things as he headed out into the night. He's done this many times and Bri, had silently let him go, hoping he'd work it out. She understood it. It was the bitterness, not just towards Ethan but towards Karl too.

Now, standing on the ridge, that's when it hit him. The principle every vintner knew: some fruit had to be dropped before harvest. Even this late, with the clusters nearly ripe, you cut away the laggards, the ones that would never catch up, that would only dilute the wine if left to hang. One weak cluster could taint the whole lot.

His brother had always been the second crop, those late clusters that never ripened properly, that hung on past their time, stealing resources from fruit that mattered. Every year you had to make the same choice: leave them and compromise the vintage or cut them away. But Karl wouldn't drop him. Wouldn't make the hard choice that every good vintner knew was necessary.

So, Ryan would.

He thought of Briana's face when she'd mentioned that day. The tremor in her voice. After all these years, Ethan still had some hold, even if she denied it. That made the cutting even more necessary.

The plan solidified as he gazed out over the land. Make Ethan prove himself. Put him in positions where he'd fail. Let the ranch itself reject him, the way a vine rejects a bad graft. And if Briana watched Ethan fail, watched him reveal his true nature, maybe those old feelings would finally die.

But another thought came, unwelcome: what if the graft took? What if Ethan had actually changed? What if his return strengthened the family vine instead of weakening it? No. Ryan had stayed. Had worked every harvest, every pruning, every day of drought and plenty. He'd earned his place by fidelity, not by charm. The ranch was his by right of sweat, not just birth.

Then as the fog pressed closer, a memory came. One of afternoon coffee in town, how it had started so simply, just needing escape from the bitterness that lingered at home. The café was warm, but the conversation was even warmer, unexpected as tasting a varietal you'd never tried before. Complex notes that lingered on the tongue. It all started with Caitlin's smile at just the right moment. The bitterness had opened spaces in him he hadn't known existed, hollow places where justifications grew like volunteers between the vine rows.

If Bri still carried that flicker in her eyes when Ethan's name came up, if his dad threw money at his brother's every whim, well. A man could only be expected to bear so much. Having sensed Bri's unspoken but underlying duplicity at Ethan's return made this memory more justifiable.

He walked back to the house, feet cold now on soil that knew his steps better than any other. The earth here was honest. It gave back what you put in, no more, no less. Not like people, who could smile and harbor old loves, who could choose favorites among sons who'd stayed and sons who'd fled.

The fog had swallowed the stars by the time he slipped back into bed. Briana moved against him, murmuring something he couldn't catch. Her hair smelled like the lavender soap she'd used for years, familiar and safe. His hand found her hip, possessive, even as guilt twisted in his chest like a corkscrew.

Tomorrow, he'd begin. Not the real pruning, that was months away. But this close to harvest, you still had to cut away the diseased clusters, the ones that would spoil the rest. Ethan was like those late season grapes that never ripened right, that threatened to taint everything they touched. Some fruit simply had to be dropped. All it would take is an attitude. Frowns instead of smiles. Bitter words at the right moment.

But Ryan wouldn't cut him out. Not yet. That would be too clean, too merciful. Instead, he'd do what his grandfather taught him with vines that didn't belong: isolate them. No shared knowledge, no decisions, no place at the table where real business was discussed. Let Ethan work the fields like any hired hand, sweat under the same sun, but never taste the wine he helped make. The ranch had ways of rejecting foreign grafts. The rootstock always knew what didn't belong.

The day would come when their father's papers would pass to him, when the deed would carry only one son's name. Then Ethan could find his own ground to fail on. Until then, Ryan would watch him the way you watched blight in a neighbor's vineyard, careful it didn't spread, patient for the season when you could finally close your borders. Some things you didn't forgive. You just waited for the earth to settle the score.

It was barely dawn, the morning after his return. Ethan's was still tired from lateness of the party, but when Tawi had appeared at the door of his room before sunrise, something in the elder's eyes had made refusal impossible.

The fog hadn't lifted yet. It clung to the hollows between hills, pooling like milk in a bowl. Ethan followed Tawi up the dirt path, boots slipping on wet grass, breathing hard in the thin morning air. The old Pomo moved with grace, never disturbing a branch, never startling the quail that burst from the brush ahead of Ethan's clumsy steps.

"You walk like a tractor off the road," Tawi said without turning, though his voice carried no harshness. "All noise and destruction."

"Sorry."

"Don't apologize. Learn." He stopped at a flat stone overlooking the valley, waiting for Ethan to catch up. The vineyards below disappeared into fog, only the highest rows visible like islands in a gray sea. "Sit."

Ethan sat. As a child, he'd found these morning lessons interesting but irrelevant, something to endure before real life began. Now, broken and returning, he understood they'd always been the real life. Everything else had been the distraction.

"First lesson," Tawi said, settling beside him with the patience of someone who had taught this before and would teach it again. "You remember how to walk, but you forget how to move. There's a difference. The earth knows when you fight against it."

He pointed to where Ethan's boots had torn the moss. "See? You push. The land pushes back. But watch." Tawi rose and took three steps, his feet finding the spaces between growing things. "Move with it, not through it. The vineyard will teach you this again, if you let it."

"I used to know this," Ethan said quietly.

"You did. And you will again." Tawi's weathered face showed something almost like kindness. "Learning the second time is different. Better, maybe. You understand now why it matters."

Tawi stood slowly, brushing dust from his worn jeans. "But walking right, that's just the beginning. Like learning to hold a pencil before you write." He gazed out over the fog-wrapped valley, hands clasped behind his back. "What I really need to teach you today is older than walking. Older than these vines your family tends."

He turned back to Ethan, and there was something ancient in his expression, like bedrock showing through soil. "Today, you start learning how to listen. Not with these," he tapped his ear, "but with everything you've forgotten you have. Life has been trying to tell you something long before you came home. Time you learned how to hear it."

"My people came to this land carrying stories," Tawi began, settling onto the stone like he'd grown from it. "Not in books. In memory. In the space between heartbeats where truth lives."

The fog began to burn away at the edges, revealing more of the ranch below. Eight thousand acres of Weinhardt land, but Tawi's people had been here first, for hundreds of years.

"Even we had writing once. Ancient marks on bark and stone. Sacred things. Long before we came to this land." His voice carried old grief. "Lost when my ancestors wandered from their roots, took up selfish ways. Burned it all, thinking new ways were better."

"Why burn it?"

"Same reason your brother wants you gone. Fear. Pride. Thinking tomorrow requires forgetting yesterday." Tawi pulled sweetgrass from his pocket, crushed it between his fingers. The smell mixed with fog and earth. "My mother taught me what survived. Not the marks, but what they meant. Treasures hidden in the heart."

A hawk circled overhead, riding thermals that didn't exist yet, waiting for the sun to create lift. Patient. Certain.

"Your family stands at a crossroads," Tawi continued. "Five generations on this land. Your father carries the values forward, but barely. Like trying to hold water in cupped hands."

"I know I failed him."

"Listen." The word cut sharp. "Your great-great-grandfather, Johann Friedrich Weinhardt, he understood. When wicked settlers came for my people, he stood between. Bought this land not for grapes but for sanctuary. The Pomo remember."

Ethan had heard pieces of this story, but never like this. Never with the weight of obligation.

"Friedrich learned from us about the land. But his real teachers were the Italians who worked these hills before him. They knew secrets. Old ways from the old country. How to listen to vines, read the fog, time the harvest by signs your universities never heard of."

"What happened to those secrets?"

"Same as always. Lost. Friedrich wrote them down, everything the Italians taught. But the journal disappeared when they built that grand house from redwood survivors of the 1906 fire. Hidden or mislaid, who knows? Prohibition came, making wine became crime. Knowledge scattered like ash."

The sun finally crested the eastern hills, turning fog to gold, then burning it away entirely. The ranch spread below them, beautiful and wounded.

"Why tell me this now?"

Tawi stood, joints creaking like old wood. "Because you came home empty. Good. Empty vessels can be filled. Your brother's too full of himself to hear what the land says. But you..." He studied Ethan with eyes that had seen too much. "You might be ready to search."

They walked back in silence, Ethan trying to move like Tawi, to leave no mark. He failed, but less than before.

CHAPTER SEVEN

WEINHARDT'S RANCH

SONOMA

"Men are like wine...some turn to vinegar,
but the best improve with age."
Pope John XXIII

The pounding on the door came at 4:47 a.m. according to the old clock on the nightstand. Ethan jerked awake, his body still trained to Silicon Valley's late starts, though two weeks home had begun to break that pattern. The old rhythms of work had been slowly settling back into his bones; walking through the vine rows at dawn, feeding cattle, his horse-riding instincts returning with each morning in the saddle. Each day had started early, but not as early as this one.

"Ethan." Karl's voice through the door. "Need you. Now. Another test, son." It seemed like there had been one each day.

The urgency cut through morning fog. Ethan pulled on yesterday's jeans, feet finding boots by muscle memory from summers long past. His old room remained exactly as he'd left it, work clothes still folded in the dresser, boots by the door, everything untouched as if disturbing it would have ended the hope that he'd come back. He'd found them waiting the night he retuned like an accusation or a prayer. Now he pulled on the familiar canvas jacket, the fabric stiff with years of waiting but already beginning to soften with use again.

In the hall, Karl was already moving. "Maverick's caught in wire. Bad."

They took the Kawasaki, Ethan hanging on as they bounced over ruts. Dawn barely cracked the eastern hills. The air bit cold, carrying copper and fear.

As the ATV jolted over rough ground, Ethan's mind flashed to his first night home. After the party, when the last truck had pulled away and the fire pit held only embers, Karl had found him on the porch.

"So. You really want to work?" His father had poured tequila into two glasses, the añejo he kept for occasions.

"I need to, Dad. Not just for money. I need to remember how things actually grow."

"This isn't coding. No quick fixes. No pivoting when things get hard."

"I know."

"Do you?" Karl had studied him over the glass rim. "Because tomorrow starts early. Every day starts early. And I won't be putting you with the field crew like Ryan expects. I want you with me. Not just the routine work, the decisions. The hard calls. If you're really back, you need to learn it all."

"Ryan won't like that."

"Ryan's not making this decision." Karl's voice had stayed steady. "You'll earn your place by showing up. Every day. No matter what."

"Some days," Karl had added, finishing his tequila, "test everything you've got."

The ATV lurched, snapping Ethan back to the present. At the corral, Jake Fisher and two other hands stood back. The young bay thrashed against fence wire wrapped around his forelegs. Blood ran dark in the dirt. Each movement tightened the wire, cut deeper.

Karl dropped to his knees in the mud beside the animal. "Easy, boy. Easy now."

Ethan crouched beside the fence, fingers digging for the wire cutters in Karl's tool bag. The colt's panic vibrated through the ground, each kick jarring his spine. Sweat beaded on his neck despite the cold. His pulse spiked, sharp, electric. For one blinding instant it felt like the club lights again, strobing behind his eyes, the rush before the crash. Adrenaline flooded his chest, the ghost of every high he'd ever chased.

Not now.

He forced his breath slow, in through his nose, out through clenched teeth, matching Karl's calm voice as his father murmured to the horse. He gripped the wire, the sting of the metal biting into his palms anchoring him to the moment.

The craving dissolved, not gone, just pushed back, replaced by the tangible, awful reality of Maverick's trembling body.

"I've got the cutters, here dad." he said, his voice steady again.

Karl looked up once, grabbed the tool. Then a quick nod, never seeing the war that had just raged inches behind his son's eyes.

The horse's eyes rolled white. Pain and panic. Karl's hands moved slow, careful, trying to find a way to cut the wire without causing more damage. But his hands trembled slightly, not from age or cold, but from something deeper.

Memory hit Ethan hard: fifteen years ago, same corral, different crisis. He was eighteen, two weeks before leaving for Stanford. The mare, Sienna,

Karl's first prize broodmare, down in the dirt, foaling gone wrong. Karl's hands working inside her, trying to turn the foal. Ethan holding the light, watching his father work through the night.

"Wrong way around," Karl had muttered. "Come on, girl. Work with me."

Hours of labor. The mare's breathing going shallow. Then finally, movement. The foal sliding free, covered in fluid and membrane. Not breathing. Karl had worked fast, clearing airways, rubbing the small chest. Nothing. Then, a gasp. The foal's first breath. Eyes opening.

"What should we call him?" Karl had asked, exhausted but smiling.

"Storm," eighteen-year-old Ethan had said. "Born in a tough night."

That colt had grown strong, steady. Became one of their best working horses. But with Duchess it was different, she threw difficult foals sometimes. Karl kept breeding her anyway, hoping.

Back in the present, the vet's truck pulled up. Dr. Sarah Wu moved with practiced efficiency. Sedative first, calming Maverick enough to examine the damage.

Behind her, Lauren Mitchell had climbed out of the passenger side, already pulling on gloves. She moved different than the vet, less clinical, more careful. Like she could feel what the horse felt. Her auburn hair caught the morning light as she knelt beside Maverick, one hand on his neck while Dr. Wu worked.

Ethan knew her. Or knew of her. The Mitchell ranch raised quarter horses two valleys over. Their families had done business back when he was a kid, but Lauren had been what, four years younger? A gap that meant everything in school, nothing now.

"Easy, boy," Lauren whispered to Maverick. The horse's breathing slowed under her touch. Even through the sedatives, even through pain, the animal responded to something in her voice.

Dr. Wu glanced at her assistant. "What do you think?"

Lauren's hands moved along the wounds, gentle but sure. Her face told Ethan everything before she spoke. "Both flexor tendons. Clean through." She looked up at Karl, and Ethan saw she'd been crying. Not dramatic tears, just wet tracks she hadn't bothered to hide. "I'm sorry."

Her face told the story before her words. "Tendons are severed. Both legs. Even if we could repair them, he'd never be sound. And with his temperament..."

Karl's jaw tightened. Maverick, born three years ago while Ethan was gone, another of Duchess's foals, her second to last. Karl had named him, maybe thinking of his absent son who'd always fought the bit. This colt had never taken to training. Threw every rider. Kicked through stall doors. Last month, Jake's ankle, seriously bruised when the horse struck out.

"Can't force a creature to be what it won't choose to be," Karl said quietly, more to himself than anyone. "That's the hardest part of loving something wild, accepting when it chooses its own destruction."

"I'm sorry, Karl," Dr. Wu said. "There's no good outcome."

Karl's face went still. But in his eyes, Ethan saw something terrible, the look of a man who'd already imagined making this choice with his own son. How many nights had Karl wondered if Ethan was dead in some valley mansion, overdosed on coke and whatever else they passed around at those parties that never ended? How many times had he prepared himself for the worst?

"I'll do it," Dr. Wu offered.

"No." Karl's voice came out rough. "My responsibility."

They moved Maverick to the oak grove, away from the other horses. Karl stayed close, hand on the colt's neck as Dr. Chen prepared the injection. The sedatives kept the horse calm now, head low, breathing steady. Lauren stayed close on the horse's other side, her hand never leaving his neck. She caught Ethan watching and held his gaze for a moment. Something passed between them, recognition maybe, or just shared grief for what was coming.

"You're Ethan," she said. Not a question.

"Yeah."

"So, you're back." Her voice stayed neutral, focused on the horse. But he caught the edge of curiosity, maybe judgment. Small towns talked. She'd have heard about the money, the crash, all of it.

"Two weeks ago."

Ethan stood back, watching his father's face. Saw the moment Karl's hand tightened on Maverick's mane, the same hand that had pulled Storm into the world, that had held hope for this one too. The slight tremor in his shoulders wasn't just grief for the horse.

The vet worked quick, professional. The horse's legs buckled. Karl guided him down, staying close, whispering something too low to hear. Then stillness. Morning light through the oaks. Birds starting their day, oblivious.

Lauren stood slower than the rest, her hand the last to leave Maverick's still form. She peeled off her gloves, movements automatic. "Every time," she said to no one in particular. "Every damn time it feels like the first time."

Dr. Wu touched her shoulder. "You did good. He went peaceful."

"Peaceful." Lauren tested the word like she didn't trust it. Then she looked at Ethan again, really looked at him. "You used to ride. I remember seeing you at the county fair. That black mare, what was her name?"

"Midnight." The memory surprised him. "That was..."

"Fifteen years ago. You won the barrel racing." A half-smile crossed her face. "I was twelve. Thought you were hot stuff."

"I probably thought so too."

"Probably?" Now she almost smiled for real. "My mom said you Weinhardts had good hands with horses but one of you, no sense with money. Guess she was half right."

The words should have stung. Instead, Ethan found himself almost laughing. "Which half?"

"Jury's still out." She headed for the truck, then turned back. "I'm sorry about Maverick. And..." She paused, seemed to reconsider whatever she'd been about to say. "Welcome home, I guess." She joined Dr. Wu in the truck and waved as they drove off.

Karl stood slow, mud on his knees, his hand coming away bloody from the wire cutters. "We'll bury him by his mother. Duchess died last winter. Another difficult birth."

The pattern laid bare. Karl breeding hope into heartbreak, again and again. Staying with each one to the end. But also, letting them choose their path, even when it led to this.

"Your mother asked me once," Karl said, not looking at Ethan, "what I'd do if you never came back. If the drugs or that life took you too far." He wiped his hands on his jeans. "I told her I'd grieve, but I'd accept it. Can't save someone who won't be saved. Love means letting them choose, even if they choose..." He gestured at Maverick's still form.

Ethan's throat closed. The weight of it, his father preparing to bury him too, if necessary. Loving him enough to let him destroy himself rather than force him home.

"Thank God you chose different," Karl continued, voice rough. "But I want you to understand, if you'd chosen the other way, part of my heart would be in that grave with you. Just like part of its going in the ground with this colt today."

They started walking back toward the house. Behind them, Jake started up the backhoe, diesel exhaust mixing with the smell of blood and earth, getting ready to dig a resting place. The machine's engine rumbled across the morning air, but it was the first bite of the blade through loam that cut into them, that mechanical scrape of metal through earth carrying the finality of it. They'd lost something special, something that couldn't be replaced by insurance claims or next season's breeding plans. The sound followed them down the hill, each scoop of earth a reminder that some choices, once made, couldn't be undone.

"You remember that night with Storm? You holding the light?"

"I remember."

"Two weeks before Stanford. You were already half gone, mind on the future. But you stayed up all night anyway. Helped bring him into the world." Karl paused. "That meant something. Even then, you could choose to stay when it mattered."

At the house, Ethan washed mud from his hands, watching brown water swirl down the drain. His father's pain wasn't abstract anymore. It had weight, history, and terrible resolve. Ten years of watching the road while prepared to accept the worst. Years of hope held alongside readiness to grieve.

Karl hadn't just been waiting. He'd been holding two futures in his heart, one where Ethan came home, one where he didn't. Ready for either. That was the real revelation: love that hoped for salvation but honored freedom, even unto death. The way Karl had stayed with Maverick to the end, present for the destruction as he'd been for the birth.

That kind of love didn't process like code. Didn't compute in the clean logic of Silicon Valley. It was messier, bloodier, more costly than any burned capital. It was divine in its terrible freedom, letting the beloved choose, even when the choice led to darkness.

And somehow, impossibly, Ethan had chosen to turn toward home. Not forced, not manipulated, but drawn by the same love that would have let him go. The miracle wasn't that Karl loved him, it was that Karl's love was strong enough to let him be lost, and patient enough to receive him when he chose return.

Part of Karl's heart was going in the ground today with Maverick. But Ethan was here, alive, muddy and present. Chosen and choosing. That was everything.

Walking back to the house, Ethan found himself thinking about Lauren Mitchell. The way she'd handled Maverick. The way she'd handled him, direct, no bullshit, but not cruel either. Like she'd already sized him up and decided to reserve judgment. He'd noticed her eyes too. Green. And her face, barely any makeup, just clean lines and natural grace. The kind of beauty that didn't ask for attention but got it anyway. He wondered what else she'd heard about him. What stories had made it back from the Valley. Probably enough to make any sane woman keep her distance.

But she'd remembered him winning that barrel race. Fifteen years ago, when everything had seemed possible and nothing hurt yet. Before he'd learned to run toward the wrong things and away from the right ones.

As the vet's truck was pulling away, dust rising in the morning light. Through the back window, he caught a glimpse of auburn hair.

Some of them just carry too much lightning inside.

Yeah. That about summed it up.

CHAPTER EIGHT

WEINHARDTS RANCH

SONOMA

"Wine is meant to be with food; that's the point of it."
Julia Child

Tawi's knife moved through onions in an even rhythm, the kind of steady work that calmed his thoughts. Garlic followed, then peppers, their colors sharp against the cutting board. He slid them into the pan where beef was already hissing, the kitchen filling with the smell before the men reached the porch.

He knew what the day had brought, grief rode back with them from the corrals, the kind that hangs in shoulders and settles behind the eyes. Food couldn't fix that, but it could steady it. It could give men something solid to hold when words fell short.

The screen door opened and shut. Karl came in first, dust clinging to his boots, his hat in his hands. Ethan followed, pale from the morning, shoulders still taut. Eden was already at the table, her coffee untouched, two extra plates set and idle at the far end, one for Ryan and one for Briana that no one moved.

Karl hung his hat on the peg. "Maverick's gone."

Eden's hand covered her mouth. "I thought as much… but how?"

"Wire cut him bad. Both tendons," Karl said, his voice flat. "No saving him."

Ethan leaned against the doorframe. His words came slowly, as though pulled out. "Lauren Mitchell was with the vet. She said he carried too much lightning inside him and no way to ground it. Dad stayed with him till the end."

The room went quiet except for the hiss of Tawi's pan. He turned the meat once, let it sear, then spoke without looking up. "That colt was fire from the day he dropped. Some you can't gentle, no matter how long you try."

Karl only nodded.

The back door creaked again, and Jake stepped in, wiping grease from his hands with a rag. "The ground's ready for Maverick, I covered him with a tarp."

"We'll head up there right after our meal," Karl replied.

"By the way, I got your Camry pulled up to the barn," Jake said, nodding toward Ethan. "Don't know how it made it this far. She's on her last legs, but I'll see what I can do."

Ethan gave a small, disbelieving laugh. "Neither do I. She was coughing the whole drive out of the Valley, running on fumes. I prayed through every hill. Didn't think she'd make it here alive. But, thanks for the effort."

Jake grinned. "Well, you and that car must have some stubborn streak in common. I'll tinker with her, see if I can squeeze out a little more."

They sat down together. Tawi brought platters of beef, vegetables still steaming, bread warm from the oven. For a while there was only the scrape of forks and the settling silence of people who needed food more than talk. Eden glanced at the other two untouched plates, then toward Ethan. "Ryan hasn't been by. Neither has Briana. Not once since you came home." She slid the extra settings a few inches back from the edge, then left them there, as if moving them farther would make it too final.

Ethan lowered his eyes. "Have you talked to them?"

"I've texted," Eden said. "No answer."

Jake tore off another piece of bread, chewing with approval. "Best meal I've had all week. Don't know how you do it, Tawi."

Karl nodded. 'This is incredible, Tawi. Whatever you're doing with those herbs..."

"That reminds me Karl, I've got to run to Sebastopol Market this afternoon and restock my pantry," said Tawi.

Eden's eyes stayed on Tawi. "That's just it. He's always been doing this for us. Ethan, do you remember the story of how Tawi came into the family?"

Ethan gave a faint smile. "So long ago, I've forgotten most of it."

Jake looked up from his plate. "I don't think I've ever heard it."

Karl chuckled, glancing at Tawi. "Then it's time someone told it again."

He leaned forward, his voice softening with memory. "Your mother, Tawi, was one of the strongest women I've ever known. Came to Eden's parents' place when times were lean. She cooked, kept the house, carried a load most men wouldn't shoulder. And she did it without complaint. When she passed, far too young. I told Eden we couldn't let you drift. You belonged here."

Eden nodded, her eyes distant. "I was so young, but I remember her baking bread. Always humming while she worked. I loved her presence more than I realized. Losing her was hard." She reached across the table, touched Tawi's hand. "When she was gone, you were twenty, but you carried on for her. Fixing things, running errands, doing what no one asked you to do. My father wanted you in the vines, but Karl saw what you carried, welcomed you to the Weinhardt's."

Karl's face broke into a small smile. "And I'll never forget that day you stepped into the kitchen when the cook left. One meal and I knew. You weren't just feeding us. You were holding us together."

Tawi shifted, embarrassed under their gaze. "I just did what I knew. Still do. Cooking's where I find myself. It's the only place I never felt like I was wearing another man's skin."

Jake looked around the table, thoughtful. "That's what makes a family, isn't it? Blood, sure. But also, the ones who hold you steady when things fall apart. Folks like that matter more than half the kin I know."

Ethan leaned back, his eyes on Tawi. "I took you for granted growing up. You were just always there, cooking, cleaning, steady. I didn't realize until now how much you gave us."

Tawi gave a small shrug. "That's the job. You feed people, you keep them standing. Everything else sorts itself out."

Karl smiled, pushing his plate back. "Wouldn't trade a day of it."

They lingered a little longer before Karl stood. "Time to bury Maverick. He'll rest beside Duchess."

Ethan rose with him. Jake stood too, folding the rag into his pocket.

The three men left together, the screen door slapping shut behind them, boots crunching gravel as they made their way toward the barn.

The kitchen grew still again. Eden's eyes lingered on the two empty place settings she had laid at the far end of the table and left untouched.

"Like I said earlier," she murmured, her voice low. "Ryan hasn't been by. Neither has Briana. Not once since Ethan came home."

Tawi stacked a plate into the sink, rinsing it under the stream. "He's stewing. Wants everyone to notice."

Eden pressed her hands against the table, her voice tight. "You know the history. Bri was torn once. Between the two of them. Ethan leaving made the choice for her, but it was never clean. She buried it, but I still see it in her face."

Tawi dried his hands, then sat across from her. "I saw it too. Back when they were young. Both boys carried a claim, though neither knew how to name it. When Ethan chose Stanford, Ryan chose to stay. Staying won her but winning that way leaves scars."

"She's loyal," Eden said quickly, then her voice softened. "But you're right. Part of her still looks over her shoulder. Sometimes I think she never stopped wondering what might have been."

"And Ryan feels it," Tawi said. "A man always knows. He may not speak it, but it eats at him. Every silence, every look, it grinds him down."

Eden's eyes filled. "That's what frightens me. His silence feels heavier than anger. And if Ethan... if Bri lets something slip..." She stopped herself, unable to finish.

Tawi's gaze held hers, steady as stone. "That's the danger of old wounds. They send out shoots that look healthy, even promising. But they drain the vine. They'll choke the fruit if you let them."

Eden's fingers tightened around her cup. "So, what do we do? Ryan's waited years to stand beside Karl, patient through everything. And now Ethan comes back, and it looks like favoritism. It's eating him alive."

"Looks cruel," Tawi said. "So does pruning. Cutting healthy shoots always does. But it's how you save the vine."

Her voice was almost a whisper. "And if it breaks them instead of saving them?"

"Then we trust the land," Tawi answered, his tone low and firm. "And the Lord who gave it."

Outside, the low thrum of the backhoe rolled in from the ridge, steady and unrelenting. Eden closed her eyes, lips moving in prayer, asking that her family, like the vineyard, might hold through the pruning still to come.

After she left, Tawi clean up and the walked to his truck. He hadn't forgotten. He needed those herbs for dinner.

The welcome home celebration had been the beginning. This family, all of them, blood and chosen, still had healing to do. But like good wine, it would take time.

The grafts need patience to take hold.

The Sebastopol Community Market always smelled like possibility, even on a busy afternoon. Caitlin pushed her cart past bins of organic apples, their waxy skins catching the filtered sunlight through the skylights. The produce section hummed with early shoppers, mostly older folks who knew the delivery schedule, knew which days brought the best deals.

She was reaching for a bag of discounted bell peppers when she heard her name. "Caitlin Ferranti?"

She turned to find Tawi standing near the herbs, a handful of fresh sage in one weathered hand. Time had added more lines to his face since she'd last seen him, deepening the grooves that bracketed his mouth, but his eyes held the same quiet warmth she remembered from childhood gatherings.

"Tawi." The name came out softer than she intended. "I didn't know you shopped here."

"Best herbs in the county." He lifted the sage slightly. "The Weinhardts expect a certain standard." His smile reached those dark eyes. "You've grown up."

She felt heat touch her cheeks. There was something in the way he looked at her, not inappropriate, but seeing. Really seeing. The high cheekbones she'd inherited from her mother's side, the olive skin from her father's Italian family, all of it mixing into something that confused most people when they tried to place her.

"How's your mother? And your sister?"

"Mom's..." Caitlin shifted the peppers in her hand. "She's getting older. Maria takes care of her now, down in Petaluma."

"Maria always was the strong one."

"She watches my daughter, Madison for me too. When I'm working and school's out."

"Madison." Tawi's expression shifted slightly, something flickering across his features. "Interesting name choice."

"Her father wanted it." The words came out flat. "Eric Krueger. We're not together anymore."

A woman squeezed past them, reaching for cilantro. The sharp green scent rose between them.

"How are things at the vineyard?" Caitlin asked, keeping her voice casual. "The Weinhardts treating you well?"

Tawi's pause lasted a heartbeat too long. "This family's been like my own for years. They're good people. Going through some changes.

She looked away, studying the price on organic carrots. "That's good. About Ryan, I mean. Working the land."

"Mmm." The sound held layers. When she risked a glance up, his eyes were on her. Not hard, not judging. Just... seeing.

"Ethan too. The land's good for him."

"Must be hard. Coming back."

"Sometimes that's what a person needs." His voice dropped lower, careful. "Home. Family. The simple things. The right things."

She busied herself with the carrots, aware of the flush creeping up her neck.

"Caitlin." Her name came soft. When she met his eyes, she found kindness there. And worry. "Some paths look easier than they are." He shifted the sage in his hand. "But you know that already. You've had enough hard roads."

She opened her mouth, closed it.

"Listen," she said quickly, needing to change direction. "Can I ask you something? About the tribal health services?"

His expression gentled, accepting the shift. Understanding why she needed it. "Of course."

"Madison needs... well, everything. Checkups, dental. And my insurance through the restaurant is terrible. I've been thinking about applying but..."

"But?"

She arranged the peppers in her cart, buying time. "I don't know. It feels like admitting I can't handle things. Like I'm taking something meant for people who really need it."

"You are people who really need it."

"I'm barely eligible. And the Italian name..."

"Your mother was Rose Pomo from Lake County. I knew her mother too. That blood doesn't thin just because you married outside." He set down his herbs, giving her his full attention. "The services are there for our children. Madison deserves healthcare."

"I just feel like I'd be judged. Single mom, can barely make rent on a waitress salary..."

"Who's judging? The aunties at the clinic?" A hint of humor touched his words. "They've seen everything. They're there to help, not gossip. Well, mostly not gossip."

Despite herself, she smiled.

"I can give you Barbara Sunrise's direct number. She runs enrollment. Good woman. Discrete." He pulled out his phone, squinting at the screen. "She'll walk you through everything."

While he looked up the number, Caitlin breathed in the mingled scents of basil and tomatoes from the next display. The market's background music played something folksy and forgettable. Normal Tuesday sounds. Normal Tuesday smells. Everything normal except the weight of secrets pressing against her ribs.

"Here." Tawi showed her the number, waiting while she entered it into her phone. "You call her. Tell her I sent you. Here's mine as well."

She typed his into her phone as well. "Thank you."

"Great, give me yours. That way, I can follow up."

After he'd type in her number, he said, "Caitlin." He picked up his sage again but didn't move away. "I want you to know something. If you need anything, anything at all, you call me. Or come by. I'm always there."

The way he said it made her throat tight. Like he knew she might need that lifeline sooner than later. Like he knew that some tangles couldn't be undone, only cut.

"I mean it," he continued. "I've watched you grow up. Watched you handle things that would break other people. You don't have to handle everything alone."

She managed a nod, not trusting her voice.

CHAPTER NINE

WEINHARDTS RANCH

SONOMA

"Bacchus has drowned more men than Neptune."
Thomas Fuller

The screen door banged open. Esther, Ethan's sister was back from her summer internship at UC Davis, her luggage forgotten in the car. "Ethan!" She practically tackled him, arms wrapped tight around his chest. They'd talked on the phone, but this was the first time she'd been home since he'd returned. She pulled back, studying his face like she needed to confirm he was really there, then hugged him again.

The rest of the afternoon she spent in the kitchen with Tawi, catching up while Ethan helped with dinner prep. They'd hand him spices as he called for them, pull roasts from the oven when the timer rang, lift lids that released clouds of steam and rosemary toward the ceiling.

The house was full of the smells of dinner, roasting meat, fresh bread, something with rosemary that made the whole kitchen side of the house smell like Sunday. Eden had just returned from the tasting pavilion. She'd spent three hours pouring for visitors in the pavilion that sat on a knoll overlooking the western vineyards.

Eden had overseen every detail of its construction years ago, insisting the wood stay unfinished, just cleaned and sealed, so visitors could see it for what it was. Something ancient, sacred to Tawi and his people, written in cambium rings too narrow to count without a lens.

Today had been typical for a Saturday in September, couples from the city, a few wine club members, one group that tried to treat it like Napa until they realized how much redwood tables weren't about tourist polish but working land. She'd poured the estate wines, told the story of the ranch's eight thousand acres stretching toward Cloverdale, the way the fog rolled in at the afternoon light bent gold across the vineyards.

Now, with her duties done and the pavilion locked until tomorrow, she'd returned to the main house, to enjoy the simple pleasure of watching her two children catch up after their years apart.

Stepping into the kitchen she watched as Ethan squeeze his sister shoulder and ask, "So U.C. was the right choice?"

"B.S. in Wine and Viticulture." She said it lightly, but pride flickered in her voice. "Four years of learning what you all do by instinct. Though I think my palate's getting better than Ryan's, don't tell him."

Eden looked up from where she sat, "She's being modest. Graduated near the top of her class. The professors knew her by name."

"Mom..."

"What? He should know." Eden's eyes moved between her children. "Your sister could work anywhere. Caymus called. Schramsberg too. She chose to come home."

Esther's cheeks colored. "This is home. Besides, someone needs to help this family realize what we're really making here. We've been underselling ourselves for years." Her fingers drummed against her leg. "I want to work with you mom on our tasting room. Maybe work toward my sommelier certification on the side."

"Educated sister," Ethan said. "Dad must be thrilled."

"He thinks I wasted money learning what he could have taught me for free." She smiled, but something tightened around her eyes. "I just need the next harvest to prove I'm more than book learning. That I can taste what matters."

"You will," Ethan said. "You always could see what the rest of us missed."

Karl entered from the porch, his shoulders carrying the long day. He had washed, but the smell of earth and diesel still clung to him. The loss of Maverick still weighed behind his eyes, even though he did not speak of it. He sat at the table as Tawi placed the platters down, his movements practiced, steady, the food steaming in the warm kitchen light.

The back door opened again. It was Briana.

Before Ethan's return she often came with Ryan for family meals bring the kids too. It was part of the rhythm of the place. But this time she was alone. For a moment she paused on the threshold, her eyes finding Ethan across the table. He stood to greet her, and in that instant, she was young again, watching him from the vineyard rows, bringing him water at harvest, just before he left and made her choice for her.

"Good to see you, Bri," Ethan said, his arms around her. She fit against him with a familiarity that pulled them both back to what might have been. For one dangerous second neither of them moved. Her perfume, something Ryan had bought her, could not mask the deeper scent that was just her, vanilla and honey, the same as that night in his truck when she had rested her hand on his thigh and he had not found the courage to close the space between them.

"You too." She pulled away first, though her hands lingered a moment on his arms. He was thinner now, worn down by what he had been through, but something in him reminded her more of the boy she had almost chosen than the man who had gone chasing another life.

Eden's voice broke the moment, carefully bright. "Come, sit. Tawi, bring an extra plate."

Briana found her seat, though her eyes flicked out the window, toward the corrals, recalling how she had seen Ethan near the fence with Lauren Mitchell was there for Mavrick. Even from a distance, she sensed the easy closeness and the look that passed between them.

Something twisted in her stomach. Not jealousy exactly, but grief for what had never been.

The meal began with the clatter of plates, Tawi moving between table and stove, serving and watching as he always had. He had set out the good plates simply, his voice carrying over the food and faces.

For a time, they ate in silence, broken only by the scrape of knives and forks, until Briana turned her gaze back to Ethan. It was the first time Bri had come to dinner since he'd returned two weeks ago. No sign of Ryan at the house, Karl had tried talking to him, Eden had gone by their place but here was Bri, a first step maybe.

"Dad told me what happened in the Valley," she said. She always called Karl "Dad," her respect for him long ago sealing her place at the table. "I know Ryan has his issues, but you're welcome here." The words came out steady, but something flickered beneath them, anger at what he'd put them through, mixed with something else she didn't want to name. Something that had no business surfacing after all these years.

Ethan kept his eyes low. "I know. Good to be home. Good to have a place to land. I told Dad I'll do whatever work needs doing. I can't blame Ryan for being bitter. I hope we can find a way through."

Her foot brushed his under the table. It might have been accident, but neither of them acknowledged it, and the spark of contact shot through her body with unwelcome memory.

Karl looked between them, his voice firm but not harsh. "I love both my sons equally. I've learned some things over the years about forgiveness. The heart wants what it wants, but the best path is to keep the family whole, working through instead of running away."

Eden saw it all, the way Bri's eyes lingered on Ethan's face, the way Ethan forced his gaze to stay on his plate, the tension carried between them like a live wire. It was a danger she had feared, and she prayed it would not unravel what fragile healing had begun.

When the meal ended, Karl stood, setting his hand on Ethan's shoulder. "North planting needs checking. Come with me, son."

He kissed Eden's cheek, squeezed Bri's shoulder in passing, and stepped out into the evening. Ethan followed, but as he passed Bri, his hand brushed her shoulder. She drew in her breath, startled, his thumb grazing the bare skin of her collarbone. Too brief to be called deliberate, but too clear to be accident. They both knew it.

He pulled his hand away and followed his father out. In the fading light his face was tight, as if he had remembered something he needed to cut off at the root. Eden caught his eye as he went. She gave a small, approving nod. He had chosen to walk away.

The ATV carried them into the vineyard. The rest of the evening slipped away in a blur of practical matters, equipment checks, reviewing the harvest schedule, Karl introducing Ethan to the new field workers who eyed him with curiosity. Now the day was nearly gone, the rows shadowed, the air cooling with the sea fog rolling in. They walked slowly, Karl's hands brushing the vines by habit, Ethan beside him listening.

"These vines are like children," Karl said at last, his voice carrying in the twilight. "You can't force them to grow the way you want. You train them, support them, prune when necessary. But in the end, they find their own shape."

They stopped where an old vine had once been cut nearly to the ground. New growth rose from the scar. Karl touched it with reverence. "Frost took this one three years ago. Could have torn it out, started fresh. But it found its own way to heal. Stronger now where it broke."

They moved on together, the rhythm of Karl's words weaving with the sounds of the night settling over the vineyard. He spoke of how he had stood at the ridge, watching the road for Ethan's return, of the hope he had held and the patience he had learned. Ethan walked in silence, humbled by the weight of it.

Later, when Ethan brought the ATV back to the equipment shed, the barn lights glowed dim against the fog. The smell of hay and oil hung heavy. Ryan stood in the doorway like a storm cloud. "So, you're back." His voice was flat, but anger pressed beneath it.

Ethan set down the wrench he had picked up. "I am."

Ryan stepped closer, boots heavy on the concrete. "I knew this would happen. Knew you'd come back when everything collapsed. And now here you are, sitting at Dad's table like nothing ever happened."

Ethan steadied himself, refusing to back away. "Yes. And I know you're angry. You have a right."

The words only sharpened Ryan's expression. His voice rose, bitter. He spoke of years of labor, of carrying the ranch, of being overlooked while

Ethan squandered what had been given. He spoke of forgiveness, of not believing in it, of resentment that would not let him go.

He stepped closer until his face was taut with fury. "And Bri," Ryan said at last, his voice dropping low. "She says she's angry at you, but I can feel it. There's still something there she can't name. Don't think I don't see it. Don't mess with that part of my life."

The words cut deep, hanging like barbed wire in the space between them. Ethan held still, refusing to strike back. Carlos, Jake's number two, appeared in the doorway, his timing merciful. "Ryan, pump in block seven is acting up."

Ryan turned without another word, walking into the night. Ethan called after him, but his brother did not turn back.

Carlos lingered a moment. "I can't say I blame him," he said. "You've got a lot to earn back. For all our sakes." He hesitated, then added, "Saw someone at the gate earlier. Fancy electric car. Asked for you by name."

Ethan felt the blood drain from his face. He walked down the drive, fog pressing close. At the gate the headlights still glowed, harsh against the dark. A Lucid Air stood waiting, its lines too sleek, too polished for this place.

The gull-wing door lifted, and Marcus Valdez leaned against the car, smiling like a predator.

"Beautiful place," Marcus called. "Can see why you came crawling back here."

The smell reached Ethan even from ten feet away, expensive cologne covering something chemical, something that promised escape and demanded its price. Marcus's smile cut in the half-light. "We need to talk."

The fog closed in; the vineyard swallowed in shadow. Ethan stood at the edge of the gate, the glow of the car alien against the dark fields, Marcus's presence like a shadow that had followed him home.

"So, Ethan," Marcus said. "Time to discuss your future."

Napa Valley

The Press Restaurant sat on the edge of St. Helena, far enough from the tourist crawl of Main Street to guarantee privacy. Cheri Morrison Krueger chose a corner table where she could watch both entrances, a habit from her consulting days that marriage to Eric hadn't broken. The old stone walls held the day's warmth against the cooling night air, and through the windows, the Mayacamas Mountains were just dark shapes against a darker sky.

Alejandro Vega arrived exactly on time, moving through the dining room like water finding its level. He'd traded his city suit for linen pants and an open collar, playing the part of weekend visitor. But his eyes stayed sharp, taking in exits, other diners, the way Cheri had positioned herself with her back protected.

"Traffic from the city heavy?" she asked as he sat.

"I came up last night. Rented an Airbnb in Calistoga for the weekend. Beautiful property. Pool, private vineyard views." He ordered wine without looking at the list. "The 2016 Scarecrow Cabernet."

"Eric thinks I'm at a spa evening with my sister." Cheri crossed her legs, silk dress whispering against the leather banquette. "She's covering for me. Again."

"Family loyalty. Useful trait." Vega waited while the sommelier poured, performed the ritual of tasting, approving. When they were alone again, he studied her over his glass. "Tell me about the progress."

"Otto's got plans to start a rumor about diluted vintage, and public media exposure. Then the offer to the workers next. He'll disrupt their harvest, throw a wrench into things at the critical moment." She took a long sip of wine; let it warm her throat. "The Kruegers have backup plans if that fails. But the real opportunity is Ryan Weinhardt. He's been seeing my husband's ex-wife."

"Eric's ex?"

"Caitlin Ferranti. Pathetic creature, really. Waiting tables in Healdsburg, living off tips because her AA degree in community development is worthless." Cheri smiled, remembering her own calculations with Eric. How easy it was to make a man believe what he wanted to believe. "But she knows the wine families. Knows what she lost when Eric divorced her. She's working Ryan hard, hoping for a second shot at being Sonoma royalty. Making him promises about what they could do together when he inherits."

"Men and their weaknesses." Vega's fingers brushed hers, deliberate now. "What else?"

"Ryan's sick of watching his father coddle Ethan. Keeps telling Caitlin that when the ranch is his, the prodigal son gets nothing. She feeds that resentment every shift she works, every cheap apartment she goes home to."

"Good. That bitterness will make him easier to move." He leaned back. "How's Hans handling our arrangement? It's been a year. I'd like an update."

"Hans appreciates where the money comes from. Always has. That kind of cash doesn't just appear." She paused. "But knowing and accepting are different things. He's asking about exit strategies."

"Then perhaps it's time to clarify their position." His voice carried weight despite its softness. "My associates don't appreciate second thoughts.

You might remind the Kruegers what happens to those who try to renegotiate."

The waiter appeared with menus. Vega ordered for both of them without asking. Oysters. Crudo. Things eaten raw, tasting of the sea.

"How direct should I be?"

"Tell them about the family in Coahuila. Respected vintners. Three generations. Until they decided our partnership was too risky." He traced the rim of his glass. "The father disappeared first. Then the eldest son. The authorities found them eventually. In separate provinces. In separate pieces."

"Hans will understand."

"He better. The younger son still runs the vineyard. Very cooperative now." His eyes met hers. "Amazing how losing everything you love improves focus."

The oysters arrived, ice and lemon and the smell of the ocean. Cheri ate one slowly, aware of his eyes on her throat as she swallowed. The restaurant was filling now, but their corner stayed private, protected by shadow and the discretion money bought in a place like this.

"Your rental in Calistoga," she said. "The one with the pool."

"Very private. The neighbors are away."

He smiled, and she remembered that first meeting at the Vintner's Gala, how he'd appeared at her elbow just as she was watching Eric flirt with another woman. How he'd known exactly what to offer.

"I have a bottle of '82 Mouton Rothschild I've been saving."

"For special occasions?"

"For new beginnings." He signaled for the check. "Ultimately, Lucien has decided that the Kruegers won't be part of our future. Too much old thinking. Too many connections to the past. But you understand evolution. Adaptation."

Cheri had seen this coming. All the more reason for a night like this with Vega.

Later as they left, Cheri touched her phone, typed quickly. Sister confirming the spa story, extending the alibi. Eric would be three drinks deep by now, wouldn't notice if she came home at all. She stood, smoothed her dress, felt the weight of the decision but not the doubt. "I'll follow you," she said.

Outside, the valley was purple with dusk. The mountains held the last light like a secret. Somewhere in those hills, the Weinhardts were checking their grapes, worrying about sugar levels and weather, never knowing the harvest was already lost. That forces were moving around them like fog, invisible until it was too late to run.

Vega's hand found the small of her back, guiding her to the parking lot. Professional. Protective. Possessive in a way Eric had never been. "Remember," he said quietly. "Fear is a vintage that ages well. Let the Kruegers taste just enough to keep them focused. Hans is smart. He'll realize the clock is ticking."

"And after? When your associates control both properties?"

"New management will be needed. Someone who understands that wine is just another business. That sentiment is weakness." He opened her car door. "The future belongs to those who aren't afraid to take it."

The drive to Calistoga took twenty minutes. Long enough to think about families torn apart, about men who thought they could change their minds after taking cartel money. Not long enough to change her mind.

Behind her, Vega's headlights stayed steady, patient. Like everything else about him, measured and certain and moving toward an outcome that felt inevitable as gravity.

The Kruegers would get their reminder. Hans would swallow his escape fantasies. Eric would drink himself deeper into uselessness. And somewhere, Ryan Weinhardt was listening to his brother's ex-wife whisper about the empire they'd build together, never knowing he was already bought and sold.

Everyone had their leverage. Everyone had their price. Cheri had learned long ago that survival meant knowing both and using them without hesitation.

CHAPTER TEN

WEINHARDTS RANCH

SONOMA

"Wine is a turncoat; first a friend and then an enemy."
Henry Fielding

So, Ethan. It's time to discuss your future.

The words hung in the night air like smoke from a distant fire. Ethan stood at the gate, the fog pressing close, the vineyard swallowed in shadow. Headlights from the Lucid Air Grand Touring threw harsh beams across the gravel, its platinum finish catching glints of the barn light far behind him. The man leaned against the car, perfectly at ease in designer jeans and a linen shirt rolled to the elbows, that practiced casual that cost more than most people's rent.

"What are you doing here, Marcus? How did you even find me?"

Marcus smiled, that connector's smile he'd perfected in a thousand Valley meetings. "Come on, hermano. You've got friends who care about you. Wasn't hard to track down where the prodigal landed." He paused, eyes drifting across the vineyard rows marching up the hillside. Something flickered across his face, not the appreciation of a wine lover, but something deeper, older.

The evening breeze carried the smell of turned earth and new growth. Marcus breathed deep, and for a moment his polished facade cracked. Ethan caught a glimpse of something raw underneath.

"My old man worked rows like these," Marcus said quietly, almost to himself. "Central Valley. Stockton. But also here in Sonoma, strangely enough. I have a little history here too."

He looked at Ethan with something like amusement. "You never knew that did you? Miguel Valdez. Died thinking I'd betrayed everything he stood for. Maybe he was right."

"Marcus...."

"But that's not why I'm here." The Valley operator reasserted itself, smooth as aged Cabernet. "There are people who miss you, Ethan. Kat's been asking about you."

The name hit like a physical thing. Kat. Her laugh in the blue haze of Neural Link. Her skin in the morning light of his Atherton place. The way she'd looked at him that last night, not with love but with the cold calculation of someone cutting losses.

"Didn't look that way when I left," Ethan managed. "She'd found other places to land long before I crashed."

"People change their minds. Regret things." Marcus pushed off the car and moved closer. The Lucid's headlights threw his face into sharp relief, shadows carving deeper lines beneath his eyes. "Besides, there are opportunities beyond just… personal reconnections."

Ethan stayed by the gate, hands gripping the wood. He could feel splinters working into his palms, real pain, honest pain, nothing like the synthetic numbness he'd chased for years.

"Your family's got a good name here," Marcus continued, "but they're not the only players. There are people, successful people, who remember what you built with Athena. Who think you got a raw deal. They'd back you again, Ethan. Real money. Real support."

"I'm done with that world."

"Are you?" Marcus reached into his jacket, casual as breathing. "You left something behind at Neural Link that night. After everything went sideways."

He held out his hand, palm cupped. Ethan didn't need to look to know what nested there, small, white, familiar as morning coffee. "Must be hell," Marcus said softly. "All this guilt. You told me what it cost your family to fund your dream. I'm sure your brother looking at you like you're poison. The workers pretending they don't know things have been lean since then. I can't imagine how you're sleeping."

The pill sat there between them, catching the last light like a tiny moon. Ethan remembered the taste, the climb, the blessed nothing that followed. His body remembered too, mouth suddenly dry, heart picking up tempo.

"There's more," Marcus said, letting his hand drop when Ethan didn't reach for it. "Things happening in this valley that might surprise you. Changes coming. The people I represent, they're looking for allies in Sonoma. Someone who understands that sometimes the old guard needs to make way for new growth."

"Get out." The words came from somewhere deep, somewhere Karl's voice lived in his bones. "Whatever you're selling, I'm not buying."

"Think about it." Marcus slipped the pill back in his jacket, pulled out a business card instead. "You really want to spend the next forty years pruning vines? After everything you've seen, everything you've built? The world's rewriting itself with AI, and you're here playing farmer?"

He held out the card. Ethan kept his hands on the gate.

Memory crashed in, Karl's hand steady on Maverick's neck as the injection went in. The weight of that choice, the terrible freedom of letting something choose its own end. His father's words: *Can't save someone who won't be saved.*

But Karl had waited. Had held possibility and grief in equal measure. Had chosen to hope even while preparing to mourn.

"The old Ethan might have been interested," Ethan said finally. "But he's dead. Had to put him down. It was time."

Marcus's smile faltered, just for a moment. Then he shrugged, set the card onto the gatepost. "We'll see. You know how to reach me when reality sets in."

The Lucid pulled away silent as fog, taillights painting the dusk red. Ethan watched it climb the hill, pause at the overlook. He could imagine Marcus up there, making his call, reporting failure.

The card fluttered in the evening breeze, expensive paper that probably cost more than a glass of their wine. Ethan plucked it off the post, tore it in half, quarters, eighths. Let the pieces fall into the dirt. But as he walked back toward the house, he could still feel it, the phantom weight of that pill in his hand, the promise of escape, the whisper that said he didn't have to carry all this weight.

Can't save someone who won't be saved.

But Karl had waited. Had held possibility and grief in equal measure. Had chosen to hope even while preparing to mourn.

And maybe that was the real miracle, not that someone could save themselves, but that grace waited patiently for them to stop running. That love held the door open, no matter how far they'd wandered. All Ethan had to do was walk through it, one step at a time.

The same grace that had brought him home now asked him to keep choosing it, day by day, vine by vine. The night settled over Sonoma Valley like a blanket, covering old wounds and new conspiracies alike. Tomorrow would bring the next move in a game that had been playing since before Ethan was born. But tonight, he walked through his father's vineyards, choosing each step, choosing to stay.

Miles away, Marcus pressed the call button on his steering wheel, the phone rang once and a then an irritated female voice filled the car. "Cheri here." Marcus could hear a man's voice background, soft jazz mixing with laughter. Cheri was clearly not happy having whatever she was doing, interrupted by this call.

"It's Valdez. I made the approach, but Ethan didn't bite."

"You made the offer?"

"Yes, I don't think he's playing. He's... different. Harder."

"Very well," came the response. "I'll take it from here."

"Understood. Will you escalate?"

"You'll be instructed." Then the line went dead.

Headlights from distant trucks cut briefly across the low fog before vanishing again. Somewhere here years ago, his father had bent his back over vines, not just in Stockton, but here in Sonoma. The same fields where the Kruegers now grew their grapes. The connection ran deeper than anyone knew.

Nearby, the Krueger estate glowed against the night, every window lit, the main house standing bright above the darkened vines. Inside, Hanns Krueger looked at the text message on his phone. It was his daughter in law. *Ethan Weinhardt's not going to work. We'll need another approach.*" That was all.

Hans turned to his sons Eric and Otto. His eyes drifted to the window, to the eastern parcels, a faint outline in the darkness, that now stretched five thousand acres. Prime land, producing some of the choicest wine in the county. Twenty acres had become an empire. He wished he could share this moment with their mother. Greta had been his wife for twenty years, his partner in building all of this from nothing. But she had died giving birth to Otto, and that void had never been filled. Not for lack of trying. There had been women since, brief affairs that burned hot and faded fast. None of them lasted. None of them could.

But all that expansion, all those perfect scores and gold medals, couldn't wash away the bitter taste in his mouth. Karl Weinhardt had "helped" them with that first parcel, played the generous neighbor, the established family lending a hand to struggling newcomers. Then watched them scrabble for respect while he kept the real treasures, the heritage sites, the century-old vines, the relationships with distributors, for his own blood. Hans had gradually grown, not just to envy the Weinhardts but hate them. That's when he'd decided to longer just to compete with them but destroy them.

Hans set down his phone, shaking his head. "The younger brother's proving difficult, Cheri just confirmed it."

"That's what I told you when Cheri suggested him," Eric said, not bothering to hide his satisfaction. "Putting all her hopes on some supposed mover and shaker in the valley? From what I hear, Ethan's over that life. But dad, I went with it since you wanted to let her try."

"The woman's got brains, Eric. Connections in the Valley," Otto said, swirling his cognac. "Where is she anyway?"

"Spa weekend with her sister."

Otto's eyes flickered with something that wasn't quite brotherly interest. "The Canyon Ranch again? That place does wonders. Worth every penny, I'd imagine."

"Ten grand for a long weekend," Eric said, leaning back with the satisfaction of a man who could afford to keep his wife polished to perfection. "Her sister's bill too. But you should see them when they come back. Like they've been dipped in gold."

"I'll bet," Otto murmured, taking another pull from his e-cigarette. "Your wife certainly knows how to... maintain her assets."

Eric's smile was all teeth. "Best investment I ever made. Happy wife, happy life. Especially when she looks like Cheri."

"She's got a good head on those pretty shoulders too," Hans added. "That Valdez idea wasn't bad. Just didn't pan out."

Eric's jaw tightened almost imperceptibly. "Since when do we run family business decisions through my wife? Used to be you'd ask your sons first."

Otto glanced between them. "She understands the tech world, Eric. Her connections...."

"I know what her connections are," Eric cut in. "I married her, remember? I'll be sure to remind her when she gets back that her little plan failed."

Otto drew deeply on his e-cigarette, releasing the smoke like a human dragon, pushing his vengeance on the Weinhardts as if it was a medieval curse. "I'm going to reach out to Rouke at the Register."

"Good." Hans moved to the window, looked west toward the Weinhardt lands. "It's time to set the second stage of our plan in motion. If we can't turn the prodigal, we'll find a way to destroy the whole family."

"Public rumors?" Eric's laugh held no warmth. "That's Otto's strategy? Dad, we need something with more... impact."

Otto studied his sibling. "You have a better idea, big brother?"

"Go ahead Otto, let it play out, but when you and dad are done with the gossip campaign, let me know. I have my own approaches."

Chapter Eleven

Healdsburg

Sonoma County

"Wine can of their wits the wise beguile."
Homer, The Odyssey

The second-floor offices of the Sonoma Register occupied a building that had survived the 1906 earthquake but looked like it might not survive the digital age. Jim Rourke sat at his desk, the morning fog still pressed against the windows, obscuring Healdsburg's historic plaza below. The newsroom smelled of burnt coffee and dying ambitions, four reporters where there used to be twelve, empty desks gathering dust like monuments to better times.

Rourke tore open the morning mail with practiced indifference. Twenty years in the wine beat, and he'd carved out a reputation as the valley's unofficial conscience, the guy who'd call bullshit on inflated scores and manufactured terroir stories. But conscience didn't pay for his kids' orthodontics or his wife's patience with late nights chasing leads that went nowhere.

"Hey Rourke," Pete Gaither called from across the room, not looking up from his screen. "You see the Healdsburg High water polo match last night? Destroyed Windsor in the semifinals."

"Yeah, saw it." Jim didn't mention he'd been at the pool, watching his son ride the bench for three quarters. Another thing that didn't pan out as promised.

He reached for his nicotine packet, three months without cigarettes, but the habit of needing something remained. The envelope in his hand felt different. Heavier paper, no return address. Anonymous mail usually meant crazy conspiracy theories about chemtrails affecting grape yields or secret Chinese buyers monopolizing vineyards. But this one made him sit up straight.

Look into the Weinhardt family operation. A former employee came to me claiming they're blending inferior Central Valley bulk wine into their estate bottles while maintaining premium prices. Their reputation for integrity might be more marketing than reality. You should investigate.

At the bottom: *For more information: truthinwine47@protonmail.com*

Jim stared at the letter. The Weinhardts. Eight thousand acres on Sonoma's western slopes, fifth-generation family operation. Karl Weinhardt was considered untouchable, the kind of old-school vintner who still believed handshakes meant something. His wines consistently scored in the mid-90s, commanded prices that made even Napa producers envious.

The timing was interesting. Just last night, Lisa had gotten off the phone with Briana Weinhardt looking shaken. They'd maintained their friendship since high school, not best friends exactly, but close enough that Briana called when she needed to vent. Their friendship had deepened over the years, especially after their kids ended up on the same soccer team. Nothing bonds mothers quite like sharing duties at weekend tournaments and commiserating over orange slice rotations.

Briana had called to unload about brother-in-law Ethan's sudden return from Silicon Valley. The prodigal son, back from his disaster, apparently looking like death warmed over. Over the years, Lisa had become Bri's sounding board for all the family drama, Ryan's resentments, Karl's stubborn optimism, the slow bleeding of assets to fund Ethan's dreams.

"Remember when I told you about the land sales?" Lisa had said, pouring herself a second glass of wine. "When Bri first told me they were selling off the Dry Creek parcels? Well, now we know why. Three million, Jim. That's what they lost on Ethan's startup. Karl sold vineyards that had been free and clear for decades. All to fund that AI company and whatever else Ethan was doing down there."

Jim had known about the land sales, public records were part of his beat. The Dry Creek parcels had gone to a Chinese investment group for well below market. At the time, he'd wondered why the Weinhardts were liquidating assets. Lisa had mentioned back then that Bri said it was for "family investments," but the details had been vague.

"Bri says Ryan's furious," Lisa had continued. "Ethan shows up after losing everything, and Karl throws a party for him like the last ten years never happened. Like those three million dollars never vanished."

Memory flickered, unwanted. Summer before senior year. Briana Larsen at the county fair, golden in the agriculture barn's dusty light. Her family, descended from Danish settlers who'd planted some of the valley's first vines, carried their own weight in local history. He'd finally worked up courage to ask her to the harvest dance. She'd looked through him like he was fog off the Pacific, turned back to her 4-H friends without a word. Later she'd dated both Weinhardt boys before marrying Ryan, the older one.

According to Lisa, that triangle had been its own drama. Briana caught between the brothers, finally choosing stability over whatever wild energy

Ethan represented. Now Ethan was back, and Bri was apparently handling it about as well as Ryan was which is to say, not at all.

Jim opened his laptop, created a new ProtonMail account. The Weinhardt story could be huge, corruption in wine country's first family, the fall of an institution. Above the fold material. Maybe even picked up by the Chronicle or the Times.

But as he typed his response to truthinwine47, something nagged at him. Anonymous sources with axes to grind rarely led anywhere good. And going after the Weinhardts meant going after everything Sonoma wanted to believe about itself, that quality still mattered, that family legacies meant something, that not everything had been corporatized and compromised.

His editor, Tom Castellanos, descended from one of the valley's original Mexican land grant families, appeared at his office door. "Morning story budget in ten, Jim. You got anything?"

"Maybe." Jim minimized his email. "Got a tip worth checking out."

"Wine business?"

"Yeah."

"Make it sexy. We need clicks. That story about the counterfeit cult Cabs did great numbers last month."

After Tom left, Jim looked back at the letter. Three million in losses. Land sold off to fund a failed dream. And now anonymous allegations of wine fraud. The Weinhardts were either victims of terrible timing or they'd found their breaking point.

Financial pressure like that could make good people consider bad options. Blending in cheap Central Valley juice to maintain cash flow while keeping up the premium facade. It would be easy enough; a few percentage points of bulk wine wouldn't change the flavor profile much but could dramatically improve margins.

Jim hit send on his email to truthinwine47, then walked to the window. The fog was lifting, revealing Healdsburg's mix of old California charm and new money polish. Teslas parked outside hundred-year-old buildings. Tasting rooms that looked like Apple stores selling wine at software margins.

The Weinhardts represented something older, more rooted. Part of him hoped the tip was wrong. Part of him, the part that remembered Briana's dismissive glance, that covered water polo matches and school board elections while dreaming of bigger bylines, hoped it was all true.

Everyone had their reasons for compromising. Maybe the Weinhardts had found theirs.

Jim returned to his desk, pulled up his files on the family. Time to dig deeper. According to Lisa's call with Bri, Ethan had been back just weeks. If the family was under enough pressure to commit fraud, his return might be the catalyst that exposed it all.

The nicotine packet had lost its kick. He reached for another, thinking about integrity, about compromise, about the stories we tell ourselves while slowly poisoning what we claim to love.

Outside, Healdsburg went about its morning rituals. Wine country's careful dance of authenticity and commerce, tradition and survival. And Jim Rourke, chronicler of its contradictions, prepared to pull another thread that might unravel it all.

Fifty miles west, where the same morning sun painted different shadows across the Weinhardt estate, another thread was already beginning to fray.

Ryan guided his bay mare along the eastern ridge, where the Weinhardt property kissed the Pacific horizon. Eight thousand acres of his sweat and sacrifice spread below him, but all he could taste was bitterness.

The morning fog had retreated to sea, leaving the air sharp with salt and eucalyptus. His phone showed one bar, barely enough, but the ridge always caught a faint signal from the tower near Jenner.

He'd needed to hear her voice.

"Hi Ryan, what's up," Caitlin's voice was warm and greeting as aways. He could hear Madison in the background chatting away about her cornflakes. "Get ready once you finished with your cereal. Mommy's got to chat with uncle Ryan. We leave for school in fifteen minutes. Why don't you wear that cute jumper you wore last week honey."

"I can't do this anymore, Cate." The words came out raw, three years of secrets bleeding through.

"It's like nothing's happened. Dad's got Ethan working beside him. Like I wasn't right. Like three million dollars didn't vanish."

"I know, baby." Caitlin's voice carried that particular frequency that had first caught him at the Wildflower Café in Healdsburg. She'd been pouring coffee, he'd been grabbing lunch between equipment runs, and something in the way she'd looked at him. She had really looked, not through him like Briana had been doing. That moment had cracked something open.

"You've given everything to that place."

The mare shifted beneath him, sensing his tension. Below, in the distance, he could see the Dry Creek parcels, or what used to be their parcels before his father sold them to fund Ethan's fantasies. Prime vineyard land, owned by Weinhardts for over a hundred years, now sporting signs in Mandarin.

"You know what kills me most?" His free hand tightened on the reins. "The way Bri reacted when she heard he was back. I saw it in her face, Cate.

That flicker. After all these years, after our kids, our life, she still carries something for him."

"Of course she does." Caitlin's voice hardened with purpose. "First loves leave marks. But that's exactly why you need to protect what's yours."

She thought of what was hers. What she'd done to claim it. Three years. Three years of stolen afternoons in Healdsburg, while Madison was at school or spending the day with her aunt. The wine sales trips that detoured through her apartment, of deleted texts and careful credit card statements.

For Ryan, it had started as comfort, someone who saw him as more than Karl Weinhardt's reliable older son and evolved into something that felt like revenge. Against Briana's distance. Against his father's favoritism. Against a world that rewarded flash over faithfulness.

"Mom keeps telling me Dad's just being compassionate," Ryan continued, guiding the mare along the ridge trail. "That we all have lessons to learn, that Ethan's learned his. But what about my lesson? Work yourself to death and watch the loser get the party?"

He could picture Caitlin in her apartment above the antique shop on Healdsburg's main drag. Probably wearing that silk robe he'd bought her last Christmas, the one Briana thought was a client gift. She'd been beautiful at thirty-two, when they'd met, divorced, bitter about her ex who'd left her for another woman, waiting tables while her A.A. credential gathered dust. Three years later, she'd hardened into something sharper. Hungrier.

"You need to fight back." Her voice dropped to that tone that used to thrill him, now sometimes frightened him. "Document everything. Every mistake Ethan makes, every time he shows up late, every decision that costs money. Build a case."

"And then what?"

"Then you go to your father with facts. Not emotions, facts. Show him Ethan hasn't changed. That he's still the same destructive force that nearly ruined everything."

The mare picked her way down toward the tree line. Ryan could see the old Zinfandel blocks from here, the ones his great-grandfather had planted. Gnarled vines that survived Prohibition, producing wine that told the story of this place. His story. Not Ethan's.

"There's a Pinot Noir showcase in San Francisco next month," he said. "I'm representing the winery. Could extend the trip a day..."

"I'll make plans." The promise in her voice should have warmed him. Instead, he felt the familiar twist of guilt and want that had become his constant companion. "We could look at apartments in the city. For when you finally leave her."

The words hung between cell towers and satellites. Leave her. Leave the mother of his children. Leave the woman who'd chosen him when Ethan left. The foundation of the life he'd built felt suddenly brittle, like frost-stressed vines ready to snap.

"I should go," he said. "Got to check the new plantings."

"Ryan?" Caitlin's voice turned silk over steel. "Remember what you told me that first night? How you'd given your whole life to that land while Ethan played startup king? How your father took out the loan against your future to fund your brother's games?"

He remembered. Remember how they sold the Dry Creek parcels to pay off the loan. Remembered the wine and the anger and the way she'd listened like he was the only man in the world. Remembered how it felt to be chosen for once, to be someone's first pick instead of the reliable backup plan.

"You deserve what's yours," she continued. "All of it. The land, the legacy, the respect. Don't let them make you feel guilty for wanting what you've earned."

After they hung up, Ryan sat on his mare, looking west toward the ocean. The mid-morning sun painted the Pacific silver and endless. Somewhere beyond that horizon, past Hawaii and across more water, lay the markets that increasingly drove California wine. Chinese investors who understood land value better than family legacy. Tech money that saw vineyards as portfolio diversification. A world where loyalty meant nothing and leverage meant everything.

His phone buzzed. Briana, texting about Karl's soccer game that afternoon. Their son, named for his grandfather. Their life, built carefully over years while Ethan burned through funds as if they were withered grape branches. But when they had discussed Ethan's return that first day, he'd seen it, that flash of something unresolved. The ghost of the girl who'd loved both brothers but chose safety over passion. Chose him by default when Ethan chose leaving.

The mare turned toward home without prompting, knowing the trail by heart. Like everything here, she knew her place, her purpose. Ryan had thought he knew his too. First son. Heir apparent. The one who stayed.

But Caitlin was right about one thing, staying wasn't the same as winning. And if Ethan thought he could waltz back into their lives, broken and needy, and reclaim what he'd abandoned, he was about to learn otherwise.

The vineyard rows flashed past as he descended, perfect lines of his labor stretching toward a horizon that suddenly felt less certain. Somewhere among those vines, his brother was probably working alongside their father, rebuilding bonds Ryan had maintained through drought and harvest, profit and loss.

You deserve what's yours. All of it.

The words echoed with each hoofbeat. What was his? What had he earned versus what he'd simply inherited? And what was he willing to do to keep it?

The answers, like the fruit on these vines, would reveal themselves in time. But unlike wine, Ryan suspected, they wouldn't improve with age.

CHAPTER TWELVE

WEINHARDT'S RANCH

SONOMA

"The best wine is the oldest, the best water the newest."
Blake

Eden sat on the west-facing porch, watching the marine layer creep inland like a slow confession. A month since Ethan's return, and the rhythms of the ranch had shifted to accommodate him, not smoothly, more like a vine graft that hadn't quite taken. The harvest was coming soon and there was lots to do. She wrapped her hands around her teacup, Earl Grey with honey, the same blend her mother had served in their Kensington flat before adventure and love had transplanted them to California soil.

This was her hour. When the men were still scattered across eight thousand acres, when the ledgers were balanced and the supply orders placed, when she could sit with her thoughts before the evening gathered them all back together. She'd spent the afternoon with Tawi, reviewing invoices for the coming harvest, then worked through the accounts Karl trusted her with. Numbers had always come easy to her, a British practicality that served well in a business where romance and reality needed constant reconciliation.

The sound of boots on gravel announced Ethan before she saw him. She'd sent word through Jake, asking for this conversation. Some truths needed telling before they calcified into assumptions.

"Mom." He climbed the steps, still moving like someone relearning his own body. The soft Valley executive was gone, replaced by something harder but not yet fully formed. Like a vine cut back to old wood, waiting to see what would grow.

She'd set out two cups, the good china they used for occasions. Not celebration exactly, but acknowledgment. This conversation mattered.

"Sit." She poured for him, watching his hands. Still trembling slightly in the late afternoon, withdrawal's long tail, or maybe just the weight of being home. "It's been good having you back, Ethan. My heart's been hoping again."

He settled into the wicker chair, his father's usually, but Karl wouldn't be back for another hour. "It's good to be back. Working the vines, the soil. Dad's been..." He paused, searching. "More gracious than I deserve."

"Your father has deep wells." Eden smiled, remembering that first glimpse of Karl Weinhardt at Valley Feed & Seed, all calloused hands and patient eyes. "I saw it when we met, before you were even thought of. That solid temperament, like granite under good soil. Of course, the rugged handsome thing didn't hurt." The memory warmed her more than the tea. "But it was his compassion that caught me. The way he'd spend an extra hour helping a struggling rancher figure out feed ratios, no thought of profit in it."

"You were quite the catch yourself." Ethan's smile carried shadows. "I got the family looks, apparently. Just none of Dad's character."

"Don't." Her voice sharpened, mother-quick. "You're more like him than you know. That same vision, just..." She looked west, where fog was beginning to pool in the valleys. "Your father's vision grew from roots. Yours tried to grow from air. There's time yet to find good ground."

The silence stretched, comfortable as old denim. Then she set down her cup, the china's small clink like a judge's gavel.

"I heard about your run-in with Ryan."

Ethan's jaw tightened. "Which one?"

"All of them." There had been at least two more since that night in the barn. Eden reached across, found his hand. His skin was rough now, small cuts from wire and wood mapping his return to physical work. "I need to be honest with you. The only way a mother can be."

Something in her tone made him straighten.

"Your father's taking you back, wants you working beside him. But Ethan..." The words tasted like medicine, necessary but bitter. "There's nothing here for you to inherit. The three million we lost, the land we sold, that was your portion. Ryan knows it. I know it. You need to know it too."

She watched it land, saw him absorb it like soil taking water. His eyes went to the vineyards, calculating worth he'd never claim.

"I know." The words came out steady, which surprised them both. "I'm just grateful for a place to land. To shake off what I became down there. Maybe learn what Dad tried to teach me before I was too proud to listen."

Eden leaned forward, her voice dropping to that register mothers use when the lesson matters most.

"But here's the thing, Ethan. Even your father can't help you if you don't learn from him. Really learn. Not just the techniques, but the connection." She paused, searching for the right words. "A branch can't bear fruit if it's not drawing life from the vine. It has to stay connected, has to let the life flow through it. Otherwise..."

She let the silence fill with meaning. Outside, a breeze stirred the nearest vines, their new growth reaching toward the dying light.

"Otherwise it withers," Ethan finished quietly. "I know, Mom. I've been that branch, trying to grow on my own strength. Look where it got me."

"The cutting away, that's already happened. The question now is whether you'll graft back properly. Whether you'll draw close enough to your father to really receive what he has to give." Eden's eyes held his, maternal love mixed with harder truths. "Because if you don't, if you just go through the motions without that deep connection, you'll wither again. And there won't be another chance to graft back."

The weight of it settled over them like fog, seeping into the spaces between words. Eden watched her son process this truth, saw him understand that salvation wasn't just in coming home, but in how deeply he rooted himself once there. The difference between mere proximity and true connection. Between working alongside his father and learning to draw life from the same source that had sustained Karl through every season.

"There are other futures," she said finally, her voice lighter but the weight of the previous words still hovering. "Other ways to build something that lasts."

"I was thinking about that." His eyes drifted east, toward the Mitchell ranch. So that spark had caught. Eden filed it away. "Maybe starting fresh somewhere. Taking what I learn here, the heritage, building something new."

"You remember our story? How we came here when I still sounded like Mary Poppins?" The memory made her smile. "My dad sold his Kensington pub right as the Beatles were conquering America. We snuck in under all that British invasion noise, landed here with big dreams and bad timing. He lost most of it on development speculation, California gold rush fever, just a century late."

Ethan knew this part, but she told it anyway. Stories needed retelling, like vines needed pruning.

"Took him fifteen years of managing Valley Feed & Seed before he could buy it. Ed Stewart gave him that chance when no one else would. By then I'd met your father, fallen for his patient heart. When Dad died, the business went to my brother Charles, primogeniture dies hard in British blood, but I had Karl. Had this." She gestured at the land, the life, the accumulated beauty of decades.

"That was enough."

"Maybe that's my path too. Earn something. Build something."

"With Lauren Mitchell?" The question slipped out before she could catch it.

Ethan's face reddened. "I barely know her. We just... connected over Maverick."

"Your father connected with me over a sick calf." Eden's smile carried decades of sweetness. "The heart finds its reasons. But Ethan," she leaned forward. "You've got things to rebuild first. Trust with Ryan, though that may take years. Respect from the crew. And Bri..."

"There's nothing there." Too quick, too firm.

"Good. Because that would break more than just your brother's heart. It would break this family." She squeezed his hand. "I can warn you about that. But there are things I can't teach you. Things you'll have to learn from the land itself, from the vines, from the rhythm of this place." She paused. "Tawi can help you see them."

"I've been listening to him."

"Good, then continue to. That man carries wisdom like other people carry worry. His people were here before any of us, reading the land like scripture. And the wisdom he's learned himself along the way. You could do worse than learning from him."

"There's no spin there," said Ethan, remembering the hype and hubris that buzzed through the Valley like bare electric wires sparking against each other.

"But Ethan, it's not just Tawi you need to draw close to. It's your father." Her voice took on an urgency that made him look up. "He's like that vine we were talking about. You can't just learn techniques from him at arm's length. You need to be with him. Really be with him. Watch how he moves through a day, how he handles setbacks, how he treats the workers when no one's counting."

She paused, her hand tightening on his. "Get close, Ethan. Close enough to see him tired, dealing with the challenges of this land. Close enough to watch him work through it all with that steady grace of his. That's where the real learning happens. Not just in the instructions he gives you about pruning or irrigation. In the silences between. In the way he touches the vines like they're old friends. In how he listens before making decisions."

The light was going golden now, that particular alchemy of fog and sun that made Sonoma light precious. Soon Karl would return, tired and satisfied. Ryan would arrive, jaw tight with fresh resentments. The careful choreography of a family holding itself together by will and prayer.

"There's something in this land," Eden said quietly. "Something each generation of Weinhardts has tended. Not just vines. Understanding. Purpose. The knowledge that some things matter more than profit."

"I felt it." Ethan's voice dropped. "Even in the Valley, even when I was so high I couldn't see straight. Something calling me back."

"Then trust it. Let it root you. Whether you stay or go, carry that with you."

Footsteps on gravel again, Tawi's distinctive gait, slightly favoring his left knee. He appeared around the corner, wiping his hands on his apron.

"Dinner's ready." His dark eyes moved between them, reading volumes. "Got a guest tonight. Karl invited Lauren Mitchell. She was here for the cattle vaccinations."

Eden caught Ethan's sharp intake of breath, the sudden alertness in his posture. She exchanged a knowing look with Tawi. Karl Weinhardt might be patient as stone, but he wasn't above a little matchmaking.

"Well then." She stood, smoothing her skirt. "We shouldn't keep her waiting."

As they walked across the broad porch, the smell of Tawi's cooking, wild mushroom risotto, if her nose was right, mingled with the evening air. Ethan walked between them, his mother and the man who's wisdom could help him, moving toward whatever future was taking shape in his father's kitchen.

Some inheritances couldn't be measured in acres. Some legacies lived in the space between what was lost and what might yet be found.

The door opened on light and voices, on the possibility of new growth from old roots. Eden watched her younger son straighten his shoulders, preparing to meet whatever waited inside. Her heart, that British-American hybrid that had learned to love like California wine, bold, complex, worth the wait, expanded to hold it all.

After dinner, the gravel crunched under their feet as Ethan walked Lauren to her Defender, the old model that predated luxury, built when utility meant everything. Tawi's dinner still lingered on their palates: wild mushroom risotto with truffle oil, grass-fed beef from their own herd, reduction sauce that tasted like concentrated memory. The 2018 estate Pinot had opened up through the meal, its cherry and earth notes speaking of the western slopes where fog met sun.

"Tawi's quite the cook," Lauren said, keys jangling in her hand but making no move toward the driver's door. The porch light threw long shadows across the yard, catching the auburn in her hair.

"I didn't always eat like this." Ethan leaned against the Defender's weathered fender. "Valley food was all deconstructed this, molecular that. Foam where sauce should be. Give me Tawi's honest cooking any day."

She smiled, that direct smile he remembered from the morning with Maverick. No artifice in it. "Must be strange, coming back to all this after..."

"After spectacular failure?" He met her eyes. "Yeah. Different world down there. Very hyper, very fast-paced, very..." He searched for the word. "Empty. Though I brought plenty of my own emptiness to it."

"Working with livestock grounds you." Lauren's hand found the Defender's door handle but didn't pull. "The animals don't care about your IPO or your user metrics. They care if you show up, if your hands are steady, if you understand their needs. There's truth in that."

The evening breeze carried salt and fog, the eternal coastal exchange. Ethan watched her profile in the half-light, the way she stood comfortable in her own skin, boots planted like she grew from this ground.

"I've got more than just the mess to overcome," he said quietly. "Got to plant new things. Root out old growth that doesn't serve." He thought of his father that morning, examining the vines. "Dad taught me that, even if I didn't listen then. Sometimes dead wood hides, you know? Looks alive enough, draws resources, but never fruits. You can overlook it for seasons until you realize it's just stealing strength from productive growth."

Lauren turned toward him fully now, the space between them charged with more than conversation. How many times had he stood like this with women in the Valley? Kat in some rooftop bar, city lights substituting for stars. Sienna against her Tesla, perfume too strong to let him smell the night. Always performing something, always conscious of the next move.

This was different. Lauren smelled like antiseptic and leather, horse sweat and honest work. No performance here, just two people breathing the same salt air.

"I'm grateful," Ethan said. "That you're here. After everything people must have told you."

"We've all got histories." Her voice dropped, thoughtful. "In veterinary work, especially with livestock, you learn something. When you're trying to get an orphan calf to take to a new mother, the success isn't in the technique. It's in the match. Good soil, like you said. But also..." She paused, choosing words with care. "Also, in the vines, in how completely the graft surrenders to the new connection. Half-measures don't take. The calf that holds back, keeps looking for what was instead of accepting what is? That's the one that fails to thrive."

The metaphors hung between them, layers of meaning Ethan felt in his chest. Complete surrender. No holding back. No keeping one foot in the old life while pretending to embrace the new.

"This soil's good," he said finally. "But this place isn't mine. Never will be. I'll have to find another way to build something. Maybe something AI can't replicate. Something that only patience and sweat can grow."

"Those are the only things worth building anyway."

The moment stretched, taut as fence wire. In the Valley, this was when you kissed, when you made the move that led to the next predictable step. But Lauren just looked at him, really looked, like she was reading his bloodlines the way she'd read Maverick's wounds. Seeing what was there, what might be there, what needed time to reveal itself.

She climbed into the Defender, the old diesel coughing to life. "Thank your family again for dinner. And you, or the conversation."

"Thank you," he said. "For not treating me like damaged goods."

"We're all damaged." She shifted into gear. "Question is what we do with the scars."

The Defender rumbled away, taillights painting the fog red. As it passed Ryan and Bri's house, movement caught Ethan's eye. Bri stood on their porch, backlit by the kitchen window. Alone. Watching.

For a moment, their eyes met across the distance. The girl who'd chosen safety. The woman who'd built a life with his brother. Mother of two, keeper of accounts, the practical choice that had seemed so clear when he'd left for Silicon Valley and all its promises.

Something twisted in his gut. Not desire exactly, more like grief for alternate histories. Then, unbidden, Kat's face flashed through his mind. That last night at Neural Link, her calculating eyes, the way she'd already moved on while he was still falling.

All these women. All these almosts and might-have-beens and spectacular failures. The dead wood he needed to prune away.

Ethan squeezed his fist tight, feeling the ghost of pruning shears, the clean cut that removed what no longer served. The memories faded but didn't disappear, retreating like fog but ready to roll back in when his guard dropped.

He turned toward the house as the marine layer began its nightly conquest, swallowing the ranch building by building. By morning, the world would be clean again, wrapped in gray possibility. But the dead wood would still be there, waiting to be recognized, waiting to be cut away.

Some surgeries you had to perform on yourself, one careful cut at a time.

CHAPTER THIRTEEN

WEINHARDT'S RANCH

SONOMA

"Wine reveals what is hidden."
Horace
Odes (Book III, 21)

The Weinhardt library occupied the height of two stories on the house's north side, built when books were wealth and knowledge was power. Floor to ceiling shelves of oak, rolling ladders on brass rails, the smell of leather and paper and time. Windows at the top let in evening light, turning dust motes into tiny stars. After saying goodbye to Lauren, Ethan found Esther there, curled in their mother's reading chair with a wine magazine. She looked up, smiled. "Remember when you used to chase me in here with garter snakes?"

"Remember when you put ponytail holders in my hair while I slept?"

"You looked pretty." She set the magazine aside. "Ryan never played our games. Too serious. Too worried about breaking something."

"He was always the stable one." Ethan moved along the shelves, running fingers over spines. Agricultural journals, German poetry, California history. His family's obsession with preserving knowledge. "Perfect firstborn son."

"Don't." Esther's voice gentled. "He saved this place while you were gone. Held it together through three bad harvests, Dad's heart scare, the endless bills. Whatever anger he carries, he earned it."

The truth of it stung. Ethan pulled a book at random, grandfather's weather journals. Twenty years of daily observations. Temperature, rainfall, fog patterns. The patience of it humbled him.

"I understand him better now," Ethan admitted. "Coming home, seeing what I left them to carry. No wonder he can't forgive me."

Esther joined him at the shelves. "He will. Eventually. Ryan holds grudges like Mom holds dinner parties. Elaborate, exhausting, but not forever."

They stood together, surrounded by their family's careful accumulation of wisdom. Then Ethan remembered.

"Tawi told me something last week. About Friedrich's journal. Our great-great-grandfather apparently wrote down everything the Italian workers taught him about winemaking. Old techniques, lost knowledge. But it disappeared when they built this house."

Esther's eyes widened. "The hiding spot. I wonder?" A long lost memory flashed through her mind, as remembering had triggered an epiphany.

"What?"

"When I was ten, maybe eleven, I climbed up there." She pointed to the highest shelves. "Hiding from Ryan after I'd scratched his bike. Behind the books on German philosophy, there was this gap. A niche that didn't match the rest of the construction. I always meant to explore it but..."

"But you grew up."

"Something like that." She was already pulling the ladder along its rails. "Help me look."

They climbed together, Ethan holding the ladder steady while Esther searched behind dusty volumes of Goethe and Schiller. Her hand disappeared into shadow.

"There's something here. A lever or..." A soft click. "Ethan!"

She pulled out a leather journal, brown with age, binding cracked but holding. On the cover, in faded gold: "Johann Friedrich Weinhardt - Familie Geschichte und Weinweisheit."

They descended carefully, treasure in hand. Spread it open on the reading table. The first pages were in German, family history reaching back to the Rhine Valley. Then entries began mixing languages, Friedrich's German giving way to halting English as he tried to capture what the Italians taught him.

"Look at this," Esther whispered, translating. "The fog speaks three languages. Morning fog is patience. Afternoon fog is warning. Evening fog is promise. Let the vines tell you which." She turned pages carefully. "And here. Never harvest by calendar. Harvest when the last cricket sings, when spiders build low, when starlings gather but don't leave."

"Agricultural superstition?"

"Or observation we've forgotten how to see." She kept reading. "He writes about fermentation timing, about using the fog itself to control temperature. About pruning by moon phases. Things that sound crazy until you remember wine was made this way for thousands of years."

Page after page of careful notes. Friedrich trying to preserve what Prohibition would soon destroy. What mechanization would mock. What his descendants would dismiss as old country nonsense while wondering why their wines never quite sang.

Then Esther stopped, her finger tracing a line. "Ethan, listen to this."

She read slowly, translating the mixed German and English: "September 28, 1912. Giuseppe taught me to watch for the three mornings when fog lifts before the church bells ring at 10. This is when the old Toscani begin crushing. Never before, never after. The wines from fog-break crushing need no sulfur, ferment steady as a heartbeat, and keep for decades. Started crushing today at 10:47 AM, fog lifted at 10:15 sharp third day running."

"Fog-break crushing?" Ethan leaned closer. "I've never heard of that."

"Neither have I. And I studied viticulture for four years." She turned the page, found more. "He calls it 'La Pausa della Nebbia.' The fog pause. Says the Italians brought it from the old country but even there it was almost lost."

They read on, Friedrich's careful notes documenting this strange technique. Three consecutive mornings when fog lifted before ten o'clock. Some correlation with atmospheric pressure, with wild yeast populations, with the exact balance of sugar and acid in the grapes. But more than science, a kind of faith. Waiting for the land to say when.

"I need to tell Dad," Esther said. "When I was at Davis, we studied how Prohibition destroyed not just wineries but knowledge. Generations of technique lost because no one could practice, no one could teach. Maybe Friedrich saved some of it."

Wind swept through the upper windows, rustling pages like whispers. The journal fell open to an entry near the end, Friedrich's English finally strong:

"The Italian Lorenzo tells me the secret is not in the doing but in the waiting. Americans always rush. But wine is made in the pause between deciding and acting. In the morning when fog holds its breath. In the moment before the grape releases from the stem. These pauses, they are where God hides the flavor."

Ethan felt something shift in his chest. All his life rushing toward the next thing, never pausing, never waiting. Maybe that's why everything he'd touched turned bitter.

"We have to try this," Esther said. "The harvest is coming. What if Friedrich was right? What if the old ways were better?"

A gentle breeze through the open window filled the library again, carrying the smell of fog and grapes and possibility. In his hands, Ethan held his family's past. In his heart, for the first time in years, he felt the stirring of a future worth waiting for.

CHAPTER FOURTEEN

HEALDSBURG

SONOMA COUNTY

"Wine gives courage and makes men more apt for passion."
Ovid

The afternoon light slanted through the windows of the Wildflower Café, catching dust motes that danced above empty tables. Caitlin Ferranti counted her tips for the third time. Seventeen dollars and thirty-five cents for the lunch shift. Not enough for groceries, let alone the dance lesson Madison had been begging for.

She glanced at the clock above the espresso machine, 2:47. School let out at three-thirty. Just enough time to finish her side work if she hustled. The café smelled of burnt coffee and the clouds of better days, when Healdsburg's old guard still gathered here for pie and gossip, before the wine bars and tasting rooms pushed them to the margins.

The morning replayed in her mind like a song she couldn't shake. Madison in the passenger seat of the old Nissan, her backpack too big for her small frame, picking at a loose thread on her jeans.

"Mom, why don't we have a house like Cousin Lacy?" The question had come out of nowhere, the way kids' questions do. "They have a pool. And a game room. And their refrigerator has ice that comes out the door."

Caitlin had gripped the steering wheel, feeling the crack in the vinyl cover catch her palm. The heater rattled, barely pushing warm air through the vents. Outside, fog still clung to the vineyards, making everything soft and uncertain.

"Apartments can be nice too, baby. Remember how we decorated your room? With the fairy lights?"

"Yeah, but..." Madison had turned to look out the window, watching the big houses roll by. "Lacy says her dad says apartments are for people who can't afford better."

The words had hit like a slap. Caitlin forced her voice steady. "Well, Lacy's dad doesn't know everything, does he? Besides, it's just you and me right now, and we're doing okay."

"Because Daddy left." Not a question. A statement, flat and matter-of-fact in that way ten-year-olds have of cutting straight to the bone.

"Oh, sweetheart. Your daddy leaving had nothing to do with you. Nothing at all. Sometimes grown-ups just..." She'd searched for words that wouldn't sound like excuses. "Sometimes they need different things."

Madison had been quiet for a moment, then: "Daddy's different now. When I see him, he doesn't really see me. Not like grandpa Hans. He always asks about school and remembers my friends' names. And the maid, Katherine makes those cookies with the jam in the middle."

"Thumbprint cookies," Caitlin had murmured, remembering Sunday dinners at the Krueger's place, back when she and Eric were first together, before everything got complicated. Hans always making sure everyone's wine glass was full, the cook orchestrating meals like small miracles.

"Yeah! And they have that big table where everyone fits." Madison's voice had brightened at the memory. "Not like our kitchen table that wobbles."

They'd pulled up to the school then, the old Nissan coughing slightly as Caitlin shifted into park. She'd watched her daughter gather her things, already transforming into the confident girl her classmates knew. Maidson had that gift, the ability to put on different faces for different worlds.

"Love you, Mom," Madison had said, leaning over for a quick kiss.

"Love you more, baby girl."

She'd watched Madison walk toward the front door, her friends calling out, surrounding her like she was someone special. Which she was. Would be even more so, someday, when things were different. When she and Ryan could finally...

The bell above the café door chimed, pulling Caitlin back to the present. Caitlin looked up from rolling silverware, and her stomach clenched.

Otto Krueger stood in the doorway like a man who owned more than he'd earned. His linen shirt cost more than she made in a week; his smile practiced as a sommelier's pour. Everything about him screamed new money trying to pass for old, from the Patek Philippe on his wrist to the calculated casualness of his stance.

"Hi, Caitlin." His eyes traveled her body with the subtlety of a combine harvester. "You're looking fine. I can understand why my brother liked you. Haven't lost that look."

The compliment slithered across her skin. She grabbed a menu, armor against whatever game he was playing. "Yeah, Otto. You were always there with the compliments. Never could tell how real they were."

His laugh had edges. "How's Madison?"

"She's thriving. Doing well in school." Caitlin kept her voice neutral, professional. Don't give him anything to use.

"My dad tells me how much he enjoys his visits with her." Otto settled into a booth, the vinyl creaking under his weight. "Family blood matters in this valley."

"What'll it be?" She held the pen like a weapon, ready to retreat to the safety of orders and coffee refills.

He picked up the menu, made a show of studying it, then set it down with deliberate care. "Before we get to food, maybe I should get to the real reason I'm here."

Every instinct screamed run. But her feet stayed planted, held by the gravity of necessity. Rent was due in a week. Madison needed new shoes. The car made that grinding noise every time she turned left.

"This isn't something your brother put you up to?" The words came out sharper than intended. "Trying to get more visitation?"

"No." Otto leaned forward, voice dropping to conspiracy level. "There's a deeper reason. The Krueger family cares for your daughter, she has our blood, after all. When Eric tossed you aside for that Instagram model..." He shrugged, letting the insult land. "I never understood it. Trading you for silicone, smarts and selfies."

The look in his eyes made her skin crawl, not quite desire, more like a butcher appraising meat.

"But Hans Krueger cares for his granddaughter," Otto continued. "And I think there's a way back into the family's good graces."

Caitlin's mind raced. Dead-end job. Half a degree. Single mother at thirty-five. The math of her life didn't add up to anything but struggle. Still, deals with devils rarely ended well.

"Ryan Weinhardt."

The name hit like a slap. Heat flooded her face, memory and shame tangled together. Three years of secrets, of stolen afternoons, of promises that evaporated like morning fog. She turned away, hands shaking. "I don't want to talk about this."

But Otto's knowing smile said he'd already won something. "We need to talk. If you're serious about a pathway back, meet me in Fitch Mountain Park after your shift. I'll be waiting by the gazebo."

The gazebo where teenagers went to smoke weed and homeless people sometimes slept. Perfect place for the kind of conversation that left stains.

"I'll think about it." The words tasted like surrender. "What do you want to eat?"

He ordered a club sandwich, tipped exactly fifteen percent, and left her with the weight of possibility crushing her chest.

Fitch Mountain Park drowsed in the afternoon heat, named for some long-dead pioneer who'd probably stolen the land in the first place. Otto sat on a bench near the gazebo, feeding breadcrumbs to pigeons like a villain in a noir film. Caitlin approached slowly, each step a small betrayal of the woman she'd hoped to become.

"I knew you'd come." He didn't look up from the birds.

"Just say what you need to say." She remained standing, refusing to settle into whatever trap he was laying.

"We know about your affair with Ryan Weinhardt."

The words hung in the air like smoke from distant fires. Caitlin's hands clenched into fists. "How could you possibly…."

"This county's smaller than you think." Otto stood, brushing crumbs from his hands. "The Weinhardts and Krueger have been circling each other for years. Old Karl playing the benevolent patriarch while we scraped for respect. Well, it's payback time."

"Ryan's not going to leave his wife for me." The admission burned coming out. "I'm not stupid, Otto. Men like him don't trade legacy for love."

"Exactly." His smile turned predatory. "Which is why you're useful. A bitter mistress can open doors that business connections can't."

"You threw me out when Eric was done with me." Old anger flared, surprising in its heat. "Haven't heard from the family since the divorce papers cleared. Now you want to use me?"

"We want to offer you opportunity." Otto's tone shifted, seller to mark. "The Krueger family is rising. There's competition in this county, and we have plans. But I need to know you're with us before I share details."

Caitlin looked across the park to where children played on swings, their laughter carrying on the breeze. Madison would be out of school now, waiting in after-care, another twenty dollars Caitlin didn't have. She thought of Ryan's promises, whispered in motel rooms and parked cars. Thought of Brianna Weinhardt's perfect life, built on the foundation of being the woman who stayed.

"What would I have to do?"

Otto's smile widened. "That's the spirit. Let's talk details."

"First, let me call my sister, I need her to pick up Madison from after-care."

"Fine."

After the call they sat on the bench, conspirators in the afternoon shade, while Caitlin sold pieces of her soul for the promise of something better than counting tips and dodging rent.

The wine cellar breathed with the patience of centuries, even though the Weinhardt family had only been making wine for five generations. Bri moved between the barrels, checking temperatures, testing for leaks, the ritual tasks that kept her hands busy while her mind churned. This was the one job Ryan had trained her in that she treasured. The cellar stayed constant, fifty-eight degrees, seventy percent humidity, while everything above ground shifted like smoke.

She loved it down here. The stone walls that held temperature like a secret. The way sound changed, became intimate, truthful. The smell of oak and wine and time working its quiet magic. Down here, she could think without the noise of children needing, husband demanding, life pressing its relentless rhythm.

Ryan had grown distant these past months. Not cruel, just absent, like a light slowly dimming. She knew the signs; her mother had worn them before her father left. Late nights that didn't quite add up. Business trips that required new cologne. The way he looked through her at dinner, seeing something else, someone else.

And now Ethan was back.

The cellar door opened, throwing light down the stone steps. Footsteps descended, measured, familiar. Not Ryan's heavy tread.

"Just checking the '22 barrels," Ethan's voice came before he fully appeared, as if announcing his presence might make it less intrusive, mumbling to himself. "Dad wants me to pull samples for...."

He stopped at the bottom of the stairs, taking in the scene. Bri alone on the tasting table, wine glass in hand, the kind of solitude that suggested she'd been here a while.

"Hi Bri, I didn't know anyone else was in here."

"Temperature swings have been brutal this spring," she said. "Ryan wanted me to check."

Ethan moved to the nearest barrel, professional instinct overriding the awkwardness. He pulled a wine thief from the rack, worked it into the bung. "The '22s are showing some volatile acidity. Not enough to worry about yet, but..." He drew a sample, held it to the light. "See the color shift? More brick than we'd like at this stage."

She moved away from her spot by the other barrels, came closer to look. "Could be the ML bacteria working overtime in the heat."

"Maybe." Ethan swirled the sample, sniffed. "Or those temperature swings are accelerating the aging. We've had what, fifteen-degree differences some days?"

"Seventeen last Tuesday," she said quietly. "Ryan's been checking twice a day."

Ethan nodded, tasted, spit into the floor drain. "It's holding, but barely. The Pinot especially; you know how sensitive it is." He moved to another barrel, the routine giving them both something to focus on besides being alone together. "This block's from the lower vineyard. Should be more stable."

He ran his hand along one of the barrels, checking its surface. "Everything's been unstable lately."

He moved closer, and she caught his scent, sweat and soil and something definitely him.

Bri broke the ice first, "How are things Ethan?"

"Ok, but moving slowly. Still, I'm settling in. Dad's welcomed me back at least. Though Ryan and I..." He paused. "Haven't seen him since the last one."

"You brother's always had your issues." She focused on the clipboard in her hands, numbers swimming. "Always seemed to work through them before. This might be the biggest one yet."

"I blew it." His voice carried weight she remembered, that mix of confidence and vulnerability that had always undone her. "Don't expect any inheritance. But I'm glad Dad's training me. I'll have to find my feet one way or another."

"That's Karl." She set down the clipboard, turned to face him fully. "Compassionate heart. The heart finds a way, as they say."

The cellar's intimacy pressed around them. She could hear his breathing, see the pulse in his throat. Memory crashed through her defenses, that night in his truck, parked above the vineyard, fog pressed against the windows like the world trying to get in. The way he'd cupped her face, thumb tracing her cheekbone. The endless moment before the kiss that never came, him pulling back, choosing leaving over staying, choosing ambition over what hung between them like ripe fruit.

"Walking through the vineyards," Ethan said softly, "gives me hope. Future. Even as it brings back memories."

The word 'memories' cracked something in her chest. "Have you ever wondered what would've been? If you'd stayed?"

"Yes." Simple. Honest. Devastating. "Especially since I've been back. But those ghosts... I can't chase them anymore. Need to find a new path."

"I saw you with Lauren the other night."

Something shifted in his face. "Yeah. I saw you watching from your porch. Wondered what you were thinking."

"Well." Tears threatened, surprising and unwelcome. "Things don't always work out how we hope."

She was talking about Ryan, about the slow dissolution of a marriage built on second choice. About standing on her porch, watching Ethan with a woman who looked at him like he was possibility instead of history.

The space between them hummed with everything unspoken. She moved closer, drawn by the gravity of old want. Ten years, two kids, a life built on being sensible, all of it fell away. She was eighteen again, choosing safety because passion had chosen leaving.

Ethan's jaw tightened. She watched him fight it, saw the moment of choice. Then he stepped back, the small distance an ocean between them.

"Bri...."

The cellar door slammed open. Ryan's silhouette filled the frame, backlit by afternoon sun.

"Well." His voice could have etched glass. "Back from town just in time to find you two together."

"Ryan, this was chance...." Ethan started.

"Nothing's going on here," Bri interrupted, hating how guilty she sounded.

"Oh yeah, brother?" Ryan descended the stairs, each step a threat. "So many reasons to hate you already. Just added another."

"Ryan, calm down." But her voice sounded weak even to herself.

"Listen, Ethan." Ryan was in his brother's face now, close enough to throw a punch. "Dad welcomed you back, but you're overstepping everywhere. Let me remind you again, you have no inheritance here. It's all mine. My kids'. You had your Valley girlfriends, your big dreams. This is real life."

"This isn't the place..." Ethan's hands came up, defensive or ready to fight, Bri couldn't tell.

A voice cut through the tension, speaking words in a language older than vineyards. Tawi stood on the stairs, his presence filling the cellar with calm authority. He continued in Pomo for several seconds, then translated: "When brothers fight over old wounds, they water the ground with blood that should feed the vine."

"You always have the right words, Tawi." Ryan's fury hadn't dimmed, just leashed. "Doesn't change my heart. Or the facts." He turned to Ethan. "I've got my eyes on you. Dad lets you stay, fine. But there's no future for you here."

He grabbed Bri's arm, not rough but possessive. "Kids are coming home."

They left together, Bri casting one look back at Ethan, seeing her own confusion reflected in his face. The cellar door closed, leaving shadows and the ghost of what almost was.

Tawi descended fully, placed a hand on Ethan's shoulder. "That was uncomfortable."

"Accidental encounter." Ethan's voice was rough.

"Sometimes accidents have deeper forces behind them." Tawi's dark eyes held knowledge accumulated over decades. "I've seen accidents become patterns. Patterns become fate."

They stood in the wine-scented quiet while Ethan's breathing slowed.

"Since I've been back," he said finally, "there's been something with Lauren. Wondering if there's a future. Not here on the ranch, but somewhere. So many relationships in the Valley were shallow. And now..." He paused, struggling. "Ryan's married. Has a family. But there are ghosts here. Bri and I, before I left... Sometimes I wonder if she married him on the rebound. And this afternoon, these old feelings..."

"There are ways to deal with what streams through our minds." Tawi's voice carried the weight of experience. "First, avoid these positions. If they happen by accident, bail out fast. Second, there's a lesson."

He settled onto an upturned barrel, storyteller's posture. "When I was young, working my mother's sheep ranch, every spring we'd bring them in. Sheep to be sheared, lambs to be branded. They'd run through a chute, and I'd sit on the fence with a lever. My job was to direct them, sheep one way for shearing, lambs the other for branding. All day, making choices with that lever."

His weathered hands mimed the motion. "Our thoughts are like those sheep. Coming fast down the chute. We choose. Let them in or throw the lever that sends them away. Can't stop them coming. Can only choose where they go."

Ethan nodded slowly, understanding beneath understanding.

"The old ones knew this." Tawi stood, brushed dust from his jeans. "They said the mind is like a river. You can't stop the water, but you can dig channels. Direct the flow. Let the good water irrigate. Send the bitter water to the sea."

He paused at the stairs. "I'm making dinner tonight. Lauren's coming back. Karl's doing, probably. Could use help in the kitchen."

A smile finally cracked Ethan's stone face. "Yeah. I'll be up in a minute."

Tawi climbed toward daylight, leaving Ethan alone with the patient barrels and the echoes of choices made and unmade. The wine slept in its oak dreams while above, the sun continued its ancient arc, indifferent to the small dramas of the hearts below.

CHAPTER FIFTEEN

WEINHARDT'S RANCH

SONOMA COUNTY

"In vino veritas, in aqua sanitas"
Pliny The Elder

"I can't believe what this hack at the Sonoma Register printed." Ryan slammed the newspaper on the dining table hard enough to rattle the wine glasses. "It's all rumor. Every word."

The great room of the Weinhardt house stretched around them, redwood beams dark with age reaching toward the vaulted ceiling. Through the west windows, the land rolled away in waves, vine rows following the natural contours like green corduroy stretched over sleeping giants. Late August light caught the leaves, some still green, others turning gold and amber. Beyond the nearest block of Pinot, the horse pastures spread toward the oak groves, where a pair of bays grazed behind split-rail fencing. Further still, the old barns stood against the horizon, weathered wood the color of dried tobacco.

Karl picked up the paper, reading slowly. His jaw tightened. "Jim Rourke's been stirring this pot for weeks. Posting stuff on social media, says he's looking for a whistle blower."

"What pot?" Ethan asked from his corner chair. He'd chosen the spot deliberately, back to the wall, clear view of both doors. Old habits from the Valley, watching for threats.

"Says we're cutting our Pinot with cheap valley wine." Ryan's voice cracked with rage. "San Joaquin swill mixed into our barrels. Says financial pressure from your disaster drove us to it." The last words hit like a slap. Ryan's eyes held more than anger. Disappointment. Disgust. The same look from fifteen years ago when Ethan left for Stanford with the family's money.

Jake Fisher, the ranch foreman, shifted his weight by the stone fireplace. Twenty-three years on the property, he knew every vine, every barrel. "No way anyone got to our wine. I'd have seen it."

"Course you would have." Karl folded the paper. "Question is, why's Rourke pushing this story now?" Eden sat quietly at the table's far end, her fingers wrapped around a china teacup, steam rising in delicate spirals. The Spode pattern, brought from England by her mother. Something flickered across her face, recognition maybe, but she kept silent. She'd learned long ago that American men needed to talk themselves out before wisdom could enter.

Brianna, spoke up. "The timing's suspicious. Right before the annual tasting."

"Exactly." Ryan turned on Ethan, shoulders squaring like a boxer. "Your failure's all over the news. CortexAI, the stolen code, everything. You come crawling home and suddenly we're under attack. Coincidence?"

"Ryan." Karl's voice carried warning.

"No, Dad. This is on him. Rourke smells blood because the golden boy crashed and burned. Now he's coming for all of us." The words hung there. Ethan felt Brianna's gaze, that old electricity still humming between them. She'd chosen Ryan, the steady one, the one who stayed. But her eyes said she remembered late nights in the barn, promises whispered against hay bales. She looked away first.

Tawi emerged from the kitchen, wiping his hands on his apron. The old Pomo had been listening, as he always did. "Truth's like good wine," he said quietly. "You can add things to the bottle, try to change what's inside. But when you open it, when you taste it, the land speaks. Can't fake what the earth knows."

Karl stood, decision made. "We're not hiding from this. Wine tasting's in a week. We'll invite everyone, the usual sommeliers, the press, and that famous one visiting from France. What's his name, Jake?"

"Henri Beaumont. Writes for Le Monde."

"Him. We'll open the barrels from last year's harvest. Let them taste what we really make." Karl's smile held steel. "Rourke wants a show? We'll give him one."

"You sure, Dad?" Ryan asked, but his eyes stayed on Ethan. "If someone has tampered, if there's even a chance..."

"No one's tampered with anything. We stand by our wine." Karl looked around the room. "All of us. Together."

The way he said 'all' made it clear. No exceptions. No matter what Ryan thought of his brother.

Tawi nodded slowly. "When the wind tries to break the oak, the tree that stands is the one with deep roots. Roots that tangle together underground, holding the earth. Even when the branches want to grow in different directions."

"One week." Eden finally spoke, setting down her teacup with British precision. "We'll need everyone working. I'll coordinate with the caterers. Brianna, we'll need the jazz quartet confirmed."

Ryan stood abruptly. "I've got work to do." He left without looking at Ethan.

The silence stretched until Brianna gathered her things. "I should help him. You know how he gets." She paused by Ethan's chair, voice dropping. "Give him time. He's protecting what you left behind."

After she left, Eden studied her younger son. "She's right, you know. Ryan held everything together while you were gone. The ranch, the business, your father's faith in this place."

"I know."

"Do you?" She picked up her teacup again. "He was right about the money. We could have been a serious disaster."

"But it wasn't."

"No. But it could have been." She stood, smoothing her skirt. "I have calls to make. The Hendersons' daughter runs a catering company now. We'll need tables, chairs, proper settings. This has to be perfect."

Five miles north, Otto Krueger stood in his climate-controlled garage, pointing at a single food-grade container filled with bulk wine from the San Joaquin Valley. Everything about the space screamed new money, from the epoxy floors to the German luxury cars to the complete absence of anything resembling actual work.

"My father's fed up with the Weinhardts'," Otto told his ranch hand, Dale Mathews. "Acting like they own the whole valley just because they've been here longer." The issues ran much deeper, but he needed to keep others in the dark. The ploy still sounded like a good excuse for revenge.

Otto examined the container like a general reviewing troops. "Tomorrow night. There's an old equipment barn on the southeast corner of their property. Leave this there, hidden but findable."

Mathews loaded the container into the truck. "What if someone sees me?"

"They won't. Everyone's focused on their precious tasting." Otto's smile belonged on something that hunted at night. "I'll make sure Rourke knows exactly where to look during his tour. One container they 'missed' when shipping the rest south. The story writes itself. The Weinhardts finally get knocked down. About time," he said, a knowing nod towards Dale.

Mathew's nodded. Agreeing with is boss had its dividends, even if he didn't completely understand all the issue between the two families.

Otto's expression darkened. "They've looked down on us for years. The Weinhardts claimed they tried to help us, but it was all phony. Now we'll see how their precious reputation handles this." Those words were the myth they told people like Dale and others.

After Mathews left, Otto brought out his cell phone and touched favorites, his dad's number popped up and he pressed it. After two rings, Hans answered, "Is everything set."

"Yes, Mathew's placing the container tomorrow night."

"You told him about our rivalry?"

"Yes, dad, like I told you before, he knows nothing about our intentions."

"Good, keep me posted."

The next days blurred into preparation. Jake's crew worked dawn to dusk, transforming the property. They strung lights through the massive oaks that had shaded generations of Weinhardts. Eden and Brianna met with vendors, tasted sample menus, argued politely about tablecloth colors.

Ethan hauled tables, repaired fencing, did whatever grunt work needed doing. The physical labor felt good, honest in a way coding never had. His body remembered this work from summers growing up, muscles finding old patterns.

Thursday afternoon, he was hanging lights in the event barn when Lauren appeared in the doorway. Jeans that had seen actual work, boots dusty from the drive, hair pulled back in a ponytail that made her look like the girl he'd known in high school.

"Thought you might need help," she said.

"Jake recruited you?"

"Eden, actually. Said you were making a mess of the decorations."

"Probably true."

They worked side by side, comfortable with shared silence. She'd been back to the ranch several times since that first visit, when she'd tried everything to save Maverick. The old stallion's death had broken something loose between them, grief opening a door that pride had locked.

"How's the clinic?" he asked.

"Busy. Dr. Wu says I'm ready for more solo calls." She tested a string of lights. "Another year and I can take over some of her practice."

"You always wanted that. Your own clients, your own schedule."

"Some of us knew what we wanted early." No judgment in it, just fact. "Others had to take the long way around."

They finished the barn as evening fog crept through the valley. Walking back to the main house, she stopped by the paddock to check a mare's swollen hock.

"She's better," Lauren said, running practiced hands over the joint. "Whatever Tawi's been putting on it works."

"He knows things."

"Yeah. Mom says his grandmother was a healer. Real medicine woman stuff, before the government made it illegal."

They watched the horses move through gathering dusk, shadows against darker shadows.

"You riding Saturday?" she asked.

"Wasn't planning to. Too much chaos."

"Your loss. Perfect weather for it."

Something in her tone made him look closer. "You asking?"

"Maybe. After the crowd clears out." She headed for her Defender, the old diesel that had seen better decades. "Think about it."

The taillights vanished into the fog, leaving only the hush of the coastal night. Ethan stood a long moment in the gravel drive, hands shoved deep in his pockets, listening to the slow retreat of the Defender's engine. When the sound was gone, the silence pressed in, the same kind that used to send him searching for noise loud enough to drown thought.

Back in his old room, the house settled around him with its familiar creaks and sighs. The evening should have left him at peace; instead his chest felt hollow. Lauren's words about broken things, about healing, circled his mind until they blurred.

Sleep came unevenly. When it did, it turned on him. He was back in the club….blue haze, glass, Kat's laughter slicing through the bass. The capsule glowed between Marcus's fingers, the promise of weightlessness. He took it, felt the rush, the light, the fall. Then the floor dropped into fire and vineyard smoke. Karl's voice called from somewhere beyond the flames, Tawi's from deeper still, but he couldn't reach either of them.

He woke with a start, breath clawing at the dark. Moonlight cut thin through the curtains, turning the familiar shapes of dresser and chair into strangers. Sweat chilled his skin. For a heartbeat he thought he heard the music still, that low electronic pulse that had once been his heartbeat. He pushed the covers aside and went to the window. Outside, the fog was thick enough to swallow the world. He opened the sash and let the cold air pour in, tasting salt and earth and something clean. "Not tonight," he whispered, voice barely audible over the wind. The words felt small but steady, carried off into the gray.

When he lay back down, the craving had retreated, but it hadn't vanished. It waited, patient as the fog itself, for weakness or morning, whichever came first.

In his cabin behind the bunkhouse, Tawi woke to Shekha's low whine, not alarm, but alert. The dog's instincts and his own ran in the same direction. He'd named her Shekha, fox in the old language, for the way she moved through the world, silent, watchful, seeing what others missed. He checked his watch: 2:17 a.m. The hour when darkness was most itself, when the veil between worlds wore thin.

He dressed and followed the dog outside, letting her lead him through fog that wrapped the ranch like wet wool. She brought him to the back porch of the main house, where he could sit and listen properly. He settled onto the bench, legs stretched toward where the sun should be. Shekha lay beside him. Something felt wrong. A disturbance in the usual rhythm, like a note off-key in a familiar song. He closed his eyes and began to pray in his grandmother's language. The words came slow, careful, addressing the Creator who watched over this land. Asking for clarity, for protection, for wisdom to see what didn't belong.

Shekha's ears pricked. She whined, nose pointing southeast toward the vineyard.

"Yeah, girl. I feel it too."

He stood, joints protesting the morning dampness. "Come on. Let's go see what doesn't belong."

They walked through lifting fog, past equipment sheds beaded with dew, toward the old barn used mostly for storage. Shekha ranged ahead, tail rigid. She stopped at a blue container tucked behind rusted cultivator discs.

Tawi knelt, opened it. The smell hit immediately, flat, industrial, wrong. He tasted a drop, spat. Bulk wine, probably fifteen dollars a case wholesale. The kind of stuff that killed brain cells and gave wine a bad name.

"Someone's playing games."

He called Karl, then Jake. Within ten minutes, the family gathered around the container.

"They're trying to set us up," Ryan said. "Plant this here, then miraculously 'discover' it during the tasting."

"Question is who." Karl examined the container. "And who'd they expect to do the discovering."

"Rourke," Eden said quietly. "He's been too confident about this story. Like he knows something."

Jake pulled out his phone. "Security cameras might have caught something."

They watched the grainy footage on Jake's screen. A truck, plates obscured. A figure in dark clothes placing the container.

"That's the Krueger ranch truck," Jake said. "I'd know that dent anywhere."

Karl's face darkened. "Hans is behind this?"

"Old wounds," Jake said quietly. "Goes back to years. Hans never forgave what he thought was our fault. Strange, sometime when you help someone, things get worse."

"What do we do?" Ethan asked.

Karl smiled, cold and certain. "We keep it right where it is. Let them think they've won. But Jake, make sure we save that footage we got tonight."

CHAPTER SIXTEEN

WEINHARDT'S RANCH

SONOMA COUNTY

"Wine is bottled poetry."
Robert Louis Stevenson

S aturday arrived perfect, one of those late August days that sold real estate and broke hearts. The fog burned off early, leaving air so clear you could see individual fence posts three ridges over. The jazz quartet, old friends of Eden's from the city, set up under the biggest oak. They opened with Autumn Leaves, because of course they did.

By 4 p.m., cars lined the drive. The wine crowd emerged in careful layers, local sommeliers greeting each other with practiced warmth, restaurant owners calculating profit margins, writers already composing opening lines. Henri Beaumont arrived in a rental sedan, somehow making it look elegant.

The food appeared in waves, each plate a small revelation. Tawi had outdone himself. Wild mushroom tartlets with herbs he gathered from the creek beds. Duck confit with a sauce that tasted like autumn mornings.

Cheeses from Andante Dairy paired with honey from their own hives and paper-thin crackers made from acorn flour, a recipe Tawi learned from his grandmother.

"Mon Dieu," Beaumont murmured, sampling a spoonful of Tawi's famous three-bean cassoulet. "This is not California cuisine. This is not French cuisine. This is..." He searched for words. "This is the land speaking through food."

Jim Rourke arrived twenty minutes late with a photographer, both trying too hard to look casual. Otto Krueger followed, nervous energy crackling off him like static. His father stayed home, too smart to show his face at the scene of the crime.

"Shall we begin?" Karl stepped forward. "We're proud to share our 2024 vintage. Jake, would you do the honors?"

Jake had staged everything in the barn, barrels lined up like soldiers, bungs already pulled. The ritual unfolded with practiced precision. He drew samples with a wine thief, filling glasses with movements handed down through generations.

Beaumont went first. The crowd hushed. He swirled, sniffed, sipped. His face revealed nothing. Another sip. A longer pause.

"This is why I come to California," he said finally. "To taste wine that could only come from this place. Cherry and earth and something else... something that speaks of fog and old trees and patience."

The tension broke. Other tasters stepped forward, murmuring appreciation. The wine showed everything Pinot should, silk and spine, power held in check.

Rourke's smile grew strained. He whispered urgently to Otto, who kept glancing toward the southeast.

"Before we continue," Rourke announced, voice too loud, "I think we should see the whole operation. Make sure what we're tasting represents everything on the property. A tour, yes?"

Karl's smile never wavered. "Of course. Jake, show our guests around."

They walked through the vineyard, Jake explaining trellising systems and clonal selections. Past the fermentation building with its temperature-controlled tanks. Toward the old equipment area where morning fog still clung to shadows.

"What's in there?" Rourke pointed at the storage barn, trying for casual and missing by miles.

"Old equipment," Jake said. "But you're welcome to look."

Rourke practically ran inside. He emerged moments later, triumphant, telling people to come and see the container. "Look what I found! Bulk wine hidden on the property. This is what they're really selling!"

Cameras appeared. The crowd murmured, uncertain.

Karl stepped forward, voice calm. "You're right, Jim. You found it exactly where someone left it Thursday night." He pulled out his phone. "I have security footage showing exactly who put it there and when. Would you like me to share it with everyone?"

The color drained from Rourke's face. Otto backed toward the parking area.

"We found it yesterday morning," Karl continued. "Thought it best to leave it for you to 'discover.' Seemed like that was the plan."

Beaumont laughed, rich and genuine. "Americans. Always such drama. The wine in the glass, that is what matters. And this wine..." He raised his glass to the light. "This wine needs no tricks."

"I think you gentlemen should leave," Karl said quietly to Rouke and his photographer. "This is a celebration, not a circus."

They left, Otto almost running, Rourke trying to salvage dignity and failing. The tasting continued, but now it felt like victory. Wine flowed, food appeared in waves, the quartet swung into something up-tempo.

Late, after most of the crowd had gone, and things had been put away, Ethan found Lauren by the horse paddock as purple dusk settled over the ranch. The last guests lingered near the barn, but out here, only the horses moved in the gathering dark.

"Still interested in that ride?" he asked.

She smiled. "Thought you'd never ask."

They saddled two horses, her movements quick and sure. A woman who'd grown up around animals, who knew them like breathing. They rode west through the vineyard, following the old fire road that wound uphill through manzanita and oak and then Redwoods.

At the top stood a barn from his great-grandfather's time, more memory than structure now. But the view remained eternal, Pacific to the west, valley to the east, everything painted in those impossible colors that came just before dark.

They tied the horses and walked to a boulder worn smooth by wind and time. Below them, an ancient apple orchard spread in neat rows, gnarled trees heavy with fruit. Harvest would be any day.

"Great-grandpa Heinrich planted those in 1903," Ethan said. "Gravenstein, Pippin, varieties you can't find anymore. Tawi makes cider from them, and this sauce that would make you cry."

"I know. He gave Mom the recipe, but it never tastes the same."

"Secret ingredients. He forages things, mushrooms and herbs. His grandmother's knowledge."

They sat quietly, watching fog creep up the valley like a living thing.

"I keep thinking about tonight," Ethan said eventually. "How Beaumont reacted to Tawi's food. 'The land speaking,' he called it."

"He's not wrong."

"What if we could do more with that? Build something here that showcases it all. The wine, obviously, but also Tawi's cooking, the whole history of this place."

Lauren turned to study him. "Like a restaurant?"

"Maybe. But not trying to be something we're not. Not molecular gastronomy or whatever's trending. Just... this." He gestured at the view, the orchard, the vines below. "Forty seats in that barn. Ingredients from the ranch, Tawi's recipes mixed with classical training. Earthy but refined. Real but elevated."

"Rooted," she said softly.

"Yeah. Exactly."

"You know what's crazy?" He picked up a pebble, rolled it between his fingers. "Even when I was at the height of everything. CortexAI on a trajectory towards two billion, parties at Neural Link, the whole Silicon Valley circus. I'd sketch this vision on napkins during board meetings. Terra/Tech, I called it. This idea that I could bring what we have here to that sterile place."

Lauren stayed quiet, letting him talk.

"The thing is that this place never left me. Not really. I'd be in some glass tower, closing deals worth millions, and I'd smell phantom traces of fog and apple wood. The restaurant was going to be my way back, I guess. My bridge between who I'd become and where I came from."

She stood, walked to the orchard's edge. "You know what those apples taste like? Not sweet like store fruit. They taste complex. Like wine grapes, almost. Like they remember every fog, every drought, every perfect day."

"That's what I want to build. Something that remembers."

She came back, sat closer than before. "It's a good dream, Ethan. The right kind."

"Different from my last one."

"Everything's different now." She met his eyes. "You're different."

He wanted to kiss her then but held back. Too much between them still, too much unknown. But when she leaned against his shoulder, watching the last light fade, he felt something in his chest unclench. Not healing yet, but the possibility of it.

"We should head back," she said finally. "Full dark soon."

They mounted up, began the descent. The horses picked their way carefully, sure-footed despite the dimness. Below them, the ranch spread like a promise, lights glowing warm against the darkness.

"This was great, Lauren," said Ethan as they reached the barn. "How about follow up?"

"Next weekend?" Lauren asked as they reached the barn. "You sure you're not too busy being the prodigal son?"

"Not for you. Besides, I've got something more I'd like to show you?"

She smiled, swung down from her horse with easy grace. "Sound interesting,"

"Good. I want to show you something. There's a meadow past the north ridge where Tawi gathers his best mushrooms. Part of the menu for the restaurant."

"Even more interesting."

She led her horse inside, began removing the saddle. He watched her work, efficient and gentle, talking soft nonsense to the mare.

"Lauren?"

"Mm?"

"Thanks. For tonight. For..." He gestured helplessly. "Everything."

She paused, curry comb in hand. "We're not kids anymore, Ethan. What we build now, it has to be solid. Has to be true."

"I know," he said. "And I need you to know something. Part of why I left, it wasn't just the tech dreams. Ryan was always going to inherit the ranch. The firstborn son, the one who stayed, who understood the land like breathing. There wasn't room for two futures here."

She turned to face him fully.

"So, I built my own empire. Thought I'd show them all what the second son could do. But now?" He laughed, bitter and short. "I've got nothing left from that world. No inheritance here, no fortune there. Just this idea that maybe, somehow, I could build something that pays back what I owe. Not in money, I'll never have that kind of money again. But in preserving what Tawi knows, in showing people what this land really means."

"Do you?" She went back to grooming. "Because I won't be another thing you leave behind when the next shiny object appears."

"There is no next shiny object. This is it. The ranch, the family, the work." He took a breath. "You."

She didn't respond, just finished with the horse, hung up the tack, closed the stall door. But as she passed him heading out, she brushed her fingers across his hand. Light as fog, but there.

"Next weekend," he said. "Don't forget."

He watched her walk to her truck, the old Defender coughing to life after three tries. She drove away, taillights disappearing into darkness.

The party had wound down. Glasses gathered on tables, the quartet packing instruments. But under the biggest oak, his parents sat with Tawi, sharing a bottle of the good stuff, the 2015 reserve they never sold.

"Join us," Karl called. "We're toasting survival."

Ethan pulled up a chair, accepted a glass. The wine tasted like coming home.

"Long day," he said.

"Good day," Eden corrected. "We showed them who we are."

"Who we've always been," Tawi added. "Just took some reminding."

They drank in comfortable silence. Somewhere in the darkness an owl called, another answered. The fog had conquered the valley now, but here in their circle of light, they were safe.

"Lauren seemed happy," Eden observed, too casual.

"Mom."

"I'm just saying. Nice girl. Always liked her."

"Eden," Karl warned, but he was smiling.

"What? I can't notice things?"

Tawi chuckled. "The boy's got eyes. Let him use them."

Ethan changed the subject. "I want to talk to you about something. An idea."

He laid it out, the restaurant concept, the integration of Tawi's cooking with wine program, the renovation of the old barn. His parents listened without interrupting.

"Interesting," Karl said when he finished. "But restaurants can be harder than tech companies. Different kind of burn rate."

"I know. But this wouldn't be about scale. Just quality. Truth."

"Truth doesn't pay bills," Eden pointed out

"No. But people pay for truth when they find it. Look at tonight. Beaumont knew immediately what was real."

Tawi spoke up. "The boy might have something. My grandmother always said food was medicine. But it's also memory, story. If he wants to tell our story through food..." He shrugged. "Worse ways to fail."

"Thanks for the vote of confidence."

"You already failed once. Makes the second time easier." Tawi's eyes crinkled. "Besides, I'm getting old. Be good to teach someone what I know before I can't remember it anymore."

"You'll outlive us all," Eden said.

"Maybe. Maybe not. But the recipes, the places where things grow, the right way to cook them... That should outlive me."

Ethan looked at Tawi. "I want to learn. Not just the cooking. How to listen like you do. How to listen to you. How you knew something was wrong the other morning."

The old man studied him. "That's not something you learn from books."

"I know."

"Takes time. Patience. Quiet mind."

"I've got time now."

Tawi nodded slowly. "We'll see. Meet me tomorrow morning, before sunrise. Bring coffee."

Karl swirled his wine, thinking. "We'll talk about it. The restaurant. Run numbers. See what's possible."

It wasn't a yes, but it wasn't a no. Ethan would take it.

Ryan appeared from the darkness, stopped at the edge of their circle. "Guests are gone. Jake's locking up."

"Sit," Karl said. "Have a glass."

"I'm good." His face stayed hard, closed. "Early morning tomorrow."

"Ryan," Ethan started.

"Save it." Ryan turned away. "You did your part today. Good for you. Doesn't change anything." He walked off into the darkness.

The silence that followed felt heavy. Eden sighed, Karl's jaw tightened, but no one spoke. Some wounds needed more than one good day to heal.

After a while, they finished the bottle and said their goodnights. Ethan walked through the fog to the barn, needing movement, needing to process the day.

The barn stood quiet, horses settled for the night. He leaned against Maverick's old stall, empty now but still carrying the ghost of the stallion's presence. Tomorrow there would be new challenges. The Kruegers wouldn't give up easily. Ryan's anger still burned hot. The restaurant idea faced a thousand obstacles. But tonight, they'd won. More than that, they'd remembered who they were. The wine had spoken true, the land had protected them, and maybe, possibly, he'd found a way forward that honored both past and future. A way that included Lauren, if he could earn it. If he could prove he'd stay this time.

The fog wrapped around the barn like forgiveness, soft and encompassing. Inside, the horses breathed steadily, safe and warm and home. Just like him, finally. Despite everything, just like him.

Miles away, in the glass and steel monument to automotive wealth that Hans Krueger called home, sleep proved as elusive as the fog was thick.

The massive house perched on Sonoma's eastern ridge like a predator surveying territory, its floor-to-ceiling windows reflecting nothing but gray emptiness in the marine layer. Inside, father and son moved through rooms that cost more than most people made in years, their footsteps echoing off Italian marble, their anger ricocheting off walls lined with abstract art neither of them understood but both had bought for effect.

Hans Krueger stood at the wine cellar's entrance, his silk pajamas catching the recessed lighting. Angelic statues that represented conquered vineyards and purchased prestige. Money laundered clean through Mexican connections had bought him this empire, transformed cartel cash into Silicon Valley gold, then wine country respectability. But tonight, the collection felt hollow. Incomplete. The Weinhardt operation remained pristine, unmarked by his schemes.

Otto appeared at the top of the cellar stairs, his own restlessness driving him through the house's cavernous spaces. At twenty-eight, he carried his father's predatory instincts wrapped in millennial entitlement, designer stubble framing a face that had never known real struggle.

"Still pacing?" Otto's voice carried barely controlled frustration. "That's not going to change what happened."

"Your brother's gone to the city," Hans said, selecting a bottle. "Two nights at the St. Regis while we clean up this Valdez mess."

"Of course he is." Otto's jaw tightened. "Ten grand for Cheri's spa weekend, now the presidential suite. All so he can savor every pampered inch of what his money bought." The words came out rougher than intended. "Those Canyon Ranch treatments... they polish a woman until she glows like marble."

Hans selected a bottle, something French and obscenely expensive, and closed the cedar door with more force than necessary. The sound echoed through the house like a gunshot.

"He should be here," Hans said flatly. "Not playing with his trophy while our plans fall apart."

Otto's laugh was bitter. "Let him go. Someone should enjoy the investment. Besides, we both know Cheri's brain works better than Eric's. Maybe we should have sent her to deal with Ethan instead of Valdez."

"Rourke was supposed to destroy them." Hans's voice was granite. "All those emails you sent, the false evidence about that container from San Joaquin. Nothing."

The study walls held photographs of Hans with politicians, celebrities, anyone whose proximity might suggest importance. A shrine to a man who had mistaken wealth for worth, power for respect. Otto sprawled in a leather chair worth more than some people's cars, watching his father pour wine with hands that trembled slightly from rage.

"The story backfired," Otto said, accepting his glass. "Made them look like victims instead of frauds."

"Victims." Hans spat the word like poison. "The great Weinhardt family, so pure, so noble. While we look like bullies attacking the innocent."

Otto took a sip, letting the silence stretch before speaking. "At least Ryan's completely hooked. Caitlin's got him believing she loves him."

Hans's laugh was bitter as winter fog. "Your brother was always an idiot about women. Abandoned his wife and daughter for some carefully sculpted tech whore. I have to admit, this second choice has its benefits," his mind dwelling on her architectural improvements.

"Caitlin thinks we're going to welcome her back," Otto said, his smile turning predatory. "Actually, believes that promise about being part of the family again."

Both men laughed then, the sound sharp and cruel in the foggy night. Hans settled into his chair, savoring the wine and the moment.

"She has no idea my lawyers are already working custody angles," Hans said. "Grandfather's rights. Unfit mother. When this is over, I'll have my granddaughter where she belongs."

"But first we need her to finish the job with Ryan."

"Oh, she will." Hans leaned forward, his voice dropping. "Because if she doesn't, she loses everything. Her daughter, her freedom, her future."

Otto set down his glass. "So, what's the plan? More newspaper stories? More fake evidence?"

"No." Hans stood, moving to the window where fog pressed against glass like searching fingers.

"I'm done with subtlety. Done with games."

"What are you thinking?"

Hans turned back to his son, eyes cold as black ice. "Remember the contacts from the old days? The ones who helped us clean money through agriculture?"

Otto's eyes widened slightly. "You're talking about calling in favors from the cartel."

"Former cartel," Hans corrected. "They're legitimate businessmen now. Agricultural supply, import-export. Very discreet."

"And what exactly would we be importing?"

Hans smiled, the expression predatory and without warmth. "Industrial herbicide. The kind that doesn't show up on standard tests. The kind that kills everything it touches."

Otto leaned back in his chair, processing. "You want to poison their vines."

"I want to erase their vines. A century of cultivation, gone overnight. Heritage rootstock, irreplaceable genetics, all of it dead."

"The timing?"

"Before harvest. Before they can celebrate another season of pretending they're better than us." Hans raised his glass. "To the end of the Weinhardt legacy and the merger that will ultimately give us everything they have."

"And after? When investigators come sniffing around?"

"Equipment malfunction. Contaminated irrigation. Disgruntled employee." Hans shrugged.

"Accidents happen in agriculture all the time. Tragic, really."

Otto's smile spread slowly across his face. "The Mexicans disappear back across the border."

"Exactly. Clean, untraceable, final."

They drank in silence, the wine coating their throats like complicity. Outside, the fog continued its ancient dance, rolling off the Pacific to bless the land that had sustained the Weinhardts for five generations. But inside the Krueger mansion, two men plotted to end that legacy with chemistry and malice.

The night was late, pushing toward dawn, but to them it felt young and full of dark possibility that would bloom with the morning sun.

CHAPTER SEVENTEEN

YOUNTVILLE

NAPA COUNTY

Wine is a seductive devil, a treasure, and a torment."
Baudelaire, Les Fleurs du mal

The Vine & Valley sat tucked into a fold of hills between Napa and Sonoma, its stone walls built from quarried local rock, ivy climbing toward windows that caught the first of September's golden light. Inside, exposed beams from century-old oaks stretched across high ceilings, while modern touches softened the rustic edges. White tablecloths, gleaming stemware, the quiet hum of serious conversation about soil and vintage and terroir.

Ethan cut into his duck breast, the meat pink and tender, accompanied by farro risotto studded with local chanterelles. His forearms trembled slightly from fatigue as he worked the knife.

Twelve hours earlier, he'd been in the vineyard pulling leaves to expose the fruit zones, his hands remembering the rhythm even after a decade away. Karl had started them at dawn, walking the upper blocks, checking seed color while the morning was still cool. Ryan worked the opposite end of the row, the two brothers maintaining careful distance. Their father moved between them throughout the day, assigning tasks that kept them apart, his presence alone preventing what everyone knew was coming eventually.

Six of them out there total. The regulars, Miguel, Carlos, Tommy, Luis, moving with practiced efficiency while Ethan struggled to keep pace. By noon his shirt was soaked through. By three, blisters had formed despite the gloves. They'd spent the afternoon going through equipment, Ethan helping Jake grease the gondolas' wheels while Ryan checked hydraulics on both tractors with Luis. Forty macro-bins inspected, stacked, ready. His father's voice calling out instructions, treating him like any other hand.

"Same as the others," Karl had said when Ethan asked about pay that first week back. "Fair day's wage for fair day's work."

The money felt different than tech money. Smaller, harder earned, more real. Enough for this dinner though, this attempt at something normal.

Across from him now, Lauren worked delicately at her lamb, raised on grasslands just twenty miles north, paired with roasted vegetables that still held the summer's heat. She was her now, the result of an actual request for a date at the end of their ride to the meadow to inspect Tawi mushrooms.

"The irony," Ethan said, setting down his fork, "is that I thought I was so much smarter than everyone else. Stanford computer science, top of my class, internships at Google before I even graduated. I had this friend, Jason, who'd started three companies before he was twenty-five. Made twenty million on an exit, bought a Ferrari the same day."

Lauren's eyes stayed on his face, reading the pain beneath the words.

"Six months later, Jason wrapped that car around a tree on Highway 17. Going a hundred and twenty in a forty-five zone." Ethan's voice went quiet. "The coroner found enough coke in his system to kill a horse."

"That's awful."

"The worst part? I was headed down the same road. Different car, same destination." He picked up his wine, a local Pinot that tasted of earth and fog. "Maybe losing everything saved my life."

Lauren nodded, her own glass barely touched. "UC Davis was hard for me too, but in different ways. Animal husbandry program was brutal, mostly men who thought I was there to find a husband." She smiled ruefully. "I actually dated one of them for a while. This cowboy type, all swagger and Marlboro masculinity. Thought he could break me like a wild horse."

"What happened?"

"I came to my senses. Realized I was attracted to the performance, not the person underneath." She touched his hand briefly. "I'm glad I'm beyond needing that kind of validation."

Ethan felt the weight of her words, the comparison she wasn't quite making. "You're talking about more than just college, aren't you?"

"I found my calling with wounded animals. There was this dog, a border collie someone had beaten half to death and dumped by the roadside. Broken ribs, infected wounds, so traumatized she wouldn't let anyone touch her." Lauren's face softened with memory. "But with patience, with consistent care, she learned to trust again. Eventually became the sweetest companion you could imagine."

The metaphor hung between them, gentle but pointed. Ethan felt his old pride bristle. "Are you comparing me to a beaten dog?"

Lauren laughed, the sound light and musical. "Maybe a little."

He stared at her, processing the sting, then found himself laughing too. "You know what? There's still a part of me that wants to argue with that, prove I'm not as broken as I was."

"Which proves you still have some breaking left to do." Her smile was kind but unflinching. "But here's the thing about taking the low road, about admitting you need healing. It's the only way back to the high ground. And the fact that your family welcomed you home, don't take any of that for granted. You've been grafted back in."

The restaurant's quiet atmosphere shattered as voices rose near the entrance. Ethan looked up to see Marcus Valdez being seated across the dining room, his silver hair catching the light, his movements predatory even in casual conversation. And beside him, dark hair spilling over bare shoulders, sat Kat.

"You've got to be kidding me," Ethan muttered.

Lauren followed his gaze, her expression shifting. "Friends of yours?"

"Former life."

Marcus spotted them within minutes, his smile sharp as a blade. He approached their table with Kat trailing behind, her red dress clinging in ways that drew every male eye in the room.

"Ethan Weinhardt." Marcus pulled out a chair beside Eathan, uninvited. "Mind if we join you? Small world, running into you here."

Kat slid into the empty seat beside Lauren, her perfume reaching across the table. The same scent that had haunted Ethan's sheets for months, that still triggered memories he thought he'd buried.

"Marcus." Ethan's voice stayed level. "This is Lauren."

"Charmed." Marcus barely glanced at her.

"This is not accidental meeting Marcus, what are you up to?"

"What no, catching up on old times? Well, if you're so eager to find out, let me get right to the point. I told you I'd be back with an offer. Goldberg's willing to drop all legal threats if you'll consult on a new AI project. Use what you remember about Athena's architecture."

"I'm not interested."

"Hear me out. Six-month contract, two million guaranteed, plus equity if we hit milestones." Marcus leaned forward. "You could buy your own vineyard with that money. Last time I was here, I was doing someone a favor. This time, it's real. The Valley wants you back. The Koreans are biting."

Kat hadn't spoken, but her eyes never left Ethan's face. When he finally looked at her, she smiled the smile that had once made him forget every rational thought.

"Hello, Ethan." Her voice was whiskey and velvet. "I've missed you."

The words hit him like a physical blow. Memories flooded back: Kat in his penthouse, naked except for his Stanford t-shirt, making coffee while markets opened in Tokyo. Kat beside him at Neural, her hand on his thigh as deals closed around them. Kat in his bed, whispering promises about futures built on ambition and endless appetite.

"Like I said, the Valley misses you too," Marcus continued. "Your reputation's rehabilitated. Everyone knows Chen was the thief. You're seen as the victim now, which plays well with investors."

Ethan forced himself to look away from Kat, to focus on the hills visible through the restaurant's windows. Those rolling slopes covered in vines that had grown here for generations, tended by hands that understood patience over profit.

"My heart's here now," he said finally. "Close to the soil, close to the vines. The ocean air that comes across these mountains each evening, the fog that rolls in from the Pacific. I tried to build something artificial, and it nearly destroyed me."

"Ethan." Kat's voice carried hurt and confusion. "You can't be serious about this small-town thing. You were meant for bigger things."

Lauren's chair scraped against the floor. "I don't know what you people are doing here," she said, looking directly at Ethan, "but I'm out of here."

She stood and walked toward the exit, her movements controlled but quick. Ethan watched her go, torn between following and staying, between the woman who saw his potential for healing and the one who'd known his appetite for destruction.

"Let her go," Kat said softly. "Some women can't handle the real you."

The words cut deeper than intended. Ethan threw cash on the table and headed for the door.

He found Lauren beside the Camry, arms crossed, staring at the hills that were already swallowing the sun.

"Listen," he started.

"I could tell there were things still lingering in your mind," she said without turning. "The way you looked at her. You need to sort that out."

They drove home in silence, the Camry's engine struggling with the hills, the air growing cooler as fog began its evening migration inland. When they reached Lauren's house, a modest cottage surrounded by her veterinary practice's outbuildings, she paused before getting out.

"I know you're a new man now," she said, looking back at him through the open door. "Don't listen to those old ghosts. Choose the right way."

The implication hung clear: choose me.

The Library, Late Evening

Karl Weinhardt sat in the leather chair that had been his father's, the one positioned to catch the last heat from the dying fire. The library wrapped around him like an old coat, familiar and worn in all the right places. Books climbed to the ceiling, their spines catching gold from the string of lights Eden had insisted on..."ambiance," she'd called it, though he'd grown to appreciate how they warmed the room. The redwood beams above had once been living trees when his grandfather was still clearing the land.

Outside, fog pressed against the windows like something alive, the same heavy mist that had soaked through his jacket when he'd walked the north vineyard at dusk. Even in late summer, the coastal air could come over the hills giving the evening a chill. His bones still carried that damp cold, the kind that crept in after nearly sixty years of working fog-wrapped mornings.

He stirred the embers with the iron poker, coaxing a few flames back to life. The oak popped, releasing the smell of smoke and resin, the scent of a thousand evenings like this one. In the firelight, the room flickered between shadow and warmth, his grandfather's surveying tools on the mantel, four generations of Weinhardt stubbornness built into these walls, beam by beam.

The leather creaked as he shifted, trying to find the angle where his back didn't protest the day's work. Old bones, as Eden liked to say. But these old bones knew every vine on the property, felt the soil's changes before any instrument could measure them. He'd been out there since the last light of evening had slipped behind the western hills.

Esther found him there, carrying the journal she'd discovered with Ethan. She settled into the chair across from him, tucking her feet under her the way she had since childhood.

"Dad, we need to talk about Friedrich's journal. I mentioned it days ago, but I don't think you really heard me."

Karl set down his reading glasses, gave her his full attention. This was his youngest, his daughter who'd gone to UC to study what he'd learned by doing. Who came back speaking of brix levels and malolactic fermentation but still knew when to pick by the weight of a cluster in her hand.

"I heard you. Just been thinking on it."

"Dad, there's something in here about harvest timing. Something we've never tried." She opened the journal carefully. "Friedrich writes about waiting for three mornings when the fog lifts before ten. He calls it fog-break crushing."

"Sounds like superstition."

"That's what I thought. But Dad, remember what they taught us about biodynamics? Everyone laughed at Rudolf Steiner's moon planting until studies showed root growth really does respond to lunar cycles. The University of Bordeaux proved it in 2016."

Karl leaned back, the chair creaking. His daughter had her mother's beauty but his stubbornness. When she got that look, like now, she wouldn't let go.

"And in Burgundy," Esther continued, "those monks everyone mocked for tasting soil? Turns out they were identifying minerality that modern spectrometers can now measure. Hundreds of years of observation validated by science."

"Ryan won't like experimenting. Not with the whole harvest."

"Ryan doesn't have to like it. Just one block, Dad. The old vine Pinot on the west slope." She leaned forward. "Remember what Grandpa used to say? That the old Italians knew things about fog that we'd forgotten?"

Karl remembered. His father spoke of it rarely, usually late at night after wine had loosened his tongue. Stories passed down but never written until Friedrich.

"The wine press will mock us. 'Weinhardt's Go Mystic' or some such nonsense."

"Let them. Since when do we make wine for critics?" She had him there. "Besides, there's precedent. In Piedmont, they still harvest Nebbiolo by the feast days, not the calendar. Everyone said it was primitive until climate data showed those feast days align perfectly with historical weather patterns."

From the kitchen came footsteps. Eden appeared in the doorway, dish towel in hand, Tawi behind her.

"We couldn't help overhearing," Eden said, though Karl knew she'd been listening on purpose. Forty-eight years of marriage taught you these things.

"The young one speaks truth," Tawi said, moving into the room with that silence he carried everywhere. "My grandmother knew about fog-break. Called it something else in our language, but same idea. When fog lifts early three days running, the earth is shifting its weight. Like a sleeper about to wake. Good time for some work. Bad for others."

"Shifting its weight," Karl said, but gently. Tawi had earned his skepticism and his respect in equal measure.

"Call it atmospheric pressure if it makes you feel modern." Tawi's rare smile creased his face. "The earth breathes in patterns. Always has. Whether you name it or not changes nothing."

Eden crossed to Karl's chair, rested a hand on his shoulder. "Remember 2018? You insisted on picking early because the ravens were gathering. Everyone said you were crazy until that heat spike hit and everyone else's fruit got cooked."

"That was different. That was observation."

"So is this." Esther held up the journal. "Friedrich observed for decades. Documented it. The Italians before him observed for generations."

Karl looked around the room. His wife, still beautiful at sixty-five, who'd stood by him through every hard season. His daughter, brilliant and stubborn, carrying forward what he'd tried to teach. Tawi, keeper of older knowledge than any of them claimed. The books rising around them, each one someone's attempt to pin down truth.

"In France," Esther pressed on, "Marcel Deiss still plows with horses on certain slopes. Says tractors compact the soil wrong. Sorbonne studied it, found he was right. The vibration patterns matter. Just because we can't measure something yet doesn't mean it's not real."

"You sound like your grandfather."

"Good. He made better wine than any of us."

That stung because it was true. Karl's father had made wine that still, forty years later, opened like a cathedral when you pulled the cork. They made good wine now, technical wine, correct wine. But not... transcendent.

"One block," he said finally. "The old vine Pinot. We follow Friedrich's method exactly."

Esther's face lit up. "Really?"

"If we're going to fail, might as well fail trying something new instead of the same old careful." He picked up the journal, felt its weight. "Or something old that might be new again."

Eden squeezed his shoulder. "Your father would be proud."

"My father would have laughed, then done it anyway." Karl stood, joints protesting. "When harvest starts, we will watch the fog pattern."

"If the marine forecast holds," Esther said.

"Then we watch. Three mornings. If fog breaks before ten each day, we pick the moment it clears on the third."

"And if it doesn't?" Eden asked.

"Then we pick like always and Ryan never has to know we almost lost our minds." But Karl was smiling now. "Tawi, you'll watch with us?"

"Someone has to make sure you see what you're looking at."

They stood together in the library as evening deepened, surrounded by all their accumulated knowledge, preparing to trust something older than any of it. Outside, the first fog of the night crept up from the coast, carrying salt and mystery and the promise of mornings when it might lift early, telling them things they'd forgotten how to hear.

Ethan lay in his childhood bed listening to the house settle, watching the fog pressing against windows, his ear to the distant sound of cattle moving through pastures. Sleep wouldn't come. Every time he closed his eyes, he saw Kat's smile, felt the old hunger stirring in places he'd thought were finally quiet.

He gave up near midnight and walked onto the porch, where he found Tawi sitting in the darkness, a cup of something steaming in his weathered hands.

"Can't sleep?" the old man asked.

"Bad dreams. Old memories."

"That's to be expected after all those years in the Valley soaking in that culture." Tawi kicked at the dry earth with his boot, eyes tracing the rows of vines disappearing into the fog. "Your sister was telling me about

~ 171 ~

something when she came home from college her first year. Called them neural pathways. Long before those professors at the university started talking about them, our people already knew about the same thing. We just called them trails in the mind."

He gestured toward the ridge where grass swayed in the wind. "When you walk the same trail every day, the grass lays down flat. The dirt hardens. After a while, you don't even have to think. Your feet remember. That's how pain works too. How destructive patterns work. You walk the same sorrow over and over, the same hunger, the same mistakes, and it becomes the only way you know."

Ethan settled into the chair beside him, feeling the truth of the words.

"But the land heals if you let it," Tawi continued. "Stop walking that trail, and the grass grows back, covers the old footprints. Then you can cut a new path. It's harder at first, rough and uneven, but each time you walk it, the way becomes clearer. The mind's no different. Creator gave us that gift, to grow new trails, even over the old scars."

He smiled faintly, tapping his temple. "So, when those university folks say we can reprogram our brains, I just nod. The old ones knew that already. We've been doing it for generations, finding our way back through the tall grass."

"But what if the old trails feel stronger? What if they're calling you back?"

"Then you sit with an old man on a porch and remember why you chose the new path." Tawi's voice carried ancient patience. "You think about your family who welcomed you home. You think about a woman who sees your healing instead of your hunger. You choose gratitude over longing."

They sat in comfortable silence, the fog thickening around them, the night sounds of the ranch settling into rhythm. Gradually, Ethan felt his breathing slow, his mind quiet. The images of Kat faded, replaced by Lauren's gentle hands tending wounded animals, by his father's tears when he'd come home, by the taste of wine made from grapes that had grown in this soil for generations.

"Thank you," he said finally.

Tawi nodded, standing with a grunt. "Sleep now. Tomorrow brings its own challenges."

But as Ethan headed inside, the old man remained on the porch, his dog emerging from the shadows to press against his leg. Something had caught the animal's attention, ears pricked toward the vineyards. Tawi strained to listen, thought he caught the sound of voices, but the wind shifted and brought only the smell of salt air from the coast.

Minutes later, the dog growled low, hackles rising. This time Tawi trusted the instinct, moving quietly to retrieve his shotgun from inside. The dog led him toward Ryan's experimental blocks; the French Pinot vines his older son had imported with such pride.

Halfway through the vineyard, shapes moved between the rows. Two men working methodically through the vines, moving with purpose but without lights. When Tawi raised the shotgun, not to shoot but to be seen, the men looked up and ran toward the ridge where a truck waited in darkness.

By the time Tawi reached where they'd been working, taillights were disappearing down the mountain road. He stood among Ryan's precious vines, sensing something was wrong but unable to identify what. The ocean breeze masked any foreign smells, and in the darkness, he couldn't see signs of disturbance.

Back on the porch, his dog settled beside him with a sigh. Tawi scratched behind the animal's ears, thinking about enemies and timing, about young men who thought they could improve on generations of wisdom.

He hoped Ethan would heed his advice about choosing new paths. Because something told him they'd all need to walk unfamiliar ground in the days ahead.

The fog swallowed the ranch completely now, wrapping them in gray silence. But somewhere in that silence, Tawi felt the presence of something patient and malevolent, waiting for morning to reveal its work.

CHAPTER EIGHTEEN

WEINHARDT'S RANCH

SONOMA COUNTY

"Even bad wine has its story."
Robert Mondavi

The early September sun hung low over the western hills, painting the vineyard in shades of gold and amber. Ryan Weinhardt stood before the gathering, his pressed shirt already showing traces of sweat despite the cooling afternoon breeze. Behind him, three oak barrels waited on stands, their contents a year in the making.

"Welcome, everyone." His voice carried across the courtyard. "Thank you for coming to share this moment with us."

The crowd was carefully curated. Local press, two sommeliers from Healdsburg, neighboring growers who understood the risk he was taking. His father Karl stood to one side, arms crossed, that careful neutrality on his face that Ryan knew too well. Dirt still clung to Karl's boots from his morning walk through the upper blocks, the daily ritual now of tasting berries, searching for that perfect balance of flavor, tannin, and color that would trigger harvest.

Eight of them working the vineyard today. The usual six, including Ethan, plus Tommy Gonzales and his cousin Luis, brought on for these critical weeks. Ryan had watched them head out at first light, his younger brother falling into step with Jake, testing the feel of seeds between his teeth, the way they crunch when approaching ripeness. Karl checking Brix levels across their fifty acres of Pinot, the ritual of testing sugar and acidity accelerating now.

The small, loose clusters hanging in the field didn't need Ryan today. Karl had mentioned yields looked to be around 2.2 tons per acre, maybe 110 tons total if they were lucky. Thick skins on berries stressed by May's wind. The kind of fruit that made decisions like this one possible, or necessary.

Eden stood beside Karl, one hand on her husband's arm. She'd probably packed sandwiches for the whole expanded crew, knowing they'd work through lunch. In the equipment shed, forty pairs of shears lay sharpened and ready, alongside new gloves, headlamps for the dawn picks, reflective vests for safety. Ethan had spent yesterday afternoon helping stage it all, then worked with Luis to position the forklift at the crush pad. Two flatbed trucks from Petaluma were already contracted for the nightly hauls to the winery once picking began. Everything and everyone ready except Ryan, who'd chosen instead to host his barrel opening.

The Weinhardts have grown wine in this valley for five generations," Ryan continued. "But tradition without innovation becomes stagnation. That's why I've spent the last three years cultivating something new. I spent a month in the Rhône Valley researching this variety, working directly with the Institut Français de la Vigne. Vidoc Noir comes from the slopes near Mont Ventoux, where they've been quietly perfecting it for decades."

He caught Bri's eye. She smiled, but he saw the tension in her shoulders. She knew what this meant to him. What failing would mean.

"I'd like my father to say a few words."

Karl stepped forward, his weathered face unreadable. "Our family came to this land when it was still wild. We learned its moods, its seasons. We've made our reputation on Pinot and Chardonnay, wines that speak of this place." He paused, glanced at Ryan. "But my son sees farther than I do sometimes. He's earned the right to try."

Then, almost as an afterthought, his eyes found Ethan. "Vision runs in this family. Sometimes it takes us away. Sometimes it brings us home. Today we celebrate the vision that stayed." The words landed like stones in still water. Ryan felt heat climb his neck. Even now, even at his moment, it came back to Ethan.

Eden stepped forward quickly, her British accent softening her words. "As another import to this valley, I can say that sometimes the best things come from unexpected places. Ryan, we're proud of what you've built here."

"Thank you, Mom." Ryan turned to the barrels, needing to move past the moment. "Vidoc Noir is hardy, complex, built for our climate. And today, we've commissioned a special label from one of our local artists." He unveiled the bottle. Hand-painted glass, the label showing fog rolling through vines. Karl's jaw tightened. Another decision made without consultation.

Eden's hand found Karl's arm again, a gentle pressure. Later, that touch said.

The first barrel was opened. Wine flowed into glasses, deep garnet catching the light. The sommeliers swirled, sniffed, tasted. Ryan watched their faces, reading every micro-expression.

Philippe Martel from the Healdsburg Inn went first. "Interesting structure. I get blackberry, wet stone, a hint of lavender." He paused, took another sip. "But there's something else. A note at the finish that's..."

"Bitter." Maria Delgado from Wine Spectator didn't soften it. "The tannins are aggressive, but beyond that, there's an underlying bitterness that overwhelms the fruit."

The words hung in the air. Ryan watched as people set down their glasses, turning instead to the carefully arranged charcuterie boards. Local cheeses, cured meats from the valley, Tawi's special pickled vegetables. They ate with determined enthusiasm, as if good food could erase the awkwardness.

"These olives are exceptional," someone murmured.

"Is this the ranch's own prosciutto?" another asked, though everyone knew it wasn't.

One by one, they drained their glasses. Not from enjoyment, but from politeness. Ryan saw it all. The sympathetic glances, the forced smiles, the way conversation turned deliberately to safer topics. The weather. The coming harvest. Anything but the wine they'd come to celebrate.

Within thirty minutes, the courtyard had emptied. Neighbors pressed his hand, murmuring encouragement that rang hollow. The press packed their cameras without asking for follow-up quotes.

"Ryan." Jake jogged up, face flushed. "Miguel just ran over from Block 12. Says you need to see something."

An hour later, Ryan stood among his dying vines. The leaves hung brown and withered. Three rows of his Vidoc Noir, poisoned.

"Herbicide, maybe." Jake knelt, examining the soil. "Or over-fertilization. But this is deliberate. Someone did this."

Tawi appeared beside them, moving with that silence he'd perfected over decades. "Three nights ago, something felt wrong in the air. You know how the land speaks when it's troubled. I walked the blocks, found footprints here between the rows. The smell of chemicals where there should be only earth and vine."

"Who would do this?" Ryan's voice cracked. "After everything I've put into this place?"

Karl and Eden arrived, Ethan trailing behind. They surveyed the damage in silence.

"It's not all lost," Karl said finally. "The other rows look healthy. We can work with what's left, adjust the cultivation."

"Your father's right," Tawi said quietly. "In the old ways, we learned that even a bitter root can be grafted onto sweeter stock. The scion takes on the strength of the new foundation. Sometimes what seems poisoned can be cut back, the soil amended, the vine given new life from better roots." He paused, looking at the damaged vines. "Bitterness doesn't have to be the end of the story."

But Ryan was past metaphors. After they left, Bri tried to reach him. "I'm here. We'll figure this out together."

"Together?" The word tasted as bitter as his failed wine. "While Dad celebrates Saint Ethan's return? While my work gets sabotaged?"

"Ryan, please."

"I need to think." He headed for his Jeep.

"Don't go to Murphy's." She knew him too well.

"I'll go wherever I want."

The door slammed. Through the window, she watched his taillights disappear down the drive. Movement caught her eye. Ethan, standing on the porch of the main house, watching her. Their eyes met across the distance. Old ghosts stirred. She turned away.

Murphy's was exactly what Ryan expected. Dark, loud enough to drown out thinking. The bar was weathered oak, sticky with decades of spilled drinks. His friends from high school were already there, deep into their second pitcher.

"Heard about the tasting," Tommy said, sliding a beer across. "Rough break."

"Dad give you the 'vision of the family' speech?" Mike asked. "While golden boy takes notes for his diary?"

"Something like that." Ryan drained half his beer in one pull.

"Your dad's always been blind about Ethan," Tommy said. "Even back in high school. Star athlete, straight A's, could charm anyone. Rest of us might as well have been invisible."

"Remember when he got into Stanford?" Mike laughed bitterly. "My mom wouldn't shut up about it for months. 'Why can't you be more like the Weinhardt boy?'"

"And now he's back." Ryan signaled for another round. "Failed startup, blown through millions, and Dad throws him a party."

"While you've been here, keeping the place running," Tommy added.

"Building something new," Mike agreed. "That Vidoc Noir, that's innovation. That's the future."

"Tell that to Maria Delgado." Ryan's laugh was hollow. "Bitter, she said. In front of everyone."

They drank in silence for a while, the bar filling with the after-work crowd. Farmers and tech workers, an uneasy mix that defined the modern valley. Someone fed quarters into the jukebox. Tom Petty sang about learning to fly.

That's when she appeared. Caitlin, sliding through the crowd with practiced ease. She wore jeans and a simple black top, but she made them look like haute couture.

"Gentlemen," she nodded to Tommy and Mike, but her eyes were on Ryan. "Heard about your tasting. Shame when hard work doesn't pay off."

"We were just leaving," Tommy said, catching Mike's eye. They knew Caitlin's reputation, knew when to make themselves scarce.

She took Tommy's vacant stool, ordered whiskey neat. "You look like a man who needs better company than beer and sympathy. Madison's with my sister, so we'll have my place all to ourselves."

Later, much later, her apartment was dark except for streetlight through cheap blinds. She poured wine, not asking if he wanted any.

"You're much more than you let yourself be," she said, apropos of nothing. "You gave those vines time, waited for them to mature."

"Story of my life," he replied. "Waiting to inherit."

"I'm serious. You stay because you think you have to. But what if you didn't?"

He didn't answer. Couldn't.

Back at the ranch, evening fog crept up from the coast. Ethan led his parents and Tawi up the ridge trail, past the old barn that overlooked everything.

"Remember when I was twelve, asking why we couldn't just grow easier grapes?" Ethan stopped at the barn's entrance. "You said the struggle made them better."

"Still true," Karl said.

"This barn's been empty twenty years." Ethan pushed open the doors, revealing the cavernous space. "But I keep seeing something else. Forty seats. Kitchen in the back. Windows cut there, facing the sunset."

"A restaurant?" Eden's voice held curiosity.

"More than that. When I talked with Lauren last week, we spent hours sketching it out. Tawi's recipes, but elevated. The ranch's ingredients telling our story. Great-grandpa's apple orchard down there, those Gravenstein and Pippins you can't find anymore. Tawi makes that sauce from them, the one that brings tears. His grandmother's knowledge of what grows wild here, the mushrooms, the herbs."

He walked them through his vision. "Even when I was drowning in Silicon Valley, I'd sketch this during board meetings. Called it Terra/Tech, this idea that I could bring what we have here to that sterile place. But I had it backwards. This place doesn't need to go anywhere. People need to come here, taste what four generations have built."

Tawi listened, nodding slowly. "The old ways, made new. Your grandmother would have understood."

"It's Ryan's land someday," Eden said carefully. "What future would a restaurant have?"

Karl was quiet, studying the space. "Maybe we give it time. See what grows. I'm learning that visions need room to breathe."

They walked back through gathering darkness, each lost in thought.

Miles away, in the Krueger estate's study, Otto poured brandy for their guest. Alejandro Vega dressed like old California money, understated elegance that whispered rather than shouted its price. Everything about him suggested careful cultivation, from his manicured hands to his patient smile.

"My associates grow concerned," Vega said mildly. "Our investments require returns."

"This alliance with the Weinhardts, specifically, young Ryan?"

"We're drawing him in," Otto said. "He's already shown interest in our operations. The boy's hungry for recognition, wants to step out of his father's shadow. But for now, we plan to hire their workers away. And if that doesn't work, the Salvadoran's are in play`. They'll be activated shortly."

Vega studied his brandy, letting the silence stretch. "We will see how your 'Salvadoran' scheme goes. Pray that it does. Our capital doesn't flow north without results." He took a slow sip. "If things get difficult, Cesar will come. And Cesar doesn't leave until problems are solved. One way or another.

"Ryan will come around," Hans insisted. "We've been cultivating him carefully. We will make him an offer soon."

Vega smiled, the expression never reaching his eyes. "For your sake, I hope so. My associates value results over promises. They tell me they want action now, or...well, others have made the mistake of taking our money and then failed, need I say more."

The threat hung in the air like a vapor from a moldy cellar.

After he left, father and son sat in silence.

"This has gone too far," Otto said finally.

Hans poured another brandy with shaking hands. "We're in too deep to stop now. It's time to approach Ryan."

Outside, fog swallowed the valley whole, hiding sins and dreams alike in its gray embrace.

CHAPTER NINETEEN

WEINHARDT'S RANCH

SONOMA COUNTY

"The harvest of a vineyard is the reward of patience."
Henri Jayer

The blue hour faded behind the coastal mountains, leaving only headlights to cut through the darkness. 10:15 p.m. Perfect. The temperature had finally dropped below sixty degrees, and the fruit would come in cool, preserving the delicate aromatic qualities that the family had spent decades cultivating.

It was late September, peak harvest season in Sonoma County, though the exact timing varied from vineyard to vineyard, dependent on sugar levels reaching that sweet spot between 21 and 25 Brix, acids maintaining their crucial balance, and tannins achieving the phenolic ripeness that separated good wine from great. Some years, harvest stretched well into October when cool weather slowed the ripening, but this year's warm summer had brought everything forward.

Thirty-five pickers moved through the vines like a slow tide, their headlamps bobbing in rhythm with the rustle of leaves and snap of stems. Karl had hired enough to bring the harvest in in two nights. The gondolas groaned between rows, shuttling fruit to the staging area where a mobile light tower blazed like an oasis in the dark.

Karl stood in the pool of light from Jake's Jeep, addressing the crew with that easy authority earned through decades of harvests. The Mexican families who'd worked Weinhardt land for generations nodded along, knowing the drill but listening anyway. Pick clean, handle gentle, watch for rot. One ton per picker per night if they kept pace.

"Temperature's holding at fifty-eight," Karl told Jake as they walked the first rows. "Perfect." He plucked a cluster, rolled a berry between his fingers, bit down. "Sugar's right. Maybe another degree Brix by morning."

The headlamps created a constellation across the hillside. Ethan worked row seven, partnered with Miguel Hernandez, whose family had been picking Weinhardt grapes since before Ethan was born. The rhythm came back slowly. Reach, cut, drop to bin. The sticky juice coating his forearms, the ache building between his shoulder blades.

"Like riding a bike, no?" Miguel grinned, his pace never slowing. "Your hands remember."

Ethan's Spanish came out rusty. "Sí, pero my back forgot how much it hurts."

Miguel laughed. "You get soft in the city. My boys, they do this since twelve years old. Makes them strong."

Down the row, one of Miguel's sons worked with his girl friend, the two of them talking quietly, picking in tandem. The sight triggered something in Ethan, a memory from when he was twelve, working his first real harvest. The Hernandez family had taken him under their wing that year, teaching him not just how to pick but how to read the fruit, how to last through the long nights. He'd envied their closeness even then, three generations working side by side, nobody trying to prove they were too good for the work.

"Hey, city boy." Ryan's voice cut through his reverie. "Pick up the pace. We're not paying you to daydream."

Ethan kept his eyes on the vines. "Just trying to match Miguel's rhythm."

"Well try harder." Ryan moved on, barking at another picker about leaving fruit on the vine.

Miguel shook his head once Ryan passed. "Your brother, he works hard but..." He made a gesture that needed no translation.

"Yeah," Ethan said. "I know."

By eleven, the fog had rolled in thick, turning the headlamps into halos. Eden appeared with Tawi and two of the younger Mexican women, wheeling carts loaded with tamales, fresh tortillas, thermoses of coffee. The pickers converged on the makeshift meal station set up between the equipment sheds.

"Eat," Eden commanded, pressing a plate into Ethan's hands. "You look ready to fall over."

The tamales were perfect, Tawi's contribution clear in the complexity of the spices. Ethan found a spot on an overturned bin, grateful for the break. His hands shook slightly as he unwrapped the corn husk.

"Good to be back out here," he said to the group nearby. "I forgot how much I missed this. The harvest, working together. Seeing families like the Hernandezes, how tight they are. Makes you appreciate what matters."

Ryan snorted from where he leaned against a tractor. "If you appreciated family so much, you wouldn't have blown three million of ours on your tech fantasies."

The conversations around them quieted.

"You're right," Ethan said. "I shouldn't have left. I'm trying to make it right."

"By playing restaurant? I heard about your little dream project with Lauren." Ryan's voice carried that particular edge Ethan remembered from childhood. "Another scheme that'll probably—"

"Ryan." Karl's voice was quiet but firm. "That's enough."

Father and son locked eyes for a moment before Ryan looked away.

"This place will be yours one day," Karl continued. "We all know that. But your brother's dreams matter too. Who knows what might come of them?"

Something passed across Karl's face, a weight in his look at Ryan. "We all lose our way sometimes. What matters is finding the path back."

Ryan stiffened, something guilty flickering in his expression before he turned away.

Karl stepped forward, his weathered hands on his hips as he surveyed the group. "Alright, people!" His voice carried that particular mix of authority and encouragement that came from years of leading crews. "We've got good momentum tonight. I see every one of you hitting your numbers if we keep this pace." He nodded toward the fog-shrouded rows. "Let's finish strong, show these vines what we're made of. Every basket counts, and you're all doing great work out here."

The pickers dispersed slowly, the tension dissipating into the fog. A few nodded at Karl's words, shoulders straightening despite their fatigue.

Ethan headed back to row seven, his mind churning. The familiar burn in his muscles felt good, clean. Different from the synthetic energy he used to chase. But as he bent to the vines, sweat running down his spine, something shifted.

The smell of crushed fruit suddenly became too sweet, cloying. The generator hum morphed into bass drops, the headlamps into strobes. He was back at Neural, the club spinning around him, Marcus nearby with that demon grin, measuring out doses like a pharmacist of oblivion.

"Just one more hit," Marcus saying. "Keep you going all night."

And Kat, beautiful Kat, leading someone else to the VIP section, looking back over her shoulder with those eyes that promised everything and delivered nothing. The music pounding, his heart trying to match it, beat for beat, the walls closing in...

"Ethan!" Miguel's hand on his shoulder snapped him back. "You okay? You dropped your shears."

Ethan bent to retrieve them, hands trembling. "Yeah. Just... something got to me."

"Is late. Almost done for tonight." Miguel studied him with knowing eyes. "The body remembers everything, no? Good and bad."

The final push carried them past two in the morning. The last bins loaded, the tractors rumbling off toward the winery. Ethan slumped against a fence post, every muscle screaming, the phantom taste of chemicals still coating his throat.

Somewhere in the fog, raised voices. Ryan and one of the Mexican workers, Enrique Navarro, near the equipment shed. Ethan couldn't make out all the words, but he caught enough. Enrique's voice, righteous and angry: "So, you're the grand jefe now, well, we work for your dad..."

Javier, a natural leader in the ranks joined the fray, "We see the way you treat your brother."

"You come off as so righteous, ...think we don't know," added Enrique. "You judge your brother but everyone knows about your little *aventuras*. At least I keep my family together..."

Ryan's response was sharp, threatening, but Enrique didn't back down. As other workers began drifting over joining the confrontation.

"Enough!" Jake's voice boomed across the yard. "Save it for tomorrow. Everyone to your trailers, breakfast's waiting and then a break. Tomorrow nights the final bush, you need the rest."

The Weinhardts had always valued their seasonal crews. For those who came from miles away, the family provided housing at no cost, rows of clean, well-kept trailers set near the vines, and made sure every worker was fed before sunrise and after dusk.

The crowd dispersed reluctantly. Ethan watched Ryan stalk toward his truck, shoulders rigid with fury. Javier spat on the ground and walked away.

As the others headed for food and rest, Ethan found himself alone on the stone wall near the old oak, too wired to eat, too tired to move. The fog wrapped around him like a blanket, muffling the sounds of the ranch settling into sleep.

Tawi appeared from the mist, moving with that silence that seemed impossible for a man his size. He settled beside Ethan, pulled a small drum from his pack. Its hide was cracked near the rim, the wood worn smooth by decades of handling.

"This old thing's been with me since I was your age," Tawi said. "Split once, years back. Some said it was finished, but my grandfather told me, 'You don't throw away a wounded drum. You thank it for surviving the storm.'"

He tapped the hide softly with his thumb, producing a sound deeper than its size suggested.

"He soaked it in river water, stretched it tight again, and played it every morning until the sound came back true. Said gratitude was what mended it. That every beat of thanks was a stitch in the tear."

Tawi looked at Ethan with those eyes that had seen too much to be surprised by anything. "Your mind's that drum. Split by the heat, by noise, by loss. But it's still got a voice. You heal it with rhythm. Steady beats of thanks, even when you don't feel them yet. That's how you keep the song alive."

He began to play, slow and even. A heartbeat rhythm that seemed to match the pulse of the fog rolling through the vines. Then he sang, low and rough, words in the old tongue that Ethan didn't understand but felt in his chest. The chant rose and fell like breath, like tides, like the seasons that turned the grapes from flower to fruit.

When the song ended, Tawi handed him the drum. "Your turn."

Ethan hesitated. "I don't know the song."

"You don't have to. Just name what you're thankful for."

The drum felt heavier than it looked. Ethan struck it once, tentative. The sound rang clear in the fog.

"For coming home," he said, and struck again. "For my father's grace." Another beat. "For another chance."

Tawi smiled, began tapping his knee in time, joining the rhythm. The simple beat carried across the vineyard, absorbed by the fog and the vines and the sleeping earth.

"The mind learns what the hands repeat," Tawi said when they stopped. "Keep beating thanks into every day, and soon that's the song your thoughts will sing on their own."

They sat in comfortable silence until headlights cut through the murk. Jake's truck, driving too fast for the hour. He jumped out, face grim.

"Tawi, Ethan. Karl needs you at the main house. Now."

The urgency in his voice killed any questions. They piled into the truck, bouncing over the rutted road. The main house blazed with light, unusual for this hour. Karl stood on the porch with Ryan, both faces set in hard lines.

"We got a problem," Jake said as they climbed out. "Miguel just called. Says the crew's talking strike. Javier's been spreading word about better wages at the Krueger place. Plus..." He glanced at Ryan. "There's been some complaints about management style."

Ryan's jaw clenched. "That's ridiculous. We pay fair wages."

"Not about the money," Karl said quietly. "Not really." He looked tired, older than his years in the harsh porch light. "Come on. We need to figure this out before morning, or we'll lose half the harvest."

They filed inside, the weight of the night's work and the brewing crisis settling over them like the fog that pressed against the windows. The drum still seemed to pulse in Ethan's hands, its rhythm a reminder that some things could be mended, but only with patience, with gratitude, with time.

CHAPTER TWENTY

WEINHARDT'S RANCH

SONOMA COUNTY

"Good wine and true friends are both born of patience."
Spanish Proverb

The fire crackled and spit, sending sparks into the darkness beyond the circle of trailers. The workers had just finished their breakfast and would have liked a much-needed nap, but something else was on the agenda.

Smoke drifted through the gathered men, carrying the smell of burning oak and something else, the acrid scent of discontent. Javier Mendoza sat forward on an overturned crate, his face half in shadow, half lit by flame.

"We've been fools too long," he said, voice carrying the practiced rhythm of a man who'd rehearsed his words. "Our fathers, they were grateful for any work. But this is not 1975. We're citizens. Our kids go to the same schools as theirs."

Miguel Hernandez shifted on his makeshift seat, a plank laid across two buckets. At fifty-eight, he'd worked Weinhardt land for thirty years. "Karl's always been fair, Javier. You know this."

"Fair?" Javier laughed, but there was no humor in it. "Fair is what they decide is fair. The Kruegers are offering twenty percent more. Health benefits. Bonuses.

Carlos Medina spoke up from where he leaned against a fence post. "My father bought our house working for the Weinhardts. Three acres on Dry Creek Road. You think he could do that now? Even with the Krueger money?"

"That's my point." Javier stood, pacing the edge of the firelight. "Costs go up, wages stay the same. These rich liberals in their Range Rovers, eating at French Laundry, they talk about justice, about supporting workers. But when harvest comes, we're still just hands to them."

"Not Karl," Miguel insisted. "When my Maria got sick, who paid for the specialist in San Francisco? When your own father needed that operation..."

"Ancient history." Javier cut him off. "And what about Ryan? Tell me he treats us with respect. Tell me he doesn't drive us like we're machines. El hijo privilegiado, born on third base thinking he hit a triple."

Luis Morales, youngest of the group at thirty-two, nodded slowly. "My daughter came home crying last week. Ryan's boy said something at school. Not racist exactly, but..." He shrugged. "The apple doesn't fall far from the tree."

"Ryan's got his problems," Miguel admitted. "But that's between him and God. What matters is the work, the pay, the history. Remember when Don César came through? El Líder sat right there," he pointed to a spot near the fire, "with Karl. Two men who didn't agree on politics but respected each other. Nuestro César saw Karl's heart."

Javier's eyes glinted. "Hearts don't pay bills. And speaking of Ryan's problems..." He paused, letting the weight of unspoken knowledge settle over the group. "Some things are better left unsaid. But we all know a man with secrets is a man who can be pressured."

The fire popped, sending up a shower of sparks. The men exchanged glances. Everyone knew there were rumors, but speaking them aloud changed things.

"That's not our business," Miguel said firmly.

"Everything's our business when it affects our families." Javier pulled out his phone, checking the time. "The Kruegers need an answer by sunup. We vote now, or we lose the offer."

The sound of approaching vehicles cut through the twilight. Headlights swept across the camp as two trucks pulled up. Karl Weinhardt climbed out first, moving with the careful precision of a man who knew these roads in full darkness. Ryan followed, jaw tight, shoulders rigid. Behind them came Jake, Tawi, and Ethan.

Ryan didn't wait for greetings. "Is it true? You're thinking of walking out on us? Right in the middle of harvest?"

The accusation hung in the smoky air. Several men stood, creating a loose semicircle. Javier stepped forward, meeting Ryan's glare.

"We're considering our options. It's called the free market. You should appreciate that."

"How could you do this to our family?" Ryan's voice rose. "We've been more than fair..."

Karl placed a hand on his son's arm. "Ryan." One word, quiet but firm. He stepped past his son, approaching the fire with open hands. "Javier. I remember sitting here with your father, Juan. You were maybe ten, hiding behind that shed, listening to everything."

A ghost of a smile crossed Javier's face before he caught himself. "Different times, Mr. Karl."

"We'd just come from meeting with César Chávez," Karl continued. "Your father and I shared a bottle of tequila, worked out wages for the season. He drove a hard bargain."

"He had you sobre un barril," Javier said. "Over a barrel, as you say. Just like you've had us."

"Is that what you think?" Karl's voice carried genuine curiosity, not offense. "That it's us against you? After three generations of working this land together?"

Miguel stepped forward. "Karl, most of us know better. But times are hard. The younger men, they see friends making tech money, working in warehouses, and wonder why they break their backs in the sun."

"Because this work matters," Tawi spoke for the first time, his deep voice cutting through the tension. "Because feeding people matters. Because the land remembers who cares for it."

Ethan started to speak. "Look, if we could just discuss this rationally..."

"Rationally?" Ryan rounded on his brother. "You've been back what, a few months? You think you have a voice here?" His laugh was bitter. "Dad might have made room for you, but you haven't earned the right to speak at this fire."

The rebuke stung, visible on Ethan's face. Karl's expression confirmed Ryan's words with a slight nod, though his eyes held sympathy for his younger son.

"He's right," Karl said simply. "Respect is earned through seasons, not blood."

Javier seized the moment. "See? Even among yourselves, there's division. Why should we trust a family that can't trust each other?"

"Because we've never lied to you," Karl answered. "Never missed a payment. Never brought in illegals to undercut your wages." He looked around the circle. "The Kruegers make big promises. Ask yourselves why. Ask what they want that's worth twenty percent more than market rate."

"Maybe they just value workers," Javier shot back, but doubt crept into his voice.

"Or maybe they value something else." Jake spoke up, his foreman's authority carrying weight. "I've been watching their crews. Vans showing up at dawn, different faces every week. You think those benefits they're promising will last past this harvest?"

The men murmured among themselves. Luis whispered something in rapid Spanish to Carlos, who nodded grimly.

"Let's vote," Javier said quickly. "All in favor of taking the Krueger offer?"

Three hands rose. Then two dropped, leaving only Javier and one of his cousins.

"All for staying with the Weinhardts?"

The rest of the hands went up. Miguel, Carlos, Luis, and all the others. Javier's face darkened, but he nodded stiffly.

Karl waited a beat, then spoke. "I didn't come here to buy your loyalty. But you've shown faith in us, in our history together. When this harvest is done, there'll be a bonus. Five percent for everyone who sees it through."

The mood shifted instantly. Men smiled, clapped backs, the tension dissolving like morning fog. But Ethan noticed Javier's expression, saw something dangerous flicker and die in his eyes.

As the gathering broke up, Karl moved amongst the men, shaking hands, sharing words of endearment in his field Spanish. Affirming his promise of a bonus.

Ethan slumped onto a redwood bench near the equipment shed, exhaustion hitting him all at once. The adrenaline of the confrontation drained away, leaving only the ache in his shoulders and the weight of everything unsaid between the brothers.

After saying final goodnight to Miguel, Karl settled beside Ethan, the old wood creaking under their combined weight. For a moment, they sat in silence, watching the crews return to their quarters. Then he spoke quietly to his son. "You know the story of the Good Samaritan?"

"Of course."

"Oil and wine," Karl said. "That's what he poured on the traveler's wounds. Oil is like love." He put his arm around Ethan's shoulder, a gentle embrace. "But wine? Wine stings. Kills the bacteria, cleans the wound. That's truth, son. And the truth is, you're back in the family, but your voice here.... That has to be earned. Truth hurts, but it heals."

Ethan nodded, throat tight. "I understand."

"Good. Understanding is the first step."

The fire died to embers as the workers settled into their temporary quarters, quiet conversations in Spanish drifting through the darkness. Ryan walked to his truck without a word to anyone.

"Going home?" Karl called out, though it wasn't really a question.

"Briana's waiting," Ryan said tersely. "Kids have school tomorrow."

Karl watched his older son drive away, taillights disappearing into the morning fog. The weight of unspoken knowledge sat heavy between those who remained.

Back at the main house, Eden waited with a tray of steaming mugs. The big kitchen glowed with warmth, a stark contrast to the tension by the fire. The old redwood beams, dark with a century of smoke and cooking oils, seemed to hold generations of conversations, arguments, reconciliations.

"Chamomile and valerian," she said, distributing the tea. "You'll need the sleep."

Jake and Tawi made their excuses, leaving Ethan alone with his parents.

Eden studied her younger son. "Lauren stopped by while you were in the middle of harvest work."

Ethan's head snapped up. "She did?"

"She poured her heart out to me about you. About your date, about Marcus and that woman showing up." Eden set down her mug, choosing her words carefully. "She cares about you, Ethan. Really cares. Not the way those city women did, all surface and appetite."

"Mom, I know..."

"Do you?" She leaned forward. "Women can allure a man, pull him in with beauty and charm. It's as old as Eve herself. But there's something deeper. 'Charm is deceptive, and beauty is fleeting," she quoted. "Lauren isn't using her beauty as bait. She sees who you could be, not just who you are.

Don't let the past poison that."

"I'm trying."

"Try harder." Her voice gentled. "That girl has vision for you. Real vision. The kind that builds a life, not just a moment. Don't let anything, or anyone, come between you and that possibility."

Ethan nodded, sipping the bitter tea. Through the window, the workers' camp was dark now, only the faint smell of woodsmoke marking where the confrontation had happened.

Later that morning in his bed, seeking a rest before the next night of harvest, sleep came slowly. His mind filled with dreams of fire and wine, oil and wounds, and the long road to earning back what had been freely given and foolishly lost. In the distance, he imagined he could hear Tawi's drum, beating out a rhythm of gratitude for hard truths and parents who loved enough to wound and heal in equal measure. But one thing lingered at the back of his mind, the look in Javier's eyes, it had spoken of something deeper, a message that the family's trouble was not over.

CHAPTER TWENTY-ONE

WEINHARDT'S RANCH

SONOMA COUNTY

"Wine... it is like a woman
It can be your salvation or your destruction."
Napoleon Bonaparte

The sun was just rising when Bri met Ryan at the porch, the scent still on him from the crush pad where hours before they'd fought to save the harvest. The air tasted different in daylight, thin, ordinary, stripped of the fog's mystery and the night's urgency. Ryan's shirt still carried purple stains from the pumpovers, and exhaustion sat in the hollows under his eyes like bruises.

Bri held a folded paper in her hands, working it between her fingers the way she did when words wouldn't come easy. The children, Sophia and little Ryan Jr., played in the dirt beneath the valley oak, building kingdoms from pebbles and imagination, unaware of the fault lines running through their parents' world.

"Enrique's wife called," Bri said without preamble. Her voice held that careful flatness that meant she'd rehearsed this conversation during the sleepless hours while Ryan worked the harvest. "Rosa. We talked for a long time."

Ryan's jaw tightened. He could feel it coming, the conversation he'd been dodging for months with longer hours in the vineyard, later nights at the equipment shed, any excuse to avoid the questions in his wife's eyes.

"She heard things in town. About a woman." Bri's fingers stilled on the paper. "About nights when you said you were at growers' meetings but your truck was parked outside a house in Healdsburg."

The porch boards creaked under his shifting weight. Down in the yard, Miguel's grandchildren had joined the play, their laughter bright and careless. Ryan watched them instead of meeting his wife's eyes.

"People talk," he said finally. The words came out rough, defensive.

"I'm not people." The folded paper trembled now. "I'm your wife. The mother of your children. I deserve more than silence and turned backs."

He wanted to deny it, to manufacture righteous anger at the accusation. But the strike crisis and Enrique's accusations had left him on edge.

"Tell me," Bri said. "Just... tell me."

But he didn't. Couldn't. The words lodged in his throat like grape seeds, bitter and impossible to swallow. He looked past her at the rows of vines marching up the hillside, each one pruned and trained by his own hands, and felt the terrible weight of being known too well to hide but not trusted enough to confess.

"I can't carry this alone," Bri said finally. The paper crumpled in her fist. "Not the wondering. Not the pretending everything's fine when the children ask why Daddy doesn't laugh anymore." She stood, moved to the door, paused with her hand on the frame. "I might leave you Ryan. For now, I just need a day or two to think. I'll be at my mother's with the kids when you figure out what matters more, your pride or your family."

She left him there with the morning sun beating down and the taste of failure bitter as unripe fruit in his mouth. The children's laughter followed her inside, then silence. Just the wind in the vines and the distant sound of equipment being cleaned, the ordinary resurrection that followed every harvest night.

Ryan sat until his muscles cramped, until the sun moved enough to throw shade across the porch. He called Caitlin. "We need to talk, I'm coming over." He got in his truck and drove to Healdsburg.

Caitlin answered the door barefoot, hair twisted up with a pencil, wearing one of his shirts from a night he'd told Bri he was reviewing contracts. Behind her, the house smelled like coffee and something else, ambition maybe, or the particular perfume of a woman tired of living in the shadows.

"You look wrecked," she said, but gently, already reaching for him.

He let her pull him inside because it was easier than standing in the doorway. The apartment was small but clean, secondhand furniture arranged carefully to make the most of the space. Nothing like the comfortable chaos of his own home. One that might lose the presence of his wife and children. The thought bit like frost on new growth.

"Is Madison here," Ryan ask, looking around the apartment."

"No, at her cousins, day off for both of them."

"The men threatened us with a strike this morning," Ryan said, slumping onto her worn couch.

"Dad was able to reason with them. It was really stressful."

"My Goodness." Caitlin's hand flew to her throat. "In the middle of the harvest?"

"If they weren't coming back it would have been a disaster."

"But they agreed?" She was already at the small kitchen counter, reaching for the bourbon. Her movements were sure, practiced. Three years of fixing his drinks had taught her exactly how much ice, how much pour.

"Yes. We held it together. Barely." He accepted the glass, the weight of it familiar in his hand. "But it was close. Too close."

She settled beside him, tucking her legs beneath her. "The Kruegers?"

"Who else?" The bourbon was good, better than what he kept at home. "They're getting bolder."

Ryan took a long pull on his drink and sank a little deeper in his chair. His weary body needed a few moments.

A knock interrupted. Three sharp raps, confident and demanding.

Caitlin's face went still. "That's Otto."

"What?"

"I called him just after to you called me. Just... hear him out. Please." She was already moving to the door.

Ryan almost bolted for the door, deeply offended that Caitlin had set him up. That she would allow this enemy into their world. But then he remembered Bri's threats. He didn't need another woman mad at him.

Otto Krueger entered like he owned the place, which Ryan supposed wasn't far from the truth given his family probably owned the building. The youngest Krueger son had that particular confidence that came from never having to earn anything.

"Ryan." Otto nodded, settling into the worn leather chair across from them. "Thanks for seeing me."

"I didn't agree to see you. You just showed up."

"Fair enough." Otto's smile was practiced, the kind he probably used on investors. "But since I'm here, maybe we can talk like civilized people. Neighbors, even."

"We're not neighbors. We're not anything."

Otto gestured toward the bourbon bottle on Caitlin's small kitchen counter. "Mind if I pour myself one? This might go easier if we're all relaxed."

Ryan watched him help himself, noting how Otto knew exactly where she kept the glasses. How many times had he been here? How comfortable was he in this space that Ryan had thought was theirs alone?

"I know what it's like," Otto said, taking a sip from his glass, "having a brother who doesn't pull his weight. Eric's been coasting on the family name since high school. Never had to prove anything, never had to earn anything. Just assumed it would all be his someday."

Ryan's jaw tightened. The parallel was too obvious to miss.

"But here's the thing," Otto continued. "Sometimes the younger son sees things clearer. Sometimes we're the ones who understand what needs to happen for the family to survive. To thrive."

"Get to the point."

Otto took a sip, considering. "A merger. Weinhardt and Krueger. Combined, we'd be the largest producer in the county. Maybe the largest in Northern California."

"My father would never..."

"Your father's still thinking like it's 1985. Small batches, family operations, handshake deals." Otto leaned forward. "But you understand scale. You understand what happened when Constellation bought Mondavi. When Gallo consolidated in the '90s. They didn't just survive, they dominated."

Ryan found himself listening despite everything. The math was seductive in its simplicity. Their combined acreage, their distribution networks, their political influence.

"Think about it," Otto pressed. "Every restaurant from here to LA would have to deal with us. Set our own prices. Control allocation. The small producers would have to sell to us or watch their grapes rot on the vine."

Otto stood, but instead of leaving, he walked to the window, looking out at Healdsburg's tree lined streets. "You know what your father doesn't see? The Chinese buyers circling. The tech money looking for vanity vineyards. In five years, Sonoma won't belong to families like ours anymore. Unless we're too big to buy."

He turned back, his eyes bright with possibility. "Imagine it, Ryan. Every wine list in California starting with our names. Senators calling us for campaign contributions. The Wine Spectator would have to create a new category just for our holdings."

"Even if I wanted this, which I don't, my father's still in charge. Nothing happens without Karl Weinhardt."

Otto's smile turned knowing. "Your father's what, sixty-eight? Still climbing into trucks, still working the crush like he's forty. Noble, sure. But for how long?" He paused, swirling the bourbon in his glass. "My grandfather worked until the day he dropped dead. Heart gave out at seventy-two. Left my father scrambling to pick up the pieces."

Ryan's face darkened, but Otto continued, his tone conversational. "I'm not wishing ill on anyone. But nature has its own timeline. And when change comes, it comes fast. The prepared inherit. The unprepared just... inherit debt and confusion."

He moved back toward the center of the room, but slowly, like a man with all the time in the world. "Your brother left for Silicon Valley, chased his dreams with family money. Three million, wasn't it? That's what, how many acres of prime vineyard land?"

"That's family business."

"Everything's family business when families share a valley." Otto set his glass down carefully. "My point is, some sons take. Other sons build. You've been building while Ethan was burning through your inheritance. But does Karl see it that way?"

The question hung in the air. Outside, a motorcycle growled past, the sound fading slowly.

"There's something else," Otto said, moving toward the door but not reaching for it yet. "The county's been nosing around about water rights again. Environmental groups making noise about sustainable farming. The small operators won't survive the new regulations. But a combined operation? We'd have the lawyers, the lobbyists, the leverage to write our own rules."

He finally reached for the doorknob, then paused. "Oh, and Ryan? This isn't just about business. This is about creating a future where people like us don't have to hide. Where relationships don't have to exist in shadows. Where a man can build a life with whoever he chooses, without shame."

Otto opened the door halfway, then looked back one more time. "Your father's a good man. Old school. Honorable. But honor doesn't protect against market forces. Tradition doesn't stop development. Sometimes the greatest respect you can show a legacy is to evolve it before someone else destroys it."

He stepped into the hallway, his voice carrying back. "Think about it, Ryan. Really think about it. I'll be around when you're ready to talk."

The door closed with finality, leaving Ryan staring at the space where ambition and possibility had stood, wearing an expensive suit and speaking uncomfortable truths.

"Bri knows," he said finally, the words scraping out of him. "About us. She's threatening to leave, take the kids."

Caitlin moved behind his chair, her hands finding his shoulders. "You knew this day would come."

"I can't lose them."

"Then maybe it's time to stop trying to have it all." She came around the chair, settling into his lap with practiced grace. Her fingers traced his jaw, forcing him to meet her eyes. "Go home tonight. Think about what Otto said. Think about what it could mean."

Her lips brushed his ear. "I've loved you in the shadows for three years, Ryan. Maybe it's time for you to step up and really love me. To choose."

The weight of her was familiar, but her words cut new paths through his thoughts. Outside, Healdsburg's traffic hummed past, oblivious to the choices being made in small apartments above storefronts.

"My father built everything we have."

"And how does he thank you? Selling land for Ethan's dreams. Welcoming him back like nothing happened." Her voice stayed soft but her grip tightened. "You deserve more than crumbs from your father's table."

She slid off his lap, standing with the grace of a woman who knew her power. "Go home, Ryan. But think about it. Think about us. Think about finally getting what you deserve."

Ryan stood, unsteady from more than bourbon. The room tilted gently, like the world had shifted on its axis while he wasn't paying attention. Everything looked the same but felt different. Caitlin, this apartment, his future, all of it suddenly uncertain and full of dark possibility. He needed to get home and get some serious rest before the heavy night that was ahead of him.

CHAPTER TWENTY-TWO

KRUEGER'S RANCH

SONOMA COUNTY

"Wine gives you courage; women give you ruin."
Ovid, Ars Amatoria

D awn had come pale; cold and fog filled to the Krueger estate. The modern house rose from manicured grounds like a glass and steel assertion, all clean lines and aggressive angles. No softness here, no century-old wood that remembered the hands that shaped it. Everything was statement and surface.

In her office, Cheri Morrison Krueger studied her reflection in the black computer screen before powering it on. Thirty-four years old, MBA from Wharton, body sculpted by the best surgeons in Beverly Hills. She'd been Eric Krueger's weakness and would be his family's downfall, though they didn't know it yet.

Her phone buzzed. The number was blocked, but she knew who it was.

"Yes?" She kept her voice low, professional.

"So, the workers stayed with Weinhardt." The voice on the other end spoke English with a slight Chilean accent. "This complicates things."

"Yes, Otto's plans failed once again but he's looking at other options."

"The timeline doesn't change."

"I understand."

"Make sure you do. Vega does. We didn't place you there to fail."

The line went dead. Cheri deleted the call log and touched up her lipstick. Eric would be looking for her soon. The family meeting was in ten minutes.

She found them in the library, though calling it that was generous. The Kruegers had books the way they had art, as investments and display. First editions behind glass, never read. The real business happened around the chrome and glass table that dominated the room.

Hans Krueger stood at the window, thick hands clasped behind his back. At seventy, he still radiated the bulky power of a man who'd taken what he wanted from life. His son Otto lounged in a leather chair, scrolling through his phone. Eric entered just behind Cheri, his hand finding the small of her back possessively.

"Ah, the lovebirds," Otto smirked. "Sleep well?"

"Can we focus?" Hans turned from the window. "Otto has news."

"About the workers, I heard Javier failed, that's not the kind of news I want to hear," snapped Eric.

"Cost us five grand for nothing, plus, whatever promises we made."

"Half," Otto corrected. "I sent him away mad. I only authorized half payment for failure."

Cheri noticed the look that passed between father and sons. These men who thought themselves sharks, circling each other even in defeat.

"The question is, next steps," Eric said. "We need leverage."

"We have it," Otto injected. "Caitlin arranged a meeting with Ryan Weinhardt this morning. I've just come from it.'

Eric looked surprised, but it didn't change his tone. "So did he bite?"

"He listened. Plus, there's Caitlin. Seems she's tired of being the other woman. Wants security, legitimacy. She is pushing him."

Eric's jaw tightened. "If Ryan caves that's good, but I don't want Caitlin anywhere near me, just want full access to my daughter."

"Don't worry, Grandpa here, has plans."

"She thinks once he agrees she'll get her dream life," said Otto.

Hans laughed. "Otto will promise a big society wedding once Eric's marriage implodes. It's the perfect ploy."

"What about Karl?" Eric asked. "He's not going to just roll over."

"Karl's getting old," Hans said. "His heart's not what it was. The stress of this harvest, family troubles, financial pressure... Nature might solve that problem for us."

"And if nature needs help?" Cheri asked carefully.

The men exchanged glances.

"We're not killers," Hans said finally. "But accidents happen. Especially during harvest. Equipment fails. Fires start. That new automated irrigation system of theirs runs on cellular controls. Easy to hack, shut down water to entire blocks during a heat spike."

"Kill the vines, kill the business," Otto nodded. "Then we offer rescue. Merger first, full acquisition shortly after that."

A knock interrupted them. The housekeeper entered with a tray of mimosas and pastries. Hans waited until she left before continuing.

"In these next weeks we keep the pressure on. Keep Caitlin reinforcing our promises. I'm confident we'll close this soon." He raised his glass. "To patience and profit."

They toasted, crystal ringing against crystal. Cheri smiled and sipped, playing her part. But she caught Eric watching her, something uncertain in his eyes. She'd been careless on the phone. He'd heard something.

"I should check on the crews," Otto said, standing. "Make sure our Salvadoran friends are settled. Our vines will be ready by the weekend."

"Salvadorans?" Cheri kept her voice carefully neutral.

"Cheaper than locals," Hans explained. "No benefits, no complaints. They're grateful just to work."

"Oh, yes and some of them have an assignment for tonight," snickered Otto. "Just a little surgery to perform. Snip, snip, tie, tie. And if that doesn't work, well I've got something even more radical."

The meeting dissolved in a dry laugh from Hans. Cheri returned to her office, but Eric followed. He closed the door behind them, leaning against it.

"Who were you talking to this morning?"

"A client." She moved behind her desk, creating distance. "From my consulting days. They still call sometimes."

"At dawn?"

"Different time zones." She met his eyes steadily. "Is there a problem?"

Eric studied her for a long moment. This woman he'd left Caitlin for, drawn by perfect curves and a razor mind. Now, in the morning light, he wondered what else he'd invited into his life.

"No problem," he said finally. "Just curious."

He left, but Cheri knew he'd be watching now. She'd have to be more careful. Lucien hadn't placed her here to be discovered by a jealous lover. There was too much at stake. Not just the Krueger lands, but the whole corridor from Napa to Mendocino. Control the water, control the wine. Control the wine, control a multi-billion-dollar industry.

She picked up her phone again, sent a coded text. "Package delayed but in transit."

The response came quickly. "Ensure delivery."

Through her window, she could see the Krueger vineyard stretching toward the hills. Neat rows of grafted vines, productive and profitable. Nothing like the wild tangle of old growth at the Weinhardt place, vines that had seen a century of seasons. Those would have to be destroyed, of course. Lucien had no use for sentiment.

But first, Ryan Weinhardt would have to cave and agree to the merger. Then his family. Then the whole careful structure of tradition and trust that held this valley together.

Cheri smiled and dialed Vega

Javier drove slowly through the morning fog, hands tight on the wheel of his Honda. The Krueger estate was behind him now, its grandeur fading in his mirrors. The heater struggled against the cold, making the old engine work harder.

Five thousand dollars. That's what Otto had promised. That's not what he got when he had reported the results of their offer. The envelope

Otto handed over held half. "You tried," Otto had said with that smirk that made Javier want to punch him. "That's worth something."

He drove without purpose, just needing movement, distance from what he'd almost done. About two miles from the estate, down a side road he'd never noticed before, Javier saw the smoke from their fires.

Curiosity made him pull over. He left the Honda running and walked toward the encampment. Through a gap in the fence, he could see them. Men huddled around barrel fires, makeshift tents and tarps strung between trees. The smell hit him first. Too many bodies in too small a space. Then he heard the voices, Spanish, but not Mexican Spanish.

"¿De dónde son?" Javier called out, approaching slowly.

The men startled, then relaxed seeing his face. Brown like theirs, working clothes like theirs.

"Salvadoran," one answered. The accent was unmistakable. "You work here?"

"Sometimes," Javier lied smoothly. "How long you been here?"

"Two days. They brought us up from Los Angeles. Promise work, place to sleep."

"This is where you sleep?" Javier looked around at the camp. No running water he could see. No proper shelter.

"Is better than the warehouse in LA," another man said. "Here is quiet. Safe."

Safe. The word stuck in Javier's throat. He asked more questions, learned what they were being paid. His stomach turned. The Weinhardts paid well, had always paid well. These men were working for scraps, probably sending most of it home.

"How many of you?"

"Twenty now. More coming tomorrow."

Twenty men. Javier thought of the promises Otto had made. Health benefits. Proper housing. Higher wages. All lies. They'd never intended to hire local crews. Just use them to break the Weinhardts, then bring in desperate men who couldn't complain.

He walked back to his car, head spinning. What Otto had told him about Ryan, the meetings with Caitlin. The way Otto had smiled when he said it. But looking back at that camp, those men sleeping rough like animals, Javier knew where his loyalty had to lie.

The Weinhardts weren't perfect. Ryan could be difficult. But they'd never done this. Never brought in desperate men to break the backs of citizens.

He drove home slowly, making decisions with each mile. That night he'd find Karl, tell him about the camp. Let him know what kind of neighbors they really had. As for the other matter, maybe some things were better left buried. Every man had to reckon with his own sins.

The sun was rising by the time he reached his house. His wife would be awake, worried. He'd tell her the truth, that the big money wasn't coming. That they'd have to make do with what honest work provided.

It wasn't much, but it was enough. And sometimes, Javier thought as he pulled into his driveway, enough was all a man could ask for. That and the ability to look his children in the eye without shame.

The morning light caught the old Weinhardt vineyards in the distance, turning the fog golden as it lifted at 9:30 a.m. One more morning like this and Esther would have her opportunity. Another day of harvest was beginning. Good honest work for good, if imperfect, people. As an act of atonement, he'd share his bribe with his compadres.

That and being back with them would have to be enough for now.

CHAPTER TWENTY-THREE

WEINHARDT'S RANCH

SONOMA COUNTY

"Wine is a turncoat; first a friend and then an enemy."
Henry Fielding

The day had passed without another incident. The workers family enjoying their children, preparing for the next night of labor. For the second night of harvest, the evening fog had rolled in early, thick as wool batting, carrying with it something more than Pacific moisture, a weight, a watching presence that made even the veteran pickers glance over their shoulders between vine rows.

That morning had been the first time the fog had lifter before 10 a.m. Two more mornings like that and Esther would get her chance. They had held off on the Old Vine Pinot just in case. But if the pattern broke tomorrow morning Karl had told Esther they'd have to have the crews go in that block tomorrow.

Karl Weinhardt stood at the edge of the crush pad, tasting the air like an old wolf. Sixty-eight years on this land had taught him to read its moods.

The fog wasn't right. Too dense, too soon. It pressed against the halogen work lights, turning them into pale islands that barely pushed back the gray. In the employee housing, modern motorhomes leased for the harvest, the families had already sent their children inside. Usually, the kids played between the rows until midnight during harvest, their laughter mixing with their parents' work songs. Not tonight.

Ryan and Ethan were back, each keeping his distance. Ryan seemed strangely subdued, his mind somewhere else. Jake noticed that the edge he'd shown with the workers was different, gentler but still all business.

Esther moved through the operation like a conductor through an orchestra, clipboard tucked under one arm, refractometer swinging from her belt. She had been encouraged by the timing on that morning's fog. Only two more and she have her opportunity.

She stopped at each bin of grapes coming in from the field, plucking berries with practiced precision. Roll them between thumb and forefinger, feeling for that perfect give, not too soft, not too firm. Bite down, let the juice flood across her palate. Sweet but not cloying, with that edge of acid that would carry through fermentation. She made notes in her quick, efficient script: *Block 7 Pinot, 24.2 Brix, pH 3.4, beautiful balance.*

"How are we looking?" Karl appeared at her shoulder, his breath misting in the sudden chill.

"Like we're racing the weather." She held out a cluster for him to taste. "The fog's dropping the temperature fast. If it gets much colder, we'll start losing aromatic compounds."

He bit into a berry, working it around his mouth with the slow deliberation of a man who'd tasted ten thousand such berries. "Tell the crews to focus on the upper blocks. Get the best fruit in first."

The destemmer-crusher hummed its metal song, purple rivers flowing into the waiting tanks. Miguel and Luis worked the sorting table, their hands dancing over the fruit, pulling out leaves and the occasional unripe cluster. They'd been doing this for twenty years, could sort in their sleep. Next to them, Ethan operated the forklift, moving bins from field truck to crush pad with newfound precision. His months back on the ranch had burned away the last of the city softness. His movements were economical now, purposeful.

Eden emerged from the kitchen trailer with a massive pot of pozole, the hominy soup steaming in the cold air. She'd been cooking since four that afternoon, pozole for the crews, sandwiches for anyone who needed a quick bite, gallons of coffee that would keep flowing until the last grape was processed. Tawi worked beside her, his gray braid swinging as he ladled soup into paper bowls, pressed them into tired hands, murmured encouragement in Spanish and English and sometimes in the old Pomo words that few remembered.

"Eat," he told Carlos, who was swaying on his feet after twelve hours in the vines. "Long night ahead."

The fog swallowed sound, muffled it, made the crush pad feel like an island floating in gray space. Workers moved in and out of the light like ghosts. The only constants were the mechanical rhythms, the pulse of the must pump, the rattle of the destemmer, the hiss of the press cycles.

Ryan prowled the catwalks above the fermentation tanks, checking temperatures, watching the cap management. During fermentation, grape skins float to the top, forming a thick cap that has to be punched down or pumped over regularly to extract color and tannin. Too little contact and you get thin, pale wine. Too much and you extract harsh, bitter compounds. It was a delicate dance, and Ryan had been dancing it since he was sixteen.

"Keep those pumpovers gentle," he called down to Javier. "We're not making Cabernet here. Pinot needs a soft touch."

Javier had arrived at sunset, quiet and careful, the way a man moves when he's not sure of his welcome. He had apologies to Karl and the others telling them about the Salvadorans and the Kruegers' greed. The elder Weinhardt had gripped his shoulder, said simply, "Good to have you back Javier. But, if you betray us again, that will be the end of it." The crew had nodded, shifted to make space, but there was still a membrane of distrust and suspicion lingered like smoke.

Now Javier worked the press, his movements precise and focused, as if perfect work could earn back what had been lost. His cousin Roberto stayed close, protective, occasionally shooting hard looks at anyone whose gaze lingered too long on Javier.

The fog thickened. The temperature dropped another five degrees. Ice crystals formed on the metal railings. Karl checked his watch: 11:47 PM. They were making good time, but something crawled along his spine, that old farmer's instinct that had saved the crop in '98 when the early frost came, that had told him to pick two days early in '08 just before the October fires.

"Jake," he called to his foreman. "Double-check the main electrical panel. This fog's got moisture in it like I've never seen."

Jake nodded, grabbed a flashlight, headed for the utility shed. The main panel fed everything, the destemmer, the press, the must pumps, the glycol cooling system that kept the tanks at precise temperatures. Lose power during harvest and you didn't just stop work, you risked losing wine. Juice sitting in pipes would oxidize. Fermentations without temperature control could spike, killing yeast, producing off-flavors. Caps without pumpovers would dry out and harbor bacteria.

Esther was in the lab, running quick analysis on the juice from Tank 6. The numbers made her frown. Temperature climbing faster than it should. The fermentation was taking off like a rocket. She made a note to increase the cooling, keep it under control. Wild ferments could produce complexity, but they could also run hot enough to cook the wine, leaving it tasting like stewed fruit.

The sound came first, a deep electrical groan, like the earth itself clearing its throat. Then a pop, sharp as a rifle shot. Then darkness, absolute and sudden. The crusher died mid-cycle. The press froze with fifty gallons of juice trapped in the bladder. The cooling system went silent.

Shouts erupted from every direction. Headlamps swung wild arcs through the fog. Someone knocked over a picking bin, and the crash echoed like thunder.

"Nobody move!" Karl's voice cut through the chaos. "Jake, status!"

"Main panel's fried!" Jake's voice came from the direction of the utility shed. "Maybe water got in through a bad seal. Hard to tell in this light."

"Backup generator?"

"Starting it now!"

The generator coughed, sputtered, caught. Two work lights flickered to life, enough to see faces, not enough to run equipment. Karl's mind raced through calculations. Tank 6 was already running hot. Without cooling, without pumpovers to keep the cap moist and the temperature distributed...

"We've got maybe thirty minutes before Tank 6 goes critical," he told Jake quietly. "After that, we're looking at a runaway ferment. Could hit 95 degrees, maybe higher. We'll lose the whole tank, that's fifteen tons of our best Pinot."

"What do you need?"

"Get that small generator hooked to the glycol chiller. One tank we can save manually if we have cooling. The rest..." He looked around at the stalled operation, thousands of pounds of grapes waiting to be processed, juice oxidizing in the pipes. "We do what we can."

Ethan was already moving, muscle memory from the old days kicking in. "Miguel, Luis, get tarps over the open bins. Wet them down first. We need to keep the fruit cool and protected." He turned to the picking crews. "Everybody with a headlamp, space yourselves around the pad. We need to see what we're doing."

Tawi appeared with Roberto and two others, carrying buckets of ice from the kitchen freezer. "For the tank," he said simply, understanding the crisis without being told. They began hauling the ice up the metal stairs, dumping it carefully onto the cap of fermenting grapes.

"The shed," someone said. "I saw someone by the shed just before it went dark."

"Who?" Ryan's voice was sharp.

"Don't know. But Enrique was heading that way..."

"I was getting a tool!" Enrique stepped into the weak light, his face flushed with anger and fear. "From my truck! Ask Eden - she saw me!"

"It's true," Eden called out. "He asked to borrow my flashlight. Said he'd left his picking knife in the cab."

But the damage was done. The membrane of suspicion had burst. Workers chose sides with their feet, very few moving closer to Enrique in support, most edging away. Ryan stood on the catwalk above, his face unreadable in the shadows.

"Enough!" Karl's voice boomed. "We've got twenty minutes to save Tank 6. Fight later. Work now."

Esther was already rigging a manual pumpover system using a sump pump and garden hoses. It wouldn't be pretty, but it would work. "I need three people," she called. "One to hold the hose, two to help me monitor temperature."

The small generator wheezed to life, Jake's cursing a steady soundtrack as he worked to connect it to the glycol chiller. One system, that's all it could power. They'd have to choose, run the press to save the fruit already crushed, or run the chiller to save the wine already fermenting.

"Chiller," Karl decided without hesitation. "We can press tomorrow if we keep the must cold. But lose that fermentation and it's gone forever."

Ethan and Miguel worked to drain the press manually, catching the precious juice in buckets, transferring it to a small tank that could be managed by hand. Every gallon saved was victory. The fog pressed closer, beading on their faces, making everything slick and dangerous.

Up on the catwalk, Ryan reached for a valve just as his boot hit a patch of condensation. His hand shot out for the rail, found it, held on as his feet scrambled against the slick metal. Everything tilted, suspended over the concrete twenty feet below.

Ethan saw it happen, was moving before thought formed. He hit the stairs running, taking them three at a time. "Don't move," he called. "Just hold on, I'm coming for you to try to help."

"I know what I'm doing!" Ryan's voice was strained but steady. "Just... get the valve. Tank 6 intake. Close it before we lose prime on the pump."

Ethan reached past his brother, their faces inches apart, and cranked the valve shut. For a moment they stayed frozen like that, Ryan hanging, Ethan braced against the rail, ready to grab him if needed. Then Ryan found his footing, pulled himself up, stood breathing hard on the catwalk.

"Thanks," he said quietly.

"Yeah." Ethan stepped back. "You good?"

"Fine. Check the shed. Someone was there. If this was sabotage..."

Ethan hesitated, then turned to go. Behind him, Ryan's voice caught him at the stairs.

"I didn't need your help."

Ethan stopped, not turning. "You were about to fall."

"I had it handled." Ryan's voice had gone cold; the momentary gratitude evaporated like morning dew. "I've been handling things for years without you playing hero."

"Ryan, I was just..."

"What? Trying to help? Like dad needs your help? Like any of us need anything from you?" Ryan wiped his hands on his jeans, the gesture sharp. "Go check the shed. Do something useful for once."

Ethan felt the words land like stones in his chest. He'd thought maybe, in that moment of crisis, something had shifted. But Ryan's face was hard as granite, his stance rigid with old resentment.

"Right," Ethan said softly. "I'll check the shed."

He descended the stairs slowly, each step echoing in the tank room. Behind him, he could hear Ryan moving along the catwalk, checking valves and gauges like nothing had happened. Like his brother hadn't just been there to catch him.

Like ten years of absence couldn't be bridged by a single moment of need.

Ethan was already heading down. At the utility shed, he met Tawi, who held up something in his weathered hand, a small handful of blue and white beads.

"Salvadoran labor contractor," Tawi said quietly. "Same as those crews working for Krueger. Found these scattered by the panel, along with cut wires."

"Blue and white beads?" Ethan asked, frowning.

Tawi rolled them in his palm. "From their bracelets, their flag colors. The workers wear them for protection, given by their families back home. 'Para que no te olvides de nosotros,' they say, so you don't forget us." He shook his head. "They wear them under their work gloves. Must have caught on the wire and snapped. Man probably didn't notice until later."

"You're sure?"

Tawi led him to a spot behind the shed where someone had cached supplies, copper wire, industrial solvent, a cheap phone with a cracked screen. The phone's case bore a sticker from a Los Angeles labor agency that specialized in undocumented workers.

"Jake must have scared them off. In their hurry they left stuff behind. The land remembers everything," Tawi said. "Footprints, scents, the way a man moves when he's carrying secrets. This wasn't Enrique. Wrong size boot, wrong pattern. Whoever did this was smaller, walked different."

They brought the evidence to Karl and Ryan, who examined it under their headlamps. Karl's jaw tightened. "Someone's trying to sabotage the harvest."

Ryan stared at the crossed wires in Karl's hands.. The fog was lifting now, not outside, but in his mind.

"Who would have done this?"

"Salvadorans," Tawi said quietly. "Found boot prints. Same tread pattern the Krueger crews wear."

Ryan felt something cold settle in his chest. *Otto's private offer. All those promises about working together.*

"Then it's the Kruegers," said Karl.

"Well, it won't work," said Ryan. "We've got Tank 6 stabilized. Temperature's holding at 78."

"Ok, we'll need to keep the manual pumps going all night, but we'll save it." Karl's voice was steady, practical. Already moving past betrayal to solutions.

Ryan nodded, but his mind was elsewhere. The generator would get them through tonight. The harvest would survive. But things were getting clearer. He was starting to realize who his real enemies where. "Good. What about the rest?"

"If we can get the main panel fixed by dawn, we can still process what's in the bins. The fruit's holding temp with the tarps and ice. Esther says we've got a six-hour window, maybe eight if the fog holds."

Karl looked around at his crew, exhausted, wet, cold, but still working. His people. His land. His wine. "Then we'd better get to it."

They worked through the night like their grandfathers had, with hand and heart and stubbornness. The small generator coughed but held. Ice buckets climbed the stairs in steady procession. Esther tasted from each tank every half hour, adjusting, correcting, conducting a symphony of fermentation by headlamp and instinct.

Just before dawn, Jake emerged from the utility shed, grinning through the grease on his face. "Got it! Bypassed the fried section, ran new wire. She's ugly, but she'll hold."

The machinery roared back to life just as the eastern sky began to pale. The fog retreated to the valleys, leaving the vineyard jeweled with dew.

They'd lost four hours, but not a single tank. The fruit had held, protected by quick thinking and old knowledge.

Esther drew a sample from Tank 6, held it to the growing light. The color was perfect, that deep garnet transparency that marked great Pinot. She tasted, let it roll across her palate, swallowed slowly. Nearby, Karl, Ryan and Ethan waited expectantly with the rest.

"Black cherry," she said, eyes closed. "River rock minerality. Bright acid. The seeds crack clean between your teeth." She opened her eyes, smiled at Karl. "This is going to be exceptional. Maybe the best since '18."

Karl tasted too, nodded slowly. "The struggle makes it stronger," he said, echoing something his own father had told him. "Easy years make boring wine."

They finished as the sun burned through the last of the fog. Every grape processed, every tank stable, every worker accounted for. The sabotage had failed.

Enrique stood with the others as Karl raised a glass of new juice in toast. The suspicion was gone, burned away by the night's shared labor. He was one of them again, fully and completely.

"To the harvest," Karl said simply. "And to the people who make it possible."

They drank deep, tasting not just grape juice but the essence of the land itself, struggle and beauty, hardship and abundance, all pressed together into something worth saving. The wine would remember this night, would carry it forward in every bottle. And years later, when someone asked about the '25 vintage, they'd say, "Ah yes, that was the year of the fog. Let me tell you the story..."

Ryan had drunk deeply too, but from another source, a flood of suspicion. He knew now the one place he should be putting his hate and it was not Ethan. The Salvadoran's were obviously put up to this by the Kruegers. Otto had made promises, but it was clear to him that his enemy wasn't his brother, but those who were drawing him into their web with their lies.

CHAPTER TWENTY-FOUR

WEINHARDT'S RANCH

SONOMA COUNTY

"Wine is a cunning tempter; it steals upon you unawares."
Plutarch

The ravine cut deep into the hillside where the property backed up against state land, a natural boundary carved by centuries of winter rain. Ethan followed Tawi in the early dawn, down a deer path he remembered from childhood, when he and Ryan would hunt for arrowheads after storms.

The old Pomo moved with surprising grace for his size, placing each foot with deliberate care.

"Why are we out here?" Ethan asked, still wound tight from the night's adrenaline. The image of Ryan on that catwalk wouldn't leave him, his brother's face in the moment before the save, surprise and something else, maybe gratitude, maybe just the ancient recognition of shared blood.

"To check the fence line," Tawi said. "And to learn something about traps."

They walked in silence until they reached a flat spot where an old game trail crossed their path. Tawi stopped, pointed to a wooden box nearly hidden in the brush. The trap was ancient, probably from the 1940s when the neighboring ranch ran sheep.

"Still here after all these years," Tawi said, squatting beside it. "Your neighbor's grandfather set this for coyotes. See how it works?" He pointed to the mechanism without touching it. "Simple spring-loaded door. Bait goes here, draws them in. They take the bait, door drops. No way out from inside."

"But coyotes are smart," Ethan said. "They'd learn to avoid it."

"Most do." Tawi stood, brushed dust from his knees. "But some coyotes, they get so hungry, so angry, they forget what they know. They see that bait and all they can think about is the satisfaction of taking it. Then...." He made a dropping motion with his hand. "Trapped by their own hunger."

Ethan felt the lesson landing, working its way under his skin. "Ryan still bitter, probably thinks I set myself up as the hero when I saved him from falling."

"Maybe he does. Maybe he's already forgotten what his eyes saw when you pulled him back." Tawi started walking again. "But that's his trap to walk into or avoid. What about yours?"

"I wanted to hit him. When he turned it all around, said he didn't need my help. Bringing up my failures again."

"He responded like that, hoping you'd take the bait." Tawi's voice carried no judgment. "To get you to react. To feed that anger until it gets so fat it can't fit through the door anymore."

They'd reached the upper fence line where the view opened up, the whole ranch spread below them, the coast beyond, fog slowly retreating towards the coast. Ethan could see figures moving in the vineyard, preparing for another night's pick.

"Those men who cut our power," Tawi continued, "they know about bait too. They want us angry, fighting each other instead of them. Want your brother suspicious of you, you resentful of him. Weak pack is easier to hunt."

"So, what do I do?"

"What the smart coyote does. Acknowledge the bait. Appreciate its craft. Then walk around it." Tawi picked up a stick, drew a circle in the dust. "Here's your anger." He drew another circle. "Here's Ryan's bitterness." He connected them with a line. "Here's the trap. You can step in it, or…" He drew a curved line around both circles. "You can take the long way. Harder path, but you stay free."

"He might never trust me."

"Maybe. Maybe not. But you control your feet, not his." Tawi tossed the stick aside. "Besides, the land is watching. It remembers who shows up, who does the work. Your brother's eyes might lie to him, but the vines know the truth. They'll tell it eventually."

They stood quietly for a moment, watching the sunset paint the fog gold and pink. Ethan felt the anger loosening its grip, not gone but managed, like pruning a vine to direct its growth.

"Thank you," he said.

"You're welcome, Thankfulness is good, but learning to avoid the traps is good too. Now come on." Tawi turned back toward the trail. "I've got breakfast to prepare."

As they walked back, Ethan looked once more at the old trap, weathered but still functional, still waiting for something hungry enough to forget wisdom. All it needed was bait. He thought of all the traps he'd walked into in the valley: pharmaceutical, financial, emotional. Each one baited perfectly for his particular hunger.

But he was home now. And maybe, if he could remember to walk the long way around, he'd stay free enough to prove himself through work instead of words. Let Ryan think what he wanted. The land would tell the truth in its own time.

The cafe sat tucked between a hardware store and a check cashing place on the back streets of Glen Ellen. Seven in the morning and already the smell of pupusas filled the narrow room. Not tortillas and refried beans like the Mexican places, but the thick corn cakes Salvadorans preferred, stuffed with cheese and pork, griddled until the edges turned crispy brown.

Cesar Zamora sat in the back booth, his clean shirt out of place among the work clothes. Three men joined him, dust still on their boots from yesterday's harvest. Hector Salazar slid in across from him while the other two grabbed plastic chairs.

The waitress brought plates without being asked. Pupusas with curtido, that pickled cabbage sharp with vinegar. Fried plantains sweet with caramelized edges. Black beans that weren't refried but whole, swimming in their own dark broth. The Salvadorans ate with purpose, men who knew hunger and treated every meal like it might be the last for a while.

Cesar picked at his food. His stomach preferred Mexican flavors, but this meeting wasn't about his comfort.

"Your men's work at the Krueger place did go as planned," Cesar said in English, watching Salazar's face.

The other two kept eating. No English meant no understanding. Just Salazar's problem.

"We did our part; we can't be held accountable for the outcome." Salazar said. His English carried the accent but came clear enough. Smart man. Careful man.

"There's another job. Bigger pay."

Salazar's hand paused halfway to his mouth. The pupusa dripped grease onto the plastic tablecloth. "How big?"

"Big enough you'll want to handle it personally. Two weeks from now. The Weinhardt cellar."

"What kind of job?"

Cesar smiled. Not friendly. Just business.

"The kind that needs special materials. The kind you'll want to scout first. Learn where things are."

The coffee arrived, strong and bitter. Salvadoran style, not the watery American kind. Salazar's companions kept eating, oblivious. One laughed at something, showing gold teeth.

"This is serious work?" Salazar ask quietly.

"Serious pay. Extra for you to lead it. Keep that between us."

They finished eating in silence. The morning sun slanted through grimy windows, catching the steam from their coffee cups. Outside, trucks rumbled past carrying workers to the vineyards. Another day in wine country. Another day of bent backs and grape juice under fingernails.

"Come," Cesar said, dropping bills on the table.

They walked out to the parking lot. Cesar's Tacoma sat clean and new beside the Salvadorans' rust-eaten Nissan with its cracked windshield and bald tires. The difference told its own story. Those who gave orders and those who took them.

Cesar popped his truck's canopy. Inside, neat as a hardware store display. Five-gallon containers that didn't need labels. Road flares that weren't for roadside emergencies. Coils of cannon fuse. Everything needed to turn wood and wine into insurance claims.

"You know what to do with these?"

Salazar nodded. His face stayed neutral but his eyes took inventory. This was cartel-level planning. Professional. The kind of people you didn't disappoint.

"I'll call you the morning of," Cesar said. "You'll have two hours to get in position."

He handed Salazar an envelope, thick enough to matter. "This is the advance. Rest when the job's done. Your bonus too, after."

Salazar tucked the envelope inside his shirt. His companions stood by their truck, smoking, waiting.

Cesar climbed into his Toyota. "Two weeks. Start learning the layout tomorrow. Don't get caught looking."

The Tacoma pulled away, clean tires on clean asphalt. Salazar walked back to his men, already pulling bills from the envelope. He counted out their shares, equal portions that made their eyes widen.

"¡Dios mío!" one whistled. "What do we have to do for this?"

"Big job," Salazar said in Spanish, keeping his voice casual. "Important people. We do it right, there's more coming."

They divided the money, each man folding bills carefully into different pockets. Protection against theft, against loss, against the poverty that drove them to stand in hardware store parking lots at dawn hoping for work.

Salazar kept his extra share hidden. The bonus Cesar promised would be even better. Enough to bring his family north. Enough to stop living five men to a room in somebody's garage.

The Nissan coughed to life on the third try. Black smoke from the exhaust, but it ran. They headed out to the day's legitimate work, picking late harvest grapes for whoever would hire them.

But in two weeks, they'd have different work. The kind that paid enough to matter.

Salazar touched the envelope through his shirt. Whatever the Weinhardts had done to earn this, it wasn't his business. His business was feeding his family. Everything else was just details.

Ryan's footsteps echoed through his empty house. Eight in the morning. The rooms felt hollow without Bri's breathing beside him, without the kids' soft snores down the hall. Just him and the silence she'd left behind. Since then, she hadn't answer any of his calls.

The hallway stretched before him, lined with photographs Bri had hung with such hope. Their wedding at the vineyard. Sophia's first steps between the vine rows. Ryan Jr. holding up a cluster of grapes, his gap-toothed grin proud as any vineyard worker. The family they'd built together, now staying at her mother's place.

He stopped at the one that hurt most. Christmas, four years ago. All of them by the tree, Bri's hand on his shoulder, the kids in their pajamas. Before the anger consumed him. Before he and Caitlin had hooked up.

The living room held evidence of their absence. Sophia's dolls arranged in a tea party she'd never finish. Ryan Jr.'s baseball glove on the coffee table. Bri's reading glasses on the arm of her chair, forgotten in her hurry to leave.

Ryan sank into his recliner, the leather cold without shared warmth. This was where it started going wrong. Right here, the night his father announced that they would sell some of the acres to fund Ethan's stupid dream. He'd come back from that meeting seething, snapping at Bri when she asked what was wrong. Started the pattern of shutting her out, choosing anger over answers.

That anger had opened doors he should have kept locked. Made him susceptible to Caitlin's interest, and even to Otto's tempting offer. He'd let strangers fill the space his family should have occupied, all because he couldn't forgive his father and brother.

The house creaked around him, too big for one person. Through the window, he could see lights on at his parents' place. Someone else awake, probably in the kitchen. That would be Tawi, starting his morning ritual.

Ryan left his empty house and walked the short distance to the main ranch house. Found Tawi kneading dough in the pre-dawn quiet, his weathered hands working steadily.

"Coffee's fresh," Tawi said without looking up.

Ryan poured himself a cup and leaned against the counter, watching the steady push and fold of the dough. The kitchen smelled like yeast and woodsmoke from the old stove.

"Couldn't sleep," Ryan said finally. "House is too quiet."

"Heavy night brings heavy morning." Tawi's voice carried rhythms older than English. "The generator still running?"

"Yeah. We'll save the wine."

"But not what troubles you."

Ryan set down his cup. Outside, an owl called from the oak grove. Tawi paused in his kneading, tilting his head as if hearing more than the bird.

"I drove them away," Ryan said. "Bri. The kids. I was so angry about everything else, I forgot what mattered."

Tawi shaped the dough into a round, movements deliberate and gentle. "Anger makes us blind. Like fog in the valley. Can't see the mountain that was always there."

"She won't answer my calls."

The old man covered the dough with a clean cloth, then turned to face Ryan fully. His dark eyes held depths that reached beyond the kitchen.

"Same way you saved the wine tonight. One pump at a time. One hour at a time. Until the power comes back."

"And if she doesn't?"

Tawi smiled slightly. "Power never really goes. Just travels through different lines. Your brother came home. Maybe other things can too."

Ryan understood. Not the words exactly, but what lived beneath them. Whatever Tawi heard in the owl's call, whatever wisdom flowed through him, it all pointed the same direction: family was the circuit that mattered. Not Otto's promises. Not Caitlin's schemes. The family he'd pushed away.

"Thank you," Ryan said.

Tawi was already back at his bread. "Sun comes in two hours. By the way, Karl's awake in the Library. It would be wise to go see him. I have words for you, but he has something deeper.

Ryan headed for the door, then paused. "Tawi? How do you always know?"

The old man's hands never stopped their work. "Same way the vines know when to bud. Same way the salmon know the river. We all got our ways of listening."

Ryan stepped out into the pre-dawn air. The stars were fading. He pulled out his phone, typed a text to Bri: "I know you're awake. The kids need their home. So, do I. I'm ready to listen now."

He didn't expect an answer. Not yet. But it was a start. Pocketing his phone, he walked towards the library.

CHAPTER TWENTY-FIVE

WEINHARDT'S RANCH

SONOMA COUNTY

From father to son, the vine remembers."
Spanish proverb

Ryan pushed open the library door. His father sat by the fire, reading. The same chair. The same gentle light on his weathered face. How many evenings had he found him here, ready to listen, ready to teach?

The room held them both. Redwood panels dark with age. Books floor to ceiling, each spine a story, a season, a harvest remembered. The fire cracked softly. Outside, fog pressed against the windows.

Karl looked up. That smile. Warm as summer soil.

"Ryan."

Something broke open in Ryan's chest. A door he hadn't known was locked.

He moved to the opposite chair. The leather sighed beneath him. Between them, the fire danced. The redwood walls seemed to lean in, listening. Waiting.

A beat. Just breathing. Just being.

"Dad, I need to tell you something."

Karl closed his book. Set it aside. His full attention now. Always his full attention when it mattered.

"I've been carrying poison." The words came hard. "About Ethan. About the money. About those acres you sold." It had been obvious to others, but finally it was being spoken honestly.

His father's eyes never left his face. No judgment there. No surprise either. Just presence.

"I thought you were throwing good money after bad. Chasing his Silicon Valley dreams while we scraped by." Ryan's hands gripped the chair arms. "I let it eat at me. Let it turn me into someone else."

The fire popped. Sparks rose and died.

"I had an affair with Caitlin."

Still Karl waited. Still, he listened. As if he'd been waiting for this moment all along.

"Otto Krueger offered us a deal. A merger. It wouldn't have cut you out at first, but..." Ryan swallowed. "I could feel where it would lead. Where Otto would take it. And I actually considered it."

His voice broke. "I became everything I hated. Unfaithful. Bitter. Self-righteous."

The redwood held their silence. Centuries of storms weathered in that grain. Centuries of standing firm.

"I never left like Ethan did. Never spent foolishly. But my heart..." Ryan met his father's eyes. "My heart's been gone for years."

Karl rose from his chair. Crossed the space between them. His hand settled on Ryan's shoulder. Heavy. Warm. Real.

"Son."

One word. Everything in it.

"I know," Karl said quietly. "I've always known."

Ryan looked up into his father's face. Saw something there that undid him completely. Love without conditions. Love without scoreboards. Love that saw everything and chose to stay.

"You knew?"

"A father knows his children. I've been waiting for this day. Praying for it." Karl's voice was gentle.

"I knew you'd find your way back. It just takes time. Different time for different sons."

"I'm the prodigal who never left home," his voice cracked.

Karl's other hand found Ryan's other shoulder. "Now the healing can really begin."

The walls blurred. Ryan stood, fell into his father's arms. Felt them close around him solid as redwood, gentle as morning mist. Years of anger dissolved. Years of distance collapsed.

They stood there while the fire burned low. Father and son. The library holding them in its ancient calm.

Another beat. Sacred. Complete.

Finally, Karl pulled back. Wiped his own eyes. That smile again, deeper now.

"Esther's up at the old growth Pinot. Wants to see if the fog breaks before ten." He squeezed Ryan's shoulder. "Go get your brother. Let's go up there together."

"Together?"

"All of us. The way it should be."

Ryan nodded. His throat too full for words.

"Ryan?" Karl called as he reached the door.

He turned.

"Welcome home, son."

The redwood panels caught the firelight. Held it. Released it slowly back into the room. Like love. Like forgiveness. Like all the things that matter most.

Ryan went to find Ethan.

The fog clung to the Krueger house like a gray curtain, shrouding the limestone facade. 8 a.m. in the morning, and the place looked exactly like what it was: money without warmth.

"So, we've heard nothing." Eric Krueger stood at the breakfast room window, coffee cooling in his hand. "Not a word from Ryan Weinhardt."

Otto shifted in his chair. "Maybe Caitlin's still working on him."

"Caitlin was supposed to have him ready to sign by now." Hans Krueger entered the room, and both sons could see the strain in his face. "That was the whole point of her being there."

"Plans change," Otto said.

"Plans fail." Hans poured himself coffee from the silver pot. His hands weren't quite steady. "The wire cutting failed. The strike threats failed. Now Caitlin's failing."

Cheri appeared in the doorway, silk robe tied loosely. "Maybe it's time to stop playing games."

"What's that supposed to mean?" Eric turned from the window.

"It means your investors are getting impatient." She moved to the sideboard but didn't take anything. "It means gentle pressure isn't working."

"Since when do you know about our investors?" Hans studied his daughter-in-law.

"Since I pay attention." She faced them all. "You think I don't hear Eric and you talk? See the stress? We need to force this merger. Now."

"Force." Hans set down his coffee cup. "That's a dangerous word."

"So is the alternative." Cheri's voice was sharp. "That's where this is heading if the Weinhardt deal doesn't happen."

"We're not there yet," Eric said.

"No? Then why Hans, did you get that call last night? The one that had you pacing until three in the morning?"

Silence. Eric and Hans exchanged glances.

"What call?" Otto looked between them.

"The Chilean." Hans's voice was quiet. "He's... concerned about our progress."

"Concerned." Cheri laughed, but there was no humor in it. "That's one way to put it."

"You don't know what you're talking about," Eric said.

"Don't I? He gave you a deadline, didn't he Hans? Made it very clear what happens if the merger doesn't go through?"

"How could you possibly...," Eric looked shocked.

"Because I'm not stupid, Eric. Because I can see what's right in front of me." She moved closer to them. "You're in too deep with people you can't control. And your amateur hour tactics aren't going to save you."

Otto stood up. "So, what do you suggest? Since you seem to have all the answers."

"Something that actually works. Something final."

"Like I said last time, I've got something radical in the works."

"Careful," Hans warned.

"Careful got us here," snarled Cheri. "Careful got us wire cutting that did nothing. Strikes that never materialized. A woman on the inside who can't even get Ryan to turn on his phone." Cheri's eyes were hard. "Time for careful is over."

"Exactly," declared Otto. "Now's time serious, and guess what, these Salvadorans will do anything for money."

The room fell silent. Outside, the last wisps of fog dissolved over the manicured lawn.

Cheri laughed. Not amused. Just cold. "You want to play cartel, Otto? You want to pretend you've got the stomach for what that means?" She leaned forward, her voice dropping. "I've seen men like you my whole life. Big talk in climate-controlled rooms. Making promises with other people's blood. But when it comes time to get your manicured hands dirty?" She stood, smoothing her robe. "You'll be at your country club working on your alibi while hired help takes the fall."

"I need some air," Cheri said. "This house feels like a tomb."

She left them there, three men staring after her.

"She's right," Otto said finally. "We're out of time."

"I know." Hans sank into a chair. "The Chilean made that very clear."

"What exactly did he say?" Eric asked.

"That we had two weeks. That his associates don't appreciate excuses." Hans rubbed his temples. "That he'd be very disappointed if he had to handle things personally."

"No more careful," Otto breathed.

"Yes."

"So what do we do?"

Before Hans could answer, they heard Cheri's voice from the hallway. Low, urgent. Speaking into her phone.

"...need to meet today. No, I can't wait... Yes, I understand... The usual place then."

Eric started toward the door but Hans caught his arm. "Wait."

They listened as her voice faded toward the back of the house.

"Who was that?" Otto asked.

"I don't know." Eric's jaw was tight. "But I'm going to find out."

Twenty minutes later, Eric found Cheri in their bedroom, dressed now, applying lipstick at her vanity.

"Going somewhere?"

"Meeting someone for lunch." She didn't look at him in the mirror. "That a problem?"

"Who were you talking to?"

"A friend."

"Which friend?"

She turned then, smiled. "You're awfully interested in my social calendar suddenly."

"I'm interested when my wife is making plans that sound like..."

"Like what?"

"Like something that involves my family's business."

"Everything involves your family's business. That's the problem." She stood, smoothed her dress. "You're so focused on the Weinhardts, you can't see the bigger picture."

"Enlighten me."

"The merger's not happening through persuasion. You know it. I know it. Time for a different approach."

"Cheri..."

"I'll be back by three." She kissed his cheek, left lipstick on his skin. "Try not to worry so much. It ages you."

Eric stood in their bedroom, her perfume still hanging in the air, and felt something cold settle in his stomach. He wiped the lipstick away and went to find his father.

The fog lay thick as wool over the old growth Pinot block, the kind of morning hush that swallowed sound and held its breath. Esther stood between the rows, boots sunk in the damp soil, fingertips brushing the cool skins of the clusters. The vines rose around her like a congregation. Behind her she heard her father's steady steps on the uneven ground and the quieter shuffling of her brothers.

Karl stopped a few feet away, hat in hand. Ethan and Ryan flanked him, both wrapped in jackets, both watching her like she might be about to call down a miracle. But there was another miracle there between the vines. Something had happened between them. It was unspoken but tension was gone. It was evident in their faces as they looked at her and then each other.

No one spoke at first. It felt wrong to break the quiet.

A faint shift stirred at the edges of the vineyard. The dark began to thin. It was subtle at first, a softening of the gray over the western ridge.

"Look," Ryan whispered.

They turned as a seam of light opened above the treetops. The fog loosened its grip, thinning just enough to show the first wash of blue. Esther checked her watch. The numbers glowed in the dim light.

"Nine fifty-five," she said.

Karl breathed out. "Third morning."

They watched as the fog pulled back like a curtain being gathered by invisible hands. Sunlight broke across the upper branches of the redwoods, then slid down the slope until it spilled over the vineyard. A faint warmth touched her face.

Ethan shook his head slowly. "I can't believe it. Three days in a row."

Karl looked at his daughter. "Feels like your great grandfather is walking the rows with us."

Esther reached for a cluster and lifted it toward her. The fruit was cool but firm. She rolled one berry between her fingers, then slipped it into her mouth. The skin gave gently. The juice was dark and bright all at once, a clean line of acid with that depth only old vines carried, something that felt as if it had been building for a century.

She closed her eyes. "They're ready. Not just by numbers. By feel. By balance."

"Just like he wrote," Ethan said. "The land speaks first."

Karl stepped closer and plucked a berry of his own. He chewed slowly, thoughtful. "I tasted this same thing with my father when I was a boy. It's strange how it comes back. Like memory in the fruit."

Esther smiled. "La Pausa della Nebbia. The fog pause. He believed the vines knew when the pause was right."

"Well," Ryan said, "they sure picked a morning for it."

The fog had retreated all the way to the far ridge, leaving the vineyard in a clean morning glow. Dew clung to the leaves. The smell of wet earth rose up around them. There was a sweetness under it, something like crushed thyme and ripe strawberry skins. Birds began to stir in the hedgerow.

Karl placed a hand on Esther's shoulder. "Ryan, have Jake call the crew. Let's bring this in now."

Ryan lifted the phone to his ear. "Jake, it's a go."

Ethan looked at her with a half smile. "You know, this feels like… I don't know. Like we're part of a story bigger than us."

She met his eyes. "We always were. We just stopped paying attention."

Ryan nodded. "Not today."

They stood together in the center of the vineyard, a small circle in the wide morning light as they waited for the workers to arrive. Esther picked another berry, then offered it to each of them in turn. It felt almost ceremonial; fruit passed from her hand to theirs. Karl tasted last, his shoulders softening as he savored it.

"This is good," he said. "This is better than good."

"It's ours," Esther replied. "And it's ready."

A breeze moved through the vines, soft and clean, lifting the last threads of fog toward the sky. The sun climbed higher. The day began to open.

Karl looked toward the house, then back to his children. "We have work ahead."

Ethan laughed under his breath. "When don't we."

"Yes, lots of work to do," whispered Ryan to himself. It would be a huge task, but he had to do it soon and it started with a meeting with Caitlin.

They began walking back through the rows, slow and unhurried, the vines brushing their sleeves. There was a sense of something beginning, something old rising up to meet something new.

The trucks came up the hill in the as the warming sun rose in the east. Fifteen pickers climbed out, their breath visible in the cool air, voices low as they gathered near the old growth block. Some had worked these vines for twenty years. They knew what this morning meant.

Canvas picking bags hung from shoulders, the wide straps worn soft from seasons of use. Curved harvest knives caught the first light as men checked the blades with calloused thumbs. Plastic lugs were stacked at the end of each row, forty pounds of fruit to a box when full. Someone had backed a flatbed trailer to the edge of the block, its wooden slats darkened with the stains of countless harvests.

Karl stood at the head of the first row, hands on his hips, studying the vines like a man reading scripture. Yes, just like they'd hope, the fog had lifted at 9:55. Third morning running. Johann would have already been cutting by now.

"We go row by row," Karl said. "Take your time with the selection. Anything with rot or bird damage goes in the drop bucket. I want clean fruit."

Ethan took his place three rows over, the picking bag now more familiar against his hip after so many years away. The weight of it brought back mornings he thought he'd forgotten. The smell of cold earth and ripe fruit. His father's voice carrying across the vines.

Ryan worked the row beside Karl, his cuts efficient and quick.

The crew moved through the block with quiet purpose. Hands reached into the canopy, lifting clusters, knives flashing. The soft thump of fruit dropping into canvas bags. When a bag grew heavy, the picker would walk to the end of the row and empty it gently into the waiting lugs.

By mid-morning the trailer held its first load, purple clusters mounded high, and one of the older workers drove it slow down the hill toward the crush pad.

Esther was waiting.

She had been up since four, hosing down the sorting table, checking the rollers on the destemmer, running sanitizer through the lines. The concrete pad was still wet, drains cleared, yellow hoses coiled and ready. She'd laid out the punch-down tools and checked the temperature on the empty fermentation tanks twice.

When the trailer pulled up, she directed the driver to the sorting table and pulled on her rubber gloves. The lugs came off one at a time, fruit tumbling onto the conveyor in a river of dusty purple. She stood at the head of the line, pulling leaves and underripe clusters, her fingers stained dark within minutes.

The destemmer hummed as the first grapes fed through, the gentle mechanical shudder separating fruit from stems. Clean berries dropped into the bin below, and Esther watched the flow with a critical eye. Too much stem material and the wine would turn bitter. Not enough and it lacked structure.

She made a small adjustment to the roller gap and nodded to herself.

Back on the hill, Ethan's shoulders had begun to ache in a way that felt almost good. Honest. The repetition of reach and cut, reach and cut, emptied his mind of everything but the work. He found himself falling into the old rhythm without thinking.

Karl moved past him, checking the fruit in his son's bag. He didn't say anything, but Ethan caught the small nod. It was enough.

The morning wore on. The fog stayed away. Row by row, the old vines gave up their fruit, and the trailers kept rolling down the hill to where Esther waited with steady hands and a knowing eye.

By early afternoon, the block was picked clean. The crew gathered in the shade of the oak at the edge of the vineyard, passing around water bottles and sandwiches someone had brought in a cooler.

Ryan found his father by the trailer, checking the weight on the last load. He waited until the foreman walked away.

"Dad, I need to go."

Karl looked at him. The kind of look that saw past whatever words were about to come.

"Now?"

"There's something I have to take care of. Today." Ryan pulled off his gloves. "It can't wait anymore."

Karl was quiet. The sounds of the crew breaking down filled the silence. Lugs stacking. Tailgates closing.

"Caitlin," Karl said.

Ryan's jaw tightened. "I'm ending it."

Karl nodded slowly, his eyes on the vines they'd just picked clean. "Some things are like the harvest. Wait too long and you miss the moment. Then the rot sets in." He turned back to his son. "Go. Do what you need to do."

"Can you and Esther handle the crush?"

"We'll manage. Ethan's here."

Ryan hesitated, then started toward his truck. He stopped and looked back. "Dad. Thank you."

"Go fix what you can fix, son. The wine will be here when you get back."

Ryan pulled away down the hill, dust rising behind him in the afternoon light. Karl watched until the truck disappeared around the bend, then turned and walked toward the oak tree where Ethan waited.

Far off, beyond the valley, beyond the groves and the cattle and the neighboring drive, the Krueger place lay in the midday stillness, waiting for its own troubles to emerge.

And the day moved toward them.

CHAPTER TWENTY-SIX

KRUEGER'S RANCH

SONOMA COUNTY

"I pray you, do not fall in love with me,
for I am falser than vows made in wine."
Shakespeare: As. You like it

C heri sat across from Vega at a restaurant in St. Helena. He'd chosen a back booth, away from windows.

"The Chilean's putting pressure on everyone," she said without preamble.

"I know." Vega sipped his water. "That's why we're accelerating things."

"Accelerating how?"

"Your brother-in-law. Otto. He's been useful with his little schemes."

"Wire cutting that accomplished nothing."

"That was practice." Vega smiled. "Now I gave him something real to do."

"Real?"

"Fifteen days from now, Ryan Weinhardt's new vintage will be in his cellar. All of it. His entire year's work." Vega leaned forward. "Shame if something happened to it."

Cheri felt her throat tighten. "You're talking about..."

"I'm talking about solving everyone's problem. No inventory means no income. No income means he needs capital immediately. Enter the merger."

"A fire."

"An unfortunate accident. These old cellars, all that wood, electrical problems..." He shrugged. "It happens."

"Eric and Hans won't agree to this."

"They don't need to know. Otto's already moved on it. Thinks it's his idea to finally do something decisive." Vega's smile was cold. "My associate from Mexico had already met with him. Making sure he understands the stakes."

"Your associate?

"Yes, Cesar Zamora from the Baja, some muscle from the cartel. He's directing things now. He's my insurance. I made Otto put him in charge. He's handling the Salvadorans Otto funded. So, when things work now, Otto gets the credit with Hans."

"These are the same Salvadorans who cut the wires?"

"Yes, that plan failed. But Cesar will put things in order. Thankfully the Salvadorans are still available. They need the money. And they're expendable if something goes wrong."

"This is..." Cheri gripped her water glass.

"This is what you signed up for when you started passing information. When you took our money." Vega checked his watch. "Fifteen days. Mark your calendar."

"What if someone's hurt? What if..."

"That's Otto's problem. And the Salvadorans'. You just need to make sure the family's positioned to offer the merger immediately after. Salvation in their hour of need."

"I can't..."

"You can and you will." His voice softened. Dangerous soft. "Unless you want Eric to know exactly who you've been talking to. What you've been sharing. How deep this goes."

Cheri stared at him. "You're threatening me?"

"I'm clarifying your position. You're either with us or you're a problem. And we solve problems."

A beat. Then his hand found hers across the table. Gentle now. The touch they both remembered.

"Cheri." Her name different on his lips. Personal. "We've shared too much to pretend this is just business."

She didn't pull away. Couldn't.

"Those nights in Napa. What we talked about. What we dreamed about." His thumb traced her knuckles. "This was always where it was heading. You knew that."

"I didn't know it would be like this."

"Because you're strong. Because you see the bigger picture." He leaned closer. "Don't lose your nerve now. Not when we're so close to everything we wanted."

"We? Or you?"

"Does it matter?" His eyes held hers. Dark. Knowing. "Love is beautiful, Cheri. But sometimes it gets in the way of what's necessary. What's inevitable."

"You used me."

"I chose you. Because you're not like them. Because you understand that real power requires real choices." His grip tightened slightly. "Don't disappoint me now. Don't become just another wine country wife who couldn't handle the truth."

She felt the trap closing. Felt the mix of threat and promise, business and bed, all tangled together.

"Fifteen days," he said, releasing her hand. "Make sure the family's ready to move on the merger the moment Ryan needs help."

"And if I refuse?"

He smiled. That smile she'd once found irresistible. Now it just looked like teeth.

"You won't. You've come too far. Invested too much. Besides, you're not the type to back down. That's what I've always loved about you."

The word hung between them. Love. Weapon and weakness both.

"This isn't love," she said.

"No. It's better. It's understanding."

"And Otto?"

"Otto will think he's proving himself. Showing daddy he can play with the big boys." Vega stood, dropped money on the table. "Let him think that. Right up until the match is lit."

"This will destroy them. The Weinhardts."

"It will save them. Through the merger. Everyone wins."

"Except Ryan."

"Ryan should have taken the deal when it was offered nicely." Vega buttoned his jacket. "Some lessons have to be learned the hard way."

Cheri watched him leave, sat alone in the booth for another ten minutes. When she finally stood, her hands were shaking.

Back at the house, she found Eric in his study.

"Good lunch?" His voice was too casual.

"Fine." She poured herself whiskey from his decanter. "Girl talk."

"Which girl?"

"Does it matter?"

"It might."

She turned to face him. "What's this about, Eric?"

"I know who you met with."

Her hand stilled on the glass. "Oh?"

"Vega. At the place in St. Helena." Eric stood, moved toward her. "Dad and I have been working with him, but how did you get in the picture?"

"Because his boss put me in the picture."

"That's why is your father shaking after one phone call? Why are you pacing at night?" She moved closer to him. "Face it, Eric. You're in over your head. All of you."

"And you're not?"

"I'm exactly where I need to be."

"Which is where? With us? With them?" His voice cracked slightly. "With me?"

For a moment, something flickered across her face. Then it was gone.

"I'm trying to save you. All of you." She touched his face. "Even if you're too proud to see it."

"Save us how?"

"By making sure this merger happens. By whatever means necessary."

"Cheri, what did Vega tell you?"

"That things are moving. That Otto's finally going to do something useful."

Eric grabbed her shoulders. "What's Otto going to do?"

"I don't know the details." The lie came easily. "Just that there's a plan. Something that will force Ryan's hand."

"When?"

"Soon."

"Cheri, if Otto's mixed up with Vega's people..."

"Then maybe for once he'll actually accomplish something." She pulled away from him. "It's obvious his wire cutting didn't work."

"This is different. Vega doesn't play games."

"Neither does your Chilean friend. So maybe it's time you all stopped pretending this is some gentleman's negotiation."

Eric stared at his wife, this woman he'd shared a bed with for five years and realized he didn't know her at all.

"And I had to drag this out of you to get the truth?"

"What truth? That your brother might actually solve your problem? That someone's going to do what you've been too afraid to do?"

"Too afraid or too decent?"

"Same thing in this world." She picked up her glass again. "The decent people lose. The ones willing to do what's necessary survive."

"And which are you?"

"I'm the one trying to keep this family from drowning." She finished her whiskey. "Even if I have to push you into deep water to do it."

"Cheri..."

"Fifteen days, Eric. That's roughly when you should be ready with merger papers. Have them drawn up. Be prepared to move fast."

"Fifteen days until what?"

"Until Karl Weinhardt needs a lifeline. And you better be ready to throw it to him." She set down the empty glass. "Or we all drown together."

She left him standing there, alone in his study, the weight of what was coming settling on his shoulders like fog that wouldn't lift.

CHAPTER TWENTY-SEVEN

HEALDSBURG CA

SONOMA COUNTY

"A good wife and a good wine, joy all the day."
Old English Proverb

Ryan stood at Caitlin's door, his hand raised to knock. The fog had lifting had been one more sign. Everything changing. His family's celebration with Esther still echoed in his chest, but this weight in his stomach wouldn't let go.

Caitlin opened before he could knock. She'd been watching from the window.

"Ryan." Her voice caught. She knew. Something in his face, the way he stood there.

"Can I come in?"

Madison's cartoons played from the living room. Caitlin glanced back at her daughter. "Madison, honey? Go play in your room for a bit."

"But Mom....."

"Please."

The little girl dragged her feet down the narrow hallway. A door clicked shut.

Ryan stepped inside. The apartment seemed smaller in daylight. He noticed things he'd ignored before. The threadbare carpet. The kitchen table that wobbled. The single window with its view of the parking lot.

"Coffee?" Caitlin asked, but she was already moving to the kitchen, needing something to do with her hands.

"No. Thanks."

She poured herself a cup anyway. Her hands trembled slightly.

"I'm turning down Otto's offer."

She stopped mid-pour. "The merger?"

"Yeah."

"But that's..." She set the pot down. "That's everything you've been working toward."

"I know."

"So why?" She turned to face him, leaning against the counter. "Did Karl talk you out of it?"

"No. It was my decision."

Something shifted in her face. Understanding creeping in. "This isn't about the merger."

Ryan looked away. A crack ran along the wall behind her, probably been there for years. "The fog lifting. My family together. It made me realize some things."

"What things?"

He forced himself to meet her eyes. "That I've been on the wrong path."

Her fingers tightened on the coffee mug. "Ryan."

"It was wrong, Caitlin. About all of it. I shouldn't have responded to you that first time. I had no right."

She set the mug down hard. Coffee sloshed over the rim. "Don't do this."

"I have to."

"No, you don't." Her voice rose, then dropped. Madison was just down the hall. "Three years, Ryan. Three years I've been waiting in the shadows."

"I know."

"Do you? Do you really?" She moved closer. "Every holiday alone. Every time you had to leave because Bri called. Every single night wondering if this would be the time you'd finally choose me."

"It was never about choosing. It was wrong from the start."

"Wrong?" She laughed, but it came out broken. "Now it's wrong? Now that the fog's lifting and everything's looking sunny at the vineyard?"

"It was always wrong."

"Then why did you…" She turned away, gripping the kitchen counter. "We talked about a future. About you leaving her. About us having a real life together."

"I know what we talked about."

"I believed you." Her shoulders shook. ".....I'm such an idiot."

"You're not. I'm the one who led you on. Who let this go on for three years when I knew….."

"Stop." She spun around. "Just stop. You're going back to her."

"I need to tell Bri the truth. She deserves that."

"And what do I deserve?" Tears ran down her face now. "What about what I deserve? I've been here for you, Ryan. When you were hurting. When things were bad with Bri. When Ethan looked like the winner and you the loser."

"I'm grateful for…."

"Grateful?" Her voice cracked. "I don't want your gratitude."

Ryan had no answer for that.

"You know what my ex said when he left?" Her voice shook. "He said I was too needy. Too much. And here you are, the second man to just..." She grabbed a coffee mug from the counter.

"Caitlin, don't."

She held it, knuckles white, then set it down carefully. "Madison's in the next room."

"I'm sorry."

"Sorry." She wiped her face with the back of her hand. "You're sorry. Well, that fixes everything. You get to go back to your big house, your perfect family, your vineyard. And me? What do I get?"

Ryan looked around the small apartment. Really looked. The mismatched furniture. The generic prints on the walls. The life she'd been living while waiting for him.

"When my dad gave Ethan that money for his startup, it did something to me. Set me on this path. And if I keep going…....."

"Oh, so now it's your brother's fault?"

"No. It's mine. All of it." Ryan moved toward the door. "I've confessed to my father. I'm trying to make things right."

"And if Bri won't take you back? If she tells you to go to hell?"

"That's the risk I have to take."

"Don't come crawling back here." Her voice turned cold. "I know where your heart is now. It was never really here anyway, was it?"

"Caitlin…"

"You used me. Just say it. You used me because you were hurting and I was easy."

"That's not…."

"Get out."

"This can be a new beginning for you too."

"Don't you dare. Don't you dare stand there and tell me this is good for me." She picked up another mug, held it like a weapon.

Ryan reached for the doorknob. He could see it now, how staying longer would only twist the knife deeper. Through the thin walls, he could hear Madison singing to herself. Some made-up song about butterflies.

He opened the door.

"I really did care about you, Caitlin."

"Go."

He left. Behind him, he heard something hit the door. Soft enough that Madison wouldn't be scared. Hard enough that he'd know.

The parking lot stretched out gray under the noon sun. He walked to his truck without looking back.

Inside the apartment, Caitlin stood alone in her small kitchen, holding herself together until she couldn't anymore.

Ryan merged onto 101 South. His hands gripped the wheel. Ten and two, like his father taught him. The highway blurred past. Dry Creek exit. Shiloh Road. The late afternoon sun hung low ahead of him, forcing him to squint against the glare. Three years of lies. His stomach turned.

Windsor, eight miles. Then six. Then four.

What would he say to Bri? The words wouldn't come. His phone buzzed. He didn't look.

The exit ramp curved ahead. Through downtown Windsor now. Past the Taco Bell. The Wells Fargo. Past Windsor Castle Park where the old English and Irish families who'd settled here after the Gold Rush used to trade goods, plant orchards, swap land. They saw the future in these oak-lined hills. Built something that would last.

Unlike him.

Her mother's house appeared. A Craftsman set back from the road, gravel drive, sagging porch posts that needed paint. Bri's car parked close to the door. He pulled to a stop, turned off the engine. Through the front window, he could see movement. Normal life happening inside.

He got out. Walked to the door. Knocked.

No answer.

Movement inside. Footsteps. Then nothing.

He knocked again. Waited. He had to. No other choice. The waiting was killing him, but he was waiting in hope.

The screen door squeaked.

Time to find out if his life was over or just beginning.

Bri stepped out, let it bang shut behind her. She stayed by the door, arms crossed. The afternoon breeze caught her hair, pushed it across her face. She didn't brush it away.

"Mom said you were here."

Ryan stood. The porch boards groaned under his boots. "Thanks for coming out."

"The kids are inside. They don't need to hear this."

"I know." He gripped the porch rail. Paint flaked under his palms. "I saw Karl. After everything went down. He helped me see some things."

She waited. "And Ethan."

"I'm working on that too."

Ryan looked out at the vineyard rows stretching beyond the property line. "There's something Tawi told me once. About houses. How people lock all the doors to keep evil out. But if you leave one door open, just one, evil gets in. Then it can open any door it wants."

The wind chimes on the porch corner played three notes.

"My bitterness." His voice caught. "That was my open door. And it let everything else in. What happened with Caitlin."

"Don't." Her voice sharp as pruning shears.

"It's over. Completely over. I need you to know that."

"You think that fixes it?"

"No." He met her eyes. "But maybe... is there any way you could find a place to forgive me?"

Bri's laugh had no humor in it. "Forgive you."

"I know how it sounds."

"Do you?" She came to the rail, kept distance between them. "Do you know what it's like? Finding out from Caitlin's friend at the grocery store? Having to smile and bag my groceries while she watched my face?"

A crow called from the walnut tree.

"Mom wants me to forgive you." Bri's knuckles were white on the rail. "Says she and Dad had their troubles. She cheated. He forgave. I never knew. Grew up thinking we were perfect."

Ryan stayed quiet.

"Maybe that's why I'm handling this better than I thought." She turned to face him. "But now it's my turn, Ryan. You were right to suspect my heart was in the wrong place. About Ethan."

His chest tightened.

"I was angry when he left. Then I married you. I did love you. I did. But things lingered. When he came back..." She shook her head. "It was hard."

The afternoon sun caught the dust motes floating between them.

"So, we both have things to forgive," she said. Yours was acted out. Mine was the heart. One's the doorway to the other." Her voice dropped. "I left that door open too, Ryan. In my heart. Maybe I never acted on it. Maybe with time I would have."

The screen door creaked. Ryan Jr.'s face appeared in the gap.

"Mom?"

"Go back inside, baby. I'll be there soon."

The door clicked shut.

Bri straightened. "The kids need us whole. Whatever that looks like."

"What are you saying?"

"I'm saying give me a month. Mom's been talking my ear off about second chances. About what matters." She pulled her sweater tight. "I think I can make that choice. But I need time."

"A month."

"A month."

The breeze picked up, rustling the old oak's leaves. Somewhere down the valley, a tractor started up.

Ryan nodded. "Okay."

Bri turned toward the house, paused with her hand on the screen door handle. "The way you talk about Tawi's wisdom. About Ethan. Something's different in you."

"Yeah."

"Hold onto that."

The screen door squeaked open. She was halfway through when she looked back. "Mom makes dinner at six. Every night. The kids would like it if you came. Once a week, maybe."

"I'd like that too."

She went inside. The door didn't bang this time. Just whispered shut.

Ryan stood on the porch, watching the shadows lengthen across the yard. A month wasn't forgiveness. But it wasn't a closed door either.

He walked to his truck, gravel crunching underfoot. The sun was lowering towards the western hills, painting the sky the color of Pinot Noir. As he drove away, he could see Bri through the kitchen window, lifting Ryan Jr. to help with something at the counter.

The road back to the vineyard stretched ahead. He'd drive it again next week. And the week after. However many weeks it took.

CHAPTER TWENTY-EIGHT

WEINHARDT'S RANCH

SONOMA COUNTY

"Where wine is shared, friendship and brotherhood grow."
Traditional Mediterranean proverb

Twelve days had passed since the first night of harvest, when the crews moved through the twenty-four acres under floodlights and the fruit came in cold and perfect. The smaller five-acre block of old growth Pinot followed two days later, picked on the morning the fog broke at 9:55 just as Esther's great-grandfather had written in his journal.

Since then, the days had been full. Sorting tables humming at dawn, the fruit sliding into open-top fermenters. The first days of cold soak, then the slow climb into fermentation with its warm energy scent rising through the crush pad.

Ryan and Ethan had found themselves side by side at the sorting table. Not talking much at first. Just nodding when good fruit came through. Shaking heads at the bad clusters. By the third day, Ethan asked Ryan about the Syrah block temperatures. Real question. Real interest. Ryan answered straight. No edge to it.

The workers noticed. Javier mentioned it to Enrique while they hosed down tanks. "You see the brothers?" he'd nodded. "About time."

By the end of the week the cap had sunk, the color had deepened, and the free-run wine whispered out of the tanks into waiting vessels. Pressing, settling, racking. The old growth fruit followed the same rhythm, only staggered a few days behind.

Karl watched from the winery door one afternoon. His sons moving together around the press. Not perfectly synchronized yet, but getting there. The fragile start of something new.

Now every lot, every experiment, every last barrel rested quietly in French oak, tucked in the cellar where time, nature, and God would knit the pieces into a whole.

With the work finally behind them, the evening shifted toward celebration. The fog held offshore and the golden hour laid a soft amber across the hills as they gathered at the long table behind the house. Eden arranged flowers from the garden, Karl uncorked a simple table wine, and Tawi moved between the grill and the kitchen with the ease of a man who had cooked for them since childhood. The scent of wood smoke and searing meat drifted over the yard.

Esther stepped out into the light, tired in the best way, knowing the year ahead would reveal whether the gamble with the old growth Pinot had been worth it. Tonight, they would eat, laugh, and breathe a little easier. The barrels were full. The work was done. The promise of next year waited in the dark below their feet.

Eden and Karl had set up tables under the massive oak that shaded the side yard, stringing lights between branches that had held similar lights for similar gatherings across five generations. The smell of mesquite smoke drifted from where Karl tended the big steel-drum barbecue his father had welded together in the sixties.

Lauren had arrived, bringing her a trunk full of tablecloths she'd somehow known they'd need. She and Eden worked in easy rhythm, setting places for what looked like half the county. The crew families were already arriving, pickups pulling into the field they used for parking, children spilling out like seeds from a pod, running toward the swing that hung from the oak's largest branch.

"Quite a spread," Ethan said, finding his mother arranging mason jars filled with late roses from her garden.

"We need this," Eden said simply. "After everything we've been through. People need to remember we're not just a business. We're a community."

The families kept coming. Miguel with his wife Maria and what seemed like a dozen grandchildren. Luis and Carlos and their wives, carrying covered dishes that hadn't been requested but appeared anyway, the unspoken law of rural gatherings. A repentant Javier with his elderly parents, who'd worked harvests here in the seventies. Even some of the newer hires, the ones who'd been watching Enrique with suspicious eyes, came with cautious smiles and contributions to the feast.

Enrique arrived last, his family clustered close like they weren't sure of their welcome. His wife Rosa carried their youngest, barely two, while their older children held tight to their father's hands. The conversation quieted when they appeared, a held breath across the gathering.

It was Esther who broke the pause, walking straight to Rosa with a smile bright as fermentation. "Rosa! I'm so glad you came. Mom's been asking for your tamale recipe for years." She took the covered dish Rosa carried, linked arms with her, and led them into the heart of the gathering like a shepherd bringing lost sheep home.

The conversation resumed, tentative at first, then warming like wine opened to air. Tawi emerged from the outdoor kitchen they'd set up near the barbecue, carrying platters that made people stop mid-sentence to stare. He'd prepared the feast with the same attention he gave to healing medicines, each dish crafted to nourish more than hunger.

There was beef from their own herd, dry-rubbed with herbs from the garden and smoke from oak that had fallen in last winter's storms. Salmon he'd somehow procured fresh that morning, grilled on cedar planks. Mountains of beans slow-cooked with ham hocks. His famous cornbread, dense and slightly sweet, that people would beg him to make for their weddings. Salads from Eden's garden dressed with Meyer lemon from the tree by the kitchen door.

"Before we eat," Karl called out, standing at the head of the longest table, "I want to say something."

The gathering quieted, children hushed by parents who recognized the tone. Karl stood there in his work clothes, he'd never changed from the previous night's crisis, looking like exactly what he was: a man who worked the land and loved the people who worked it with him.

"Nearly two weeks ago someone tried to break us. Cut our power, threatened our harvest, hoped we'd turn on each other." He paused, looked directly at Enrique. "We didn't. We came together. We saved the fruit. We proved what I've always known, this ranch isn't about the family name on the deed. It's about every hand that tends these vines, every back that bends to pick, every voice that calls out in the fog to guide us home."

He raised his mason jar of last year's Pinot. "To the harvest. To the families who make it possible."

The toast rang across the gathering in Spanish and English and languages in between. Enrique's eyes filled, and Rosa pressed her face into his shoulder. Their children, sensing the shift, let go of their parents' hands and ran to join the other kids at the swing.

"All right then," Tawi called out. "Eat before it gets cold and I take it personal."

The feast unfolded like all the best gatherings, chaotic, joyful, excessive. Children ran between tables stealing cookies. Teenagers clustered at their own table, pretending not to notice each other while noticing everything. The old-timers gathered near the barbecue, telling stories that grew more elaborate with each glass of wine.

Ethan found himself at a table with Miguel and Luis, listening to stories about his grandfather, about harvests from before he was born when they still picked everything into wooden boxes and sorted on tables made from old doors. The stories wound around each other like vines, each memory supporting the next.

"Your brother," Miguel said quietly at one point, nodding toward where Ryan had appeared at the edge of the gathering, standing uncertain in the shadows. "He's a good man. Just carries too much weight."

Ethan watched his brother at the periphery, saw Bri's absence like a hole in the fabric of the evening. Before he could think too much about it, he stood, grabbed a plate, loaded it with food.

Ethan crossed the patio. Tri-tip, salad, Tawi's cornbread. Set it down by Ryan's elbow.

"Thanks." Ryan looked up from the harvest reports.

"You need to eat." Ethan pulled out a chair. The evening light caught the vineyard rows stretching west. "How'd it go yesterday?"

Ryan knew he meant Bri. "Better. She let me stay for dinner."

"That's good."

They sat in the quiet. Somewhere nearby, Esther was laughing at something Eden had said. Normal sounds. Family sounds.

"I know you're hurting, bro." Ethan leaned back. "My coming back hasn't helped. It upset a lot of things. The investment. The pressure I put on you. On dad. On this place."

Ryan picked up his fork. Put it down and listened.

Ethan continued. "I've tried to show it in how I've been. But I need to say it straight." He looked out at the vines. "Forgive my arrogance. I know what I did to you."

"When it comes to forgiveness, I'm first in line for needing it." Ryan's voice came quiet. "Bri's been..." He stopped. Started again. "She's been amazing. More grace than I deserve."

"Yeah."

"Like someone great once said. If you don't forgive, you can't be forgiven."

The truth of it settled between them like dust after harvest.

From the porch, Karl watched his sons. Eden came up beside him, drying her hands on a dish towel.

"Look at them," she said softly.

Karl put his arm around his wife. His boys at the same table. Talking. Really talking. The family finding its way to something new. Something better.

"Thank God," he said. And meant it.

As the evening deepened, someone brought out guitars. Music rose with the smoke from the dying coals: Mexican ballads, country songs everyone knew, even some rock that made the teenagers look at their parents with new respect. Esther's clear voice led a harmony on an old hymn their grandmother had loved, the sound carrying across the vineyards like a blessing.

"This is what it's about," Eden said, finding Ethan during a quiet moment. She leaned against him the way she had when he was young, and he put his arm around her. "Not the wine, not the money. This."

"I know, Mom. I forgot for a while, but I know."

The party wound down slowly, families departing with sleepy children and promises to see each other. Enrique was among the last to leave, approaching Karl with formal dignity.

"Thank you," he said simply. "For believing. For the trust."

Karl gripped his shoulder. "You're family. Family takes care of family."

The last of the trucks pulled away. Taillights disappearing down the drive. The BBQ pit still glowed orange. Empty beer bottles lined the picnic tables.

Ethan found Lauren helping Eden stack chairs.

"Want to take a ride?"

She looked up. "Now?"

"Moon's breaking through."

Twenty minutes later they were saddled up. The horses eager, dancing sideways at the barn gate. The fog had torn into patches. Moonlight spilled through.

They rode up the old trail. No talking at first. Just the creak of leather. The horses' breath clouding white.

"Good party," Lauren said finally.

"Dad knows how to throw one."

"All those families. The Gonzalez clan must have had thirty people."

"At least." Ethan shifted in his saddle. "Makes you think."

"About what?"

"Having one. A family like that."

She didn't answer right away. Her horse picked its way over a fallen branch. The ocean smell rode in on the breeze. Salt and kelp and distance.

"You want that? Kids? The whole thing?"

"Yeah. Someday." He glanced over. "You?"

"Maybe. With the right person."

They crested the ridge. The valley spread below. Patches of fog caught in the hollows like cotton.

"How's Ryan doing?" she asked.

"Better. I talked with him about her at the party."

"That's good."

"They've got work ahead of them. Ghosts to deal with." Ethan's horse snorted, shook its head. "I've got my own share."

"We all do."

"I want to stay here. In Sonoma. Maybe the restaurant idea."

"You still thinking about that?"

"If things work out." He reined in his horse. Looked at her straight. "I'm learning to let go of the old stuff. Choose what's ahead instead. A future here."

The fog shifted. Closed. Opened again.

"One with you. If you'll be patient while I figure things out."

Lauren's horse stepped closer. Their knees almost touched.

"I can be patient."

"Yeah?"

"For the right things."

They sat there. The moon bright then hidden then bright again. The horses stamped, ready to move. Somewhere below an owl called.

Not a promise exactly. Not yet. But hope. Each in their own way carrying it.

"Come on," Lauren said. "Let's ride."

They turned the horses back toward home. The fog closing behind them like a door.

Salazar was working on his second beer at Los Tres Hecheras bar in Petaluma, when his phone vibrated. He nodded to the two men next to him and stepped outside.

"Yeah?"

"Tonight's the night." Cesar's voice came low through the phone.

Salazar lit a cigarette. Watched a couple stumble out of the bar across the street. "You sure?"

"Wine's all in the cellar. They just threw that big party. Whole family's there. Workers. Everyone."

"So?"

"So, they'll be dead tired. Maybe drunk. Sleeping hard."

The street was quiet. Just the neon buzz from the bar signs. Salazar pulled on his cigarette.

"You been there before," Cesar continued. "You know the layout."

"I know it."

"Three a.m. That's the sweet spot."

"Yes, that's what I planned?"

"No mistakes this time." Cesar's voice turned sharp. "I heard the rumors. Workers talking about finding some Salvadoran bracelet last time."

Salazar flicked ash onto the sidewalk. Said nothing.

"None of that tonight. You want your bonus? Do it clean. In and out. Nothing left behind."

"I got it."

"Three a.m."

The line went dead.

Salazar stood there. Finished his cigarette. Ground it under his boot. Inside the bar, someone had turned up the music. Accordion and guitar spilling into the street.

Three hours to wait.

He went back inside. Ordered another beer. The two men looked at him. He shook his head slightly. Not yet.

The clock above the bar read midnight.

CHAPTER TWENTY-NINE

KRUEGERS RANCH

SONOMA COUNTY

"Wine is a mocker, strong drink is raging."
Proverbs 20:1

The headlights cut through darkness like accusations. Engine still running, rattling like Caitlin's thoughts.

She pounded again. Fist against oak. "Open up!"

The door swung wide. Maria, the housekeeper, stepped back as Caitlin shouldered past. Bourbon and something sharper, desperation, trailing in her wake.

"Where is he? Where's Otto?"

The great room opened before her. Hans sat deep in leather, crystal tumbler catching firelight. The whiskey looked like liquid amber. Expensive. Everything here was expensive.

"Caitlin." Not a greeting. A statement of fact.

"Don't." She swayed. Caught herself on the doorframe. "Ryan won't do it. Your precious connection to the Weinhardts? Gone."

Otto emerged from the shadows. Always lurking, that one.

"We know." Otto's voice, smooth as the whiskey his father nursed. "You told me the day Ryan told you."

"But does *he* know?" She pointed at Hans. Finger shaking. "Does he know his big plans all fail? He can't win against the Wienhardts."

Hans took another sip. Savored it. The room smelled of leather and wood smoke and money. So much money.

"Sit down before you fall down."

"I don't want to sit." She stumbled forward. "You know what your other son did?

Eric? Got me pregnant. Married me. Then ran off with that…" She caught herself.

"Left me with Madison. You send presents at Christmas. Little trinkets. Like that makes you family."

The fire crackled. Hans watched her over his glass.

"Where is my granddaughter?"

"My sister's. Like you care."

She turned to Otto. Got close. Too close. His cologne couldn't mask what she saw in his eyes. Had always seen.

"I've watched you watching me. Even when I was married to Eric." The words tumbled out. "I'm not proud. Take me. We'll get married. Keep it all in the family."

"You're drunk."

"So?"

Movement from the hallway. Eric appeared first, bare feet on hardwood. Cheri behind him, silk robe hastily tied. Their hair still mussed from sleep or something else.

"What the hell...."

"There she is." Caitlin's laugh came out broken. "The upgrade."

Cheri's eyes narrowed. "Get her out of here."

"Don't tell them what to do in their own house."

"My house too." Cheri stepped forward. Everything about her was polished. Sculpted. The kind of beautiful that required maintenance. Regular appointments. A surgeon's skill.

Caitlin was beautiful too, but hers was natural. Fading now under stress and alcohol and single motherhood.

"Your house until the next upgrade comes along."

Cheri moved fast. Eric caught her arm.

"Miguel!" He shouted toward the back of the house. "Miguel, get in here!"

The gardener appeared, still pulling on his jacket.

"Drive Ms. Ferrente home. Make sure she gets inside safe."

"I can drive myself."

"No." Eric's voice went hard. "You can't."

Miguel took her arm. Gentle but firm. She let herself be led. At the doorway, she turned back.

"This isn't over."

"Yes," Hans finally spoke. "It is."

The door closed. They heard the car start. Headlights swept across windows as Miguel backed her Nissan around.

Silence settled like dust.

"This is your mess, Eric." Hans hadn't moved. "Clean it up."

"It's not the first time." Otto's smile held no warmth.

They dispersed. Eric and Cheri back to their wing. Her voice carried down the hallway. Sharp. Accusatory.

In their bedroom, she rounded on him.

"If this fire plan Otto cooked up doesn't work...."

"It'll work."

"The Chilean called again. His men were here. Watching."

"I know."

"We need something permanent. Something final."

Eric collapsed on the bed. "I have a plan."

"What plan?"

But he was already fading. The booze he'd had before bed pulling him under.

Cheri watched him breathe. Waited until the rhythm steadied. Deep. Even.

She picked up her phone. Moved to the bathroom. Closed the door.

"It's me." Soft. Careful. "These Kruegers are driving me crazy."

"Patience, Cheri." Vega's voice like smoke. "Soon."

"You promise?"

"I'm looking forward to driving you crazy too. But in a much different way."

She smiled at her reflection. Perfect teeth. Perfect lips. Perfect surface.

Underneath, something else entirely.

The Weinhardt house rose from the earth like it had grown there. Redwood timbers, dark with age. Majestic but not imposing. Stately but lived in.

Through the entry, the staircase curved upward. Hand-carved banister worn smooth by generations of hands. Two hallways branched off, east wing where the boys had grown up, west wing where Esther had played with dolls and the ones that would belonged to her daughters one day.

The great room opened beyond. Stone fireplace tall enough to stand in. Windows that brought the valley inside. Against the far wall, a grandfather clock of Black Forest oak measured out the silence, its face reading two-thirty in the morning, its pendulum swinging with the unhurried certainty of something that had kept time longer than anyone in the house had been alive. Past the offices where Eden managed the business of soil and grape. Past the kitchen where Tawi created his masterpieces.

Into the library.

Floor-to-ceiling books. Agricultural journals mixed with poetry. Business texts beside Scripture. The smell of leather and paper and time.

Karl sat near the dying fire. Ryan across from him. Both men holding silence like wine in a glass.

"I've been thinking about what you said earlier." Ryan finally spoke. "About Ethan."

Karl waited.

"He's like the prodigal. I never left, just my heart." Ryan shifted in his chair. "But I think I understand now. Something I missed before."

"What's that?"

"Your heart. The part that waits. That watches the road." Ryan met his father's eyes.

"All these years, I thought I knew you. Learned the business. The legacy. The proper way to prune, to harvest, to age."

The fire settled. Sparks rose.

"But I kept my distance from the other part. The compassion. Thought it was..." He searched for words. "Thought caring too much was weakness. That Ethan hanging around you all the time, wanting to be close, I thought that was soft."

"Love isn't soft. It's the hardest thing there is."

"I'm starting to see that." Ryan stood, moved to the shelves. Touched book spines like memories. "If I'd gotten closer, really close, I would have learned. Would have understood why you keep his room ready. Why you still walk to the road some evenings."

"You understand now."

"Maybe. Some." Ryan turned back. "You told me I'm still your heir. That all this will be mine."

"You've earned it. Stayed when things were hard."

"But maybe there's still something for Ethan. Not the portion he sold. Something else. He is my brother. That matters more than deeds and accounts."

Karl studied his son. The boy becoming the man he'd hoped for.

"That's wisdom talking."

"That's you talking. Finally heard."

They sat with that truth between them. The fire dying to embers.

"Can't sleep?"

"Too much in my head."

"The porch helps. Always has."

Ryan sat on the great house porch.

Three AM.

The valley spread below. From this height, the ranch revealed itself completely. Three hundred feet down, the barns stood geometric against darkness. The stables where bloodlines traced back to Spain. Cattle dotting the far pastures. The vines, empty of their fruit, soon to be pruned back, waiting for spring's resurrection.

And the cellars. Built into the hillside itself. Where the wine became itself in darkness

Down at the cellars, metal scraped against metal.

Salazar examined the lock. Nodded to his men. Two Salvadorans. Young. Eager to prove themselves. One would stay outside. Watch.

The lock gave way.

Inside, the air hung thick. Fermentation's sweet decay. Tomorrow's fortune sleeping in oak.

"Cuidado." Careful.

They moved with purpose. Accelerant splashed precise as paint strokes. Not too much. Evidence was evidence. Old rags positioned where they'd burn hottest.

One man stumbled. Caught himself against a barrel.

"Idiota! Leave no marks."

They worked five more minutes. Ten. The smell of gasoline overwhelming the wine's perfume. Everything ready.

No timer. No fancy setup. Cesar had pocketed the money for that. Otto too cheap to check. Everyone cutting corners.

Just rags. Gasoline. A road flare from someone's truck.

Out through the broken door.

Now, with all three of them outside. The two Salvadorans beside him. Waiting.

Salazar pulled the flare from his jacket. Struck it against the striker. Red flame sputtered to life.

He smiled. Tossed it through the doorway.

The explosion blew him backward.

Back on the porch, Ryan sat with his thoughts. Bri. His father. Ethan home now, the prodigal returned, sleeping in his old room. The strange mathematics of family, how absence could equal presence, how distance measured more than miles.

Movement caught his eye. Down by the cellars. Shadows where shadows shouldn't be.

Then, a figure at the cellar door. The spark of a flare. Red against black.

The figure threw something…

The burst came instant. Orange erupting from the cellar doors. The concussion visible even from the hillside. Flame climbing into night.

The dinner bell hung beside him, ancient brass, his grandmother's. Never rung at night except….

He grabbed the rope. Pulled hard. The bell's voice shattered the valley's sleep.

Then he ran. The three mysterious figures were heading his way, but they'd have to reach the junction first before turning toward the front gate, he had seconds, maybe less.

Ethan jolted awake. That bell. Memory crashed through, eight years old, his father pulling on clothes, mother already calling the fire department. The vines burning.

Everyone running.

Never ring the bell at night unless.

He yanked on jeans. Bare feet on cold floor. Out the door.

Orange light flickered through his window. The cellars.

Outside, Ryan. Running downhill. And below, by the flames, figures. Moving.

Ethan ran. His body still soft from Silicon Valley's excesses. Lungs already burning. But his brother was struggling with two dark shapes in the firelight.

Down the hill. Feet finding the path by memory. The fire growing with each stride.

Ryan hit the first one without slowing. They went down hard, rolling in dirt. The man was young. Strong. A fist caught Ryan's jaw.

The second Salvadoran circled, looking for an opening. The third figure sprinted away, through the gate and into the darkness.

Ryan drove an elbow back. Felt ribs give. Rolled free. On his feet now, but they were closing in.

"Gringo's fast."

They moved together. Practiced. One high, one low.

Then, impact from the side. Ethan, running full speed. Took the second man down.

The bell still rang in the distance. Help coming. But not yet.

Ethan's man recovered fast. Too fast. Straddled him. Something in his hand, a pry bar from the cellar tools.

Ryan lunged. Caught the man's wrist as the bar descended. They struggled. The first Salvadoran grabbed Ryan from behind.

Ethan bucked. Threw his man off balance. Ryan broke free, spun, connected with a cross that dropped the first man.

The one with the pry bar raised it again. Aimed at Ethan's head.

Ryan's kick caught him in the ribs. He crumpled. Both Salvadorans scrambled up, saw the situation changing. Workers appearing from the bunkhouse. Karl somehow already there.

They ran. Vanished into darkness where Salazar had gone.

"You okay?"

Ethan tasted blood. Nodded. "The fire..."

Already, others were arriving. Miguel from the bunkhouse with buckets. More workers with hoses. Neighbors who'd heard the bell.

Smoke billowed from the cellar. Thick. Chemical. Fed on accelerant and old timber.

They formed a line. Buckets passing hand to hand. Water splashing on ancient wood. Steam rising like ghosts.

Ryan and Ethan worked side by side. No words. Just movement. Just purpose.

The fire fought back. Hungry. Greedy for the old redwood beams. For the barrels. For everything.

"The ceiling's catching!"

More water. More bodies. The community pouring in, neighbors, workers, family. The line extended. Buckets flying. Women from the worker houses. Teenagers. Everyone.

Time stretched. Compressed. Existed only in the space between buckets.

Ryan's hands blistered. Ethan's lungs burned. Still, they worked. Brothers again.

Karl appeared beside them. Directing water where it mattered most. His life's work burning. His face carved from stone.

The fire roared. Fed on years of wine-soaked wood. On accelerant. On hatred.

Then, slowly it began to starve.

Smoke still. Thick. But less orange in it now. More gray. The hungry sound dying.

Finally it was quiet.

They stood there. Soot-covered. Exhausted. Steam rising from the cellar mouth like the earth's last breath.

"The barrels?" Someone asked.

"Morning will tell."

They stood there. The community. The family. Everything uncertain except this, they'd fought together. The bell had rung, and they'd answered.

Ryan looked at Ethan. Ethan looked back. No words needed.

The bell finally stilled. Its voice silent now.

But its call had been heard.

CHAPTER THIRTY

WEINHARDT'S RANCH

SONOMA COUNTY

"Wine is a fire in the veins."
Henry Wadsworth Longfellow

Morning light filtered through the cellar's ventilation grates. Smoke smell still thick. Char and wet stone and burned wood.

Karl stood back, hands in his pockets. Watching. His daughter moved between the barrels with her testing equipment. He could have done this inspection himself. Done it many times. But this was how it worked. Fourth generation teaching the fifth.

"Start with the damaged rows," he said quietly.

Esther nodded. Professional. The way U.C. Davis taught her. The way he'd taught her before that. Saturday mornings in this same cellar. His hands guiding hers on the wine thief. "Pull smooth, dear one. Let the wine tell you its story."

Ryan and Ethan followed behind. Ryan knew these barrels as well as anyone. He and Ethan had helped press the grapes. But this was Esther's moment. Other wineries had already come calling after her graduation. Silverado Creek. Kendall-Jackson. She could write her ticket anywhere in the valley.

She chose home.

"How bad?" Ryan asked.

She ran her hand along a charred barrel. This year's harvest. "The new vintage took the worst of it. These five rows."

"All of them?" Ethan stepped closer.

"The ones closest to where it started." She tapped the wood. Still solid. "But they didn't burst. Fire scorched the outside, probably heated the wine inside, but the barrels held."

Karl watched her work. Methodical. Sure. The way he'd taught her.

"You know what happened after the 1906 quake?" She kept her voice careful. Not wanting to give false hope.

They all knew. But Karl understood why she needed to say it. Work through it out loud. Test the theory against the evidence.

"Some wine cellars burned in some of the big houses. But the barrels that got touched by fire without breaking..." She paused. "Some of those wines became famous. The smoke, the heat. It changed them."

"Changed how?" Ethan asked.

"Nobody knows exactly. But collectors paid a fortune for those bottles." She touched another barrel. Warm still. "The thing is, we won't know what we have until we open these next year."

Karl spoke up. "Your grandfather used to tell stories. Tasted one of those fire wines once. Said it was like nothing else."

Esther pulled out her notebook. Same leather journal he'd given her when she left for Davis. Started sketching the damage pattern. "Could be ruined. Could be something else. These idiots who did this, they had no idea what they were playing with."

"Idiots?" Ryan's jaw tightened.

"Look at the burn pattern. Random. Amateur." She moved to the next row. "Hit our newest barrels. This year's Pinot, we just pressed."

Karl nodded. She was reading it right. Seeing what he saw. No strategy to the destruction. Just thugs with accelerant and a flare.

"So, we wait," Ryan said.

"We wait." She closed the notebook. "Next year when we rack these, we'll know. Could be a total loss. Or..."

"Or?"

"Or these morons might have accidentally given us something special." She looked at her father. "Fire does things to wine. Sometimes terrible things. Sometimes..."

Karl finished for her. "Sometimes magic."

The cellar felt different now. Not just damaged. Changed. Five generations of wine knowledge standing in the smoke-scarred space. Looking at barrels that held either disaster or providence.

"Want me to call the insurance?" Ryan asked.

Karl shook his head. "Not yet. Let's see what we have first." He looked at his daughter. Pride clear in his eyes. "Esther will monitor them. Test them when it's time."

She straightened. Understanding the weight of that trust. The other wineries could wait. This was her cellar. Her responsibility now.

"One way or another," she said quietly, "next year's going to be interesting."

Karl smiled. Same thing his father had said after the frost of '72. Same thing every generation said when weather or fire or chance changed the game.

That was wine. Always had been.

"Dad." Ryan's voice cut through the quiet. "Those guys last night. The ones who started this."

Karl turned from the barrels. Waited.

"Hispanic. Maybe Salvadoran." Ryan glanced at Ethan. "The way they talked. The accent."

Ethan nodded. "Krueger's been hiring crews like this. Same type of guys that Tawi suspect. The bracelets."

"We should go after them." Ryan's hands made fists. "The Kruegers. Make them pay for this."

Karl studied his sons. The anger burning in them like accelerant. Natural. Expected. But dangerous.

"You know what happens to wine in the dark?" He moved to an undamaged barrel. Ran his hand along the wood. "It hides. Good qualities, bad qualities. All hidden."

They waited. Knowing a lesson was coming.

"But light?" He tapped the barrel. "Light shows everything. Every flaw. Every strength. That's why we rack wine. Move it from barrel to barrel. Expose it to air and light."

"Dad...."

"The Kruegers want us in the dark. Want us angry. Reactive." He looked at the charred barrels. "But time and light expose everything. Just like with wine."

"So, we do nothing?" Ryan's jaw worked.

"We document. We watch. We let them think they're winning." Karl smiled. Thin but certain. "Light always finds its way in. And when it does, everyone sees what's really in the barrel."

Ethan understood first. "Evidence. Build a case."

"Better than revenge." Karl headed for the stairs. "Revenge spoils like wine in heat. Justice ages properly."

The brothers exchanged looks. Their father's way. Always the long game. Always patience over passion.

Above them, morning sun slanted through the cellar door. Light doing what light does.

Exposing everything.

The news reached the Krueger compound by breakfast. Otto's phone had been ringing since dawn.

"Salazar called at five this morning." Otto set down his coffee. "The Weinhardt boys jumped them. Right as the fire started. That's why the damage stayed minimal."

Hans looked up from his newspaper. The patriarch studying both his sons. Waiting.

"The housekeeper heard it from her friend on their crew." Otto continued. "Ryan and Ethan fought them off. Salvadoran muscle versus valley boys. Guess who won."

"You're playing like a little leaguer." Eric leaned against the counter. Calm. T-shirt and jeans. "Still thinking matches and gasoline solve problems."

Otto's face darkened. "At least I'm trying something."

"Boys." Hans's voice cut through. Tired. But something else there too. Interest maybe. His eldest finally showing some backbone.

"Fire burns barrels." Eric sipped his coffee. "But putting the Weinhardts on the wrong side of the law? That burns everything."

Cheri watched from the doorway. Interested, now that Eric was finally planning something.

"We all know about Ryan and Caitlin." Eric set down his mug. "She thought he'd marry her. He broke it off instead. Remember when she showed up here? Drunk. Screaming about promises?"

"Pathetic display." Hans nodded.

"Desperate." Eric corrected. "And desperate people do desperate things. Illegal things. The kind that brings in the law."

The kitchen went quiet. Morning light through windows. Too bright.

"What are you thinking?" Otto studied his brother. Something shifting between them.

"I'm thinking Caitlin's ready to crack. Ready to do something that puts Ryan in handcuffs." Eric pushed off from the counter. "His little affair? Big mistake. Huge."

"Eric." Cheri's voice carried warning.

He looked at her. Steady. "This is chess, not checkers. The Weinhardts want to play? Fine. But we play to win."

Hans folded his newspaper. "What do you need?"

"Salazar's contact information."

"The cartel soldier Vega brought me?" Otto frowned. "Why?"

"Because things are going to get messy." Eric's eyes went cold. "And when Caitlin finally tells her story about what Ryan did to her, we need to make sure it's... convincing."

Otto's eyes narrowed. Understanding dawning. "Salazar's still pissed about this morning."

"Good. I need men who are motivated." Eric waited. "Men who know how to handle delicate cargo."

Hans and Otto exchanged looks. The old man nodded slowly. Finally seeing what he'd waited years to see. Eric thinking like a Krueger.

Otto pulled out his phone. Scrolled through contacts. "He won't be gentle."

"Gentle doesn't get results."

While Otto found the number, Eric moved to the window. Looked out at their own vineyards. Beyond them, somewhere past the hills, the Weinhardt property. All those perfect rows. All that careful cultivation.

"Ryan's going to learn," he said quietly. "Some mistakes you can't take back. Some women you shouldn't touch."

Cheri left the room. Her footsteps fading down the hall.

Otto handed over the number. "You'll need a place. Somewhere quiet."

"Already thought of that." Eric pocketed the information. "The old packing shed off Lovall Valley Road. Nobody uses it anymore."

"How long?"

"Long enough for her to understand her role. To practice her lines." Eric headed for the door. "Long enough for bruises to look fresh when she surfaces."

Hans watched his eldest son leave. Finally ready to do what needed doing.

The morning had shifted. No longer about failed arson. About something worse. Something that would bring badges and warrants. Legal eyes on valley business.

And a woman, once convinced of her role, would make it clear that crossing the Kruegers carried a price.

The coffee tasted like regret. Caitlin set the mug down, hand shaking slightly. Morning light through the kitchen window. Too bright. Making her head pound worse.

The apartment showed every bad decision. Secondhand couch with the spring that poked through. Water stain on the ceiling from the upstairs neighbor's leak. Landlord still hadn't fixed it. Three months now. The dining table she'd bought at Goodwill. One leg shorter than the others. Had to wedge cardboard underneath.

"Mom, have you seen my purple hairband?"

Madison's voice from the bathroom. Sweet. Clear. Nothing like the fog in Caitlin's head.

"Check your backpack, baby."

Her sister's words from last night came back in pieces. Maria carrying her up the stairs. "You can't keep doing this, Cait. She needs you whole." The disappointment in her voice. The worry.

Madison appeared in the doorway. Seven years old and perfect. Hair in pigtails with that little curl at the end that never stayed put. No matter how much Caitlin smoothed it down. Her daughter's smile. Gap where the tooth fairy had visited last week. The way it lit up her whole face.

"Found it!"

Caitlin's throat tightened. This beautiful child. The one good thing from all the wreckage. Eric hadn't wanted her. Signed away rights before Madison could even walk. Ryan had pretended to care. Brought her little gifts. Played stepdad until it got too real. Too complicated.

Bastards. All of them.

"You want cereal or toast?"

"Toast please. With the strawberry jam."

Caitlin moved to the kitchen. Each step careful. The hangover sitting heavy in her bones. While bread toasted, she watched Madison at the table. Homework folder open. Practicing her letters. The way she wrote her name. Big careful M. The little dip in the middle of the d. Tongue poking out in concentration.

Everything Caitlin did was for her. Every double shift. Every bad job. Every compromise.

She thought of Tawi suddenly. That day at the market. His kind face. The way he'd looked at her. Not judging. Just seeing. "If you need anything, anything at all, you call me."

Her phone sat on the counter. She picked it up. Scrolled to the number he'd given her. Barbara Sunrise at the tribal clinic. But his number was there too.

Her thumb hovered over it.

What would she even say? That she was drowning. That Ryan had promised things he never meant. That she'd believed him because she needed to believe someone might actually choose her.

"Mom, it's getting burnt."

The number rang once, then she dropped the phone, cutting off the call. She rescued the toast. Spread jam carefully. Cut off the crusts the way Madison liked.

"There you go, sweet girl."

Madison took a big bite. Jam on her chin. Happy. Safe. Loved.

That's what mattered. Not the threadbare carpet. Not the empty wine bottles she'd hidden in the recycling. Not the men who'd walked away. This child. This morning. This moment.

"Time to brush teeth," Caitlin said. "Don't want to be late."

While Madison got ready, Caitlin looked around the apartment one more time. The cracked outlet cover. The cabinet door that wouldn't close right. The photos on the wall. All of Madison. Baby pictures. First day of kindergarten. Last Christmas.

Her whole world in a two-bedroom apartment that smelled like old carpet and new hope.

"Ready, Mom!"

Madison stood by the door. Backpack on. Shoes tied. That smile again.

Caitlin pulled her close. Breathed in her strawberry shampoo smell. Her daughter hugged back. Fierce. Like she knew her mom needed it.

"Love you, baby."

"Love you too."

They walked to the car together. Caitlin's old Nissan. More rust than paint now. But it started. Most days.

As she buckled Madison in, Caitlin felt something shift. All the bitterness. All the anger. It didn't matter. Eric could have his new wife. Ryan could have his family vineyard. The Kruegers could have their money and their schemes.

She had Madison.

The only treasure worth keeping. The only love that hadn't lied.

"Can we listen to the happy songs?" Madison asked.

"Of course, baby."

Caitlin turned the key. Engine coughed but caught. They pulled out into morning traffic. Madison singing along to the radio. Off-key and perfect.

Everything else had fallen apart. But this. This remained.

Her daughter. Her reason. Her only truth in a world full of broken promises.

Her phone rang. The display lit up. Eric.

Her stomach turned. What now? What could he possibly want after her night of rage?

She let it go to voicemail. Kept her eyes on the road. Madison still singing. Still perfect. Still safe.

For now.

CHAPTER THIRTY-ONE

WEINHARDT'S RANCH

SONOMA COUNTY

"Wine and debt make sorrow twin brothers."
French Proverb

October light slanted through the tall windows. First real cool day since spring. Karl added another log to the fire. The pop and hiss of resin. Smoke curling up the chimney. The library smelled like leather and old paper. Redwood beams overhead, dark with age. Shelves reaching to the ceiling. Books collected over lifetimes.

Eden carried in the tea service. Proper British china. The set her mother brought from Surrey in '65. Steam rising from the pot. Earl Grey. Some traditions you didn't let go.

"Everyone here?" Karl looked around at his children. Ryan in the leather chair by the window. Ethan on the couch. Esther cross-legged on the carpet like when she was little.

"Present and accounted for." Esther grinned.

Eden poured. The ritual of it. Sugar for Ryan. Milk for Ethan. Esther took hers black. Strong. Like everything about their daughter.

"We wanted to talk about the future." Karl settled into his chair. The one his father used. His grandfather before that. "About what comes next. For all of us."

The fire crackled. Outside, wind moved through the bare vines. Harvest done. The work of waiting begun.

"Your mother and I..." Karl reached for Eden's hand. Forty-five years and still reaching. "We've watched you all these past months. Seen you change. Grow."

Ryan shifted. They all knew what he meant. The affair. The almost-loss of Brianna. The slow work of rebuilding.

"Ryan, you're letting go of the bitterness. That's not easy. Ethan, you've come home. Really home. Not just physically."

"And Esther hasn't messed up yet." Eden's eyes crinkled.

They all laughed. Esther loudest. "Give me time. Though there is this guy from Davis..."

"Is he worthy?" Karl's voice went stern. Playing at it.

"We'll see."

The moment settled. Comfortable. Family finding its shape again after the storms.

"I want to tell you something." Karl stood. Moved to the window. "Something that happened in this room. 1934."

They waited. Even Eden, who'd heard it before.

"Your grandfather. Bill. Told me what happened to my great grandfather, Heinrich August Weinhardt." Karl touched the window frame. Same wood Bill's hands had touched. "Bill was old by then. Arthritis had twisted his fingers. Years of vine work. Started when he was twelve."

Karl could see him still. Grandfather Bill in that same chair. Hands that couldn't hold a wine glass steady anymore. But eyes still sharp.

"He told me about 1930. Heinrich August, his dad was twenty then. Young. Stupid. Full of himself." Karl turned back to his children. "He'd been gambling. Cards mostly. Sometimes horses. Owed money to the wrong people."

The fire popped. Sparks rising.

"These men came to the ranch. Threatened him. Threatened the family. My great-grandfather, Johann Friedrich, met them at the door. Him and two ranch hands. He had carved this ranch out of bare ground. He wasn't about to backdown to anyone."

Karl smiled slightly. "Donnybrook, they called it then. Fists and blood. German stubbornness against city muscle."

"Who won?" Ethan asked.

"Everyone lost something." Karl moved back to his chair. "But Johann Friedrich made his point. Then he made Heinrich promise. No more gambling. Ever."

Eden poured more tea. The sound of it. Civilized. Careful.

"Then he asked the men how much. The debt. They told him. He went to his room. Came back with a leather pouch. Gold coins. From Germany. His whole savings."

The library went quiet. Just the fire talking.

"Paid it all. Every cent. Then never mentioned it again. Not once in all the years after."

Karl looked at each of his children. "Bill said that moment changed everything. Not the payment. The trust. His father believing he could be better. Would be better."

"That's why Grandpa Heinrich filled this library." Eden's voice soft. "All these books. Learning. Making up for those wild years."

"It lived in him." Karl touched his chest. "Lives in me. In all of us. That's what family does. Pays debts we can't pay. Believes when we can't believe."

Ryan's jaw worked. Thinking of Brianna. Her forgiveness. The door still open.

"The fire in the cellar." Karl continued. "All we've been through. It's like that moment in 1930. Crisis that shapes us. Makes us better."

"Or breaks us." Ethan said quietly.

"No." Eden's voice firm. "Not this family. We bend. We burn sometimes. But we don't break."

Esther uncurled from the floor. Went to her brothers. Hand on each shoulder. "Mom taught me something when I was little. About having two brothers."

They looked up at her.

"She said they'd try to push me out. Natural order. Boys and their clubs." She squeezed. "But you never did. Not once. Made room. Made me part of everything."

"You earned it." Ryan's voice rough.

"By being smarter than both of us combined." Ethan added.

More laughter. The good kind. Family finding its rhythm.

"Next year when we open those fire-touched barrels." Karl stood again. "We'll see what we have. Maybe ruined. Maybe something extraordinary. Like Heinrich after 1930. Like all of us after this year."

The October light was fading. First stars appearing. The library held them all. Four generations of stories in these walls and a fifth one building now. Pain and redemption. Loss and finding.

Eden looked around at her family. Her boys becoming men worth knowing. Her daughter strong and sure. Her husband still dreaming after all these years.

"More tea?" she asked.

They all said yes. Even Esther, who never had seconds.

Because this moment. This room. This family knitting itself back together. You didn't rush that. You sat with it. Let it steep like good tea. Like wine in oak. Like forgiveness in the heart.

The fire burned lower. Shadows dancing on the redwood beams. Outside, the first fog of evening crept up from the valley. But inside was warm. Was whole.

Was home.

"Speaking of family..." Ethan cleared his throat. "Could we have Lauren to dinner tonight? It's kind of important."

Karl and Eden exchanged glances. That parent look. Knowing.

"Of course," Eden said. "I'll set another place."

"Always like having that gal here." Karl's eyes held something. Approval maybe. "She's good people."

"Ethan." Esther sat up straighter. "What's this about?"

"Yeah." Ryan leaned forward. "What's so important it can't wait?"

Ethan's face went red. Looked at his parents. "It's about what I asked you for. From Grandma's collection."

"Oh." Ryan's eyebrows shot up. "OH."

"Wait." Esther looked between them all. "Grandma's... you didn't. You did!"

Ethan stood. Headed for the door. "I need to change before she gets here."

"Ethan James Weinhardt." Esther's voice followed him. "You cannot just drop that and leave!"

"Watch me." But he was grinning as he escaped.

Laughter filled the library. Real laughter. The kind that came when life surprised you with joy in the middle of ordinary moments.

Karl reached for Eden's hand again. Squeezed.

Another story for these walls. Another chapter in the long book of their family.

The good chapters. The ones you read again and again.

The apartment still smelled like the mac and cheese she'd made Madison for after-school snack. Caitlin kicked off her work shoes. Feet aching from the lunch rush. Double shift tomorrow.

Madison was in her room. Homework probably. Or drawing. Always drawing these days.

Her phone rang. Eric again.

She almost let it go. Then picked up. "What do you want?"

"Caitlin." His voice different. Softer. "I've been thinking about that night. When you came to the house."

Her face burned. The memory fuzzy but the shame sharp.

"Eric, I don't want to..."

"No, listen. Please." He sounded... concerned? "It hit me after. You're Madison's mother. I haven't been... I know I haven't been there."

"You signed away your rights."

"I know. And Dad, Hans, he's been more of a grandfather than I've been a father. You're right about that."

She sat down. Where was this going?

"Look, Caitlin. I know you think I'm shallow. And maybe Cheri isn't your favorite person." He paused. "But she's helped me grow a spine. Made me see things differently."

"Like what?"

"Like how Otto tried to use your relationship with Ryan. To manipulate things. I don't like that. You got caught in the middle of Otto's schemes."

The late afternoon sun slanted through her kitchen window. Dust motes floating. Everything tired and gold.

"Why are you telling me this?"

"Because I think I have a solution. Something that could help you settle things. All those years you gave Ryan. His empty promises."

Her chest tightened. "What kind of solution?"

"Meet me tonight. Murphy's Bar. Neutral ground. 12:30 tonight. This has to be confidential." His voice stayed calm. Reasonable. "It's time the Weinhardts and Kruegers found level ground. And you might be the catalyst."

"I don't know..."

"Caitlin, you can't keep living like this. Paycheck to paycheck. Madison deserves better." He played his trump card. "Hans is part of this. He wants something good for his granddaughter. For both of you."

Hans. The old man had always been kind. Sent birthday cards. Christmas money.

"Just drinks? Just talk?"

"Just talk. About the future. About making things right."

She looked toward Madison's room. Her daughter humming some song from school. Happy. Safe. But for how long? How long before the bills crushed them? Before she had to choose between rent and medicine?

"Fine. 12:30."

"Good. You won't regret this."

She hung up. Dialed Maria immediately.

"Hey, sis. Can you watch Madison tonight?"

"Of course. Everything okay?"

"It's... there might be an opportunity. For Madison's future. I can't really explain yet."

"I'll be there in twenty."

Caitlin went to check on Madison. Found her at her little desk. Drawing flowers. Purple and yellow. Careful crayon strokes.

"You're going over to Aunt Maria's tonight."

"Yay! Maybe she'll make cookies?"

"I'm sure she will."

The old growth Pinot stood bare against the late October sky. Twisted vines. Gnarled wood. Decades of seasons written in every trunk.

Lauren walked beside Ethan through the rows. Work clothes still on from the vet clinic. The smell of an animal still on her.

"Dad's thrilled you're here," Ethan said. "Set an extra place before I even asked."

"Your father's always been kind to me."

The sun hung low. Golden hour painting everything warm. The time when vineyards showed their bones. Their truth.

"Remember the day Maverick died?" Ethan stopped walking.

She nodded. Of course she remembered. The stallion thrashing. Dr. Wu's calm hands. The moment when wildness left those dark eyes.

"You were there. Steady. While I was falling apart." He turned to face her. "Something happened that day. Like the rebellious part of me died with him. And you saw it. Saw me."

"Ethan..."

"No, let me say this." He took her hand for the first time. Callused fingers against hers. "That ride to the barn that time. You didn't try to fix anything. Just sat with me in it. Then the restaurant idea, your great input..."

Wind moved through the bare vines. Whispered promises of spring.

"The way you handled Marcus and Kat at Vine and Valley. Made that stand." His voice roughened. "I knew then. This is what I want. Someone real. Someone who sees what matters the way I do now."

Lauren's breath caught. The light making everything golden. His face. The vines. This moment.

"I've been thinking about it for weeks. How you make everything clearer. Better. How you understand what matters."

He reached into his pocket. Her heart stopped.

"I talked to Mom and Dad yesterday." He was sinking to one knee. Right there in the dirt between the vines. "Asked for Grandma's ring."

The box opened. Simple setting. Old gold. Diamond catching the last sun.

"I know I don't have an inheritance anymore. Know the future's uncertain. But I've got the right heart now. The right dreams." His voice broke slightly. "And with you, I don't want them to be dreams. I want them to be real."

The whole world held its breath. The vines. The valley. Everything waiting.

"Lauren, will you marry me?"

She looked down at him. This man who'd found himself in losing everything. Who'd chosen land over comfort. Work over ease. Her over anyone else.

The ring caught the light. Threw tiny rainbows.

Somewhere a hawk called. The wind picked up. Moved through the vineyard like a blessing. Like an answer waiting to be spoken.

The sun sank lower. Painting shadows between the rows. Time suspended in amber light.

Everything possible in that pause. Everything hoped for. Everything real.

The vines stood witness. Patient. Knowing what they'd always known.

That the best things grew slowly. In the right soil. With the right care.

Under the right light.

CHAPTER THIRTY-TWO

SANTA ROSA

SONOMA COUNTY

"False friends drink your wine and speak you fair."
English Proverb

Murphy's smelled like spilled beer and old wood. Almost closing time. Guinness signs glowed in the windows. The crack of pool balls from the back room. Light laughter rising and falling like waves. Only a few clients there, most of them wouldn't know either Eric or Caitlin. Eric planned it that way.

They sat in the corner booth. Furthest from the noise. Her second whiskey sat half empty. She'd promised herself one. But Eric kept talking, kept painting pictures of a better life.

"Like I said." He leaned forward. Still nursing his first beer. "Hans wants to pay for everything. Tutor. After-school programs. That private school in Napa."

"St. Helena Prep?" Her voice caught. "That's fifteen thousand a year."

"Drop in the bucket for Hans. He wants his granddaughter to have chances."

The whiskey burned warm. Made everything softer. More possible.

"And Ryan?" she asked.

"I'll confront him myself. Tell him what an ass he was for dropping you. Let the whole county know how he played house for three years then walked away."

"His wife won't..."

"Brianna? No. But he was Madison's surrogate dad. He owes her something. The family owes her something."

A group near the bar erupted in song. Irish voices. American beer. The mix that made Murphy's what it was.

"This weekend." Eric signaled the waitress. Another round. She shouldn't but... "Come to the house. All of you. Madison can swim. Pool's heated. Chef's planning something special."

"Eric, I don't know..."

"Spa day for you. Masseuse coming for the whole family. Hans insisted."

It sounded like a dream. Like everything she'd wanted those nights lying awake. Worrying about Madison's teeth. Her school. Her future.

"Why now?" The question slipped out.

"Because I grew up. Finally." He looked sincere. Those eyes that had charmed her once. "Because Madison deserves better than our failures."

The third whiskey appeared. She shouldn't. But hope tasted like amber fire. Made her forget the water stain on her ceiling. The car that might not start tomorrow.

"Let me walk you to your car." Eric threw cash on the table. Too much. Like always.

Outside, the October air bit sharp. Cleared her head some. Not enough.

The parking lot was mostly empty. Her Nissan sat under the broken streetlight. Of course.

"So, this weekend?" Eric touched her elbow. Gentle. "Madison will love the pool."

"I'll think about..."

Movement in the shadows. Fast. Too fast.

Hands grabbed her from behind. Rough. Foreign voices. Spanish but different. Salvadoran accent.

The scream caught in her throat. Hand over her mouth. Chemical smell. Her keys hitting asphalt.

"No!" Muffled. Desperate.

Eric stepped back. Calm. Like he'd expected this.

The betrayal hit harder than the hands dragging her.

Van doors opening. Dark inside. She fought. Kicked. Useless.

"Lovall Valley Road." Salazar's voice to Eric. Matter of fact. "The old packing shed."

They threw her in. Face hitting metal floor. Tape across her mouth before she could scream again.

The last thing she saw was Eric. Standing there. Adjusting his jacket like nothing had happened.

Then doors slamming. Engine starting. The smell of fear and motor oil.

Moving. Fast. Away from lights. Away from help. Away from Madison.

Tears came hot. The tape cutting into her skin.

All lies. All of it lies.

And she'd believed. Again.

God help her, she'd believed.

The kitchen held a hundred years of meals. Cast iron pans hung from hooks forged by the first Weinhardt. Tawi dried the last plate. Set it in the cupboard where Eden's grandmother's china lived.

Through the doorway, voices. Esther and Eden. One more cup of tea before bed. The ritual between mother and daughter. He smiled. Good sounds in this house tonight. Laughter from the library earlier. Karl's voice telling the old story. Debts that couldn't be paid. Love that paid them anyway.

The kitchen spotless now. Counters wiped. Floor swept. Everything in its place.

Something nagged at him. Like a pebble in a shoe.

The phone call.

One ring from Caitlin's number. Then nothing.

He dried his hands on the old towel. Stepped out to the porch. His chair waited. Same chair twenty years. The boards creaked familiar under his weight.

Dog came from nowhere. Always did. Grey muzzle now. But still faithful. Settled by his feet with a sigh.

Stars sharp tonight. No fog yet. The vineyard sleeping all around. Vines bare. Waiting for spring.

"Something's wrong, old friend."

Dog's tail thumped once. Understanding.

Tawi closed his eyes. Let the night sounds come. Owl in the oak. Coyotes distant on the ridge.

The land breathing slow and deep.

Then the words came. Old words.

Pomo words his grandmother taught him.

"Aw shee-oo kah-yah."

Watch the one who is lost.

"Heh-oo shah-well kohm ehl."

Bring her home safe and well.

"Kah-oo eh-way-lah koh-tay."

Guard the child who waits.

The prayer moved through him. Through the night.

Carried on wind that knew these hills before vines.

Before fences.

Before any of this.

He thought of Caitlin at the market. That desperation behind brave words. The way she'd looked when he mentioned Ryan, like someone drowning who'd given up on shore.

"Cha dun al miye." ·

Let the darkness pass.

"Bate kun xa che."

Dawn always comes.

Dog pressed against his leg.

Warm. Solid.

Inside, the house settling into sleep. Family healing. Finding its way back. The fire that hadn't destroyed them. The betrayals forgiven. The son coming home. All of it weaving together like basket reeds. Stronger for the bending.

But somewhere out there. Caitlin. That single ring like a cry cut short.

"Xa le ma sha." I am listening.

"Ko ma tal." Show me the path.

The prayer finished but he stayed. Watching. Waiting. The way his people always had. Patient as stone. Ready as water.

Dog whined soft. Nose pointing toward the valley.

"I know." Tawi's hand found the grey head. "I feel it too."

Tomorrow he'd check. Call the number back. Drive by her apartment maybe. But tonight all he had was prayer. Old words for new troubles.

The fog started its crawl from the coast. First wisps like ghosts walking.

He stood. Bones creaking like the porch boards. "Come on, old friend."

They went inside.

The packing shed breathed with wind through broken slats. October cold seeping through gaps where walls met floor. Abandoned twenty years. Maybe more. Smelled like rat droppings and rotted wood.

Caitlin's head throbbed. Blood from her lip. Metallic taste. The chair creaked when she tried to move. Rope cutting wrists.

"Finally awake." Eric's voice from the shadows.

She tried to speak through the gag. Only muffled sounds.

He stepped into the dim light from the single bulb. Clean still. Like violence didn't touch him. Never had.

"Salazar's boys got carried away." He studied her face. "Nothing permanent though. You'll heal."

The shed groaned. Old timbers remembering weight they no longer carried.

"Here's what happens now." He pulled up a crate. Sat facing her. "I know how much you love Madison. Beautiful girl. Smart like her mother."

Ice in her veins. Not Madison. Please.

"Some of what I promised? The school, the help? That could still happen." He leaned forward. "But you have to earn it."

She watched his face. Looking for the man she'd once married. Gone. If he'd ever existed.

"You hate Ryan. After what he did. Using you. Dropping you." His voice stayed conversational. "Well, we're going to make him pay. Together."

He reached over. Pulled the gag down.

"Eric, please..."

"Listen." Sharp now. "When the police find you, here's your story. Ryan called. Wanted to meet. One more time. Hinted at starting things up again."

"No one will believe..."

"They will. Because you came here. Because of this." He gestured at her face. "Ryan did this. Beat you when you wouldn't give him the photos."

"What photos?"

"The ones of you two together. Intimate ones. Videos too. He's scared his wife will find out. Wanted them destroyed. Got violent when you refused."

The wind picked up. Somewhere metal scraped against metal. Ghost sounds.

"Here's the important part." Eric leaned closer. "When the sheriff asks how you ended up here alone, you tell them Ryan got an emergency call. From his father. Some crises at the vineyard. He had to leave suddenly. Said he'd come back. Wanted to give you time to think about handing over the photos."

"That's insane..."

"Is it? Man panics after beating his mistress. Gets a call. Family emergency. Leaves her tied up while he deals with it." Eric shrugged. "Happens all the time."

Caitlin's mind raced. Looking for holes. Ways out.

"And here's the clever part." Eric smiled. "You tell them you left your phone connected to Maria when you met Ryan here. Wanted someone to know where you were. Smart woman meeting an ex-lover. She heard the whole conversation. That's how she knew where to send help."

"She won't..."

"Salazar's with her right now. Making sure she understands her part. She'll wait a bit. Then call the sheriff. Worried sister. Haven't heard from you. Knows you went to meet Ryan at the old packing shed because she heard it on the phone."

"That will never work, Eric. Bringing my sister into this. I won't do this. I can't."

"Yes, you will. It will work."

"This is insane."

"You will," Eric stepped close. Raised his hand. The slap cracked loud. His knuckles split on her cheekbone. Blood now. His and hers.

"Shit." He shook his hand. Red drops on the floor.

He grabbed her jaw. Forced her to look at him. "Do we understand each other?"

One choice. Only ever one choice.

"Yes."

"Say it. All of it."

"Ryan called me. Asked me here. Beat me. Wanted photos destroyed. Got an emergency call from his dad. Left me here to think about it. I left my phone connected to Maria so she could hear. That's how she knew where I was." The words tasted like ash.

"Good girl." He pulled the gag back up. "Remember. Madison's future depends on you sticking to this story. But if you don't..."

He didn't need to finish. She knew. These men. What they could do. Where they could take a little girl.

Eric was offering her a choice. Simple. Clean. Brutal. Do what he asked, play the part, and Madison stays safe. Refuse, and her daughter disappears into a world no child ever comes back from. Sold. Traded. Gone. Just another face on a missing poster that nobody looks at anymore.

There was no choice. There never had been.

"Think about that while you wait." He headed for the door. Stopped. "You know the saddest part? You actually believed me at Murphy's. Still so desperate for someone to save you."

Then gone. Car doors. Engines fading.

Alone with the wind. The cold. The knowing that Madison's safety now hung on a lie.

Time passed. Hard to tell how much. Everything hurt.

The call came into Sonoma County Sheriff's dispatch at 2:47 PM.

Maria's voice shaking. "My sister. She went to meet someone at the old packing shed. Lovall Valley Road. I heard it on the phone. She left it connected. That was hours ago. Please."

"We'll send someone right away, ma'am."

Deputy Martinez found her twenty minutes later. Tied to a chair. Face swollen. Blood on the floor.

And a story that would burn through the valley like wildfire.

Just like Eric planned.

CHAPTER THIRTY-THREE

SANTA ROSA

SONOMA COUNTY SHERIFF'S OFFICE

"Wine makes men reveal what discretion hides."
Ovid, Ars Amatoria

S herrif Homas Hendricks pressed the button, the recorder's red light blinking to life.

"Interview Room 3. Sheriff Thomas Hendricks, badge 1425. Present: Ryan Weinhardt and Deputy Maria Gonzalez, badge 3892."

The metal chair was cold. Ryan had been waiting forty minutes. Tom's call had been vague. Something about needing help with an investigation. Maybe the Lovall Valley fire from last month.

"Ryan, you understand this conversation is being recorded?"

"Sure, Tom."

"For the record, please state your full name and date of birth."

"Ryan Michael Weinhardt. March 12th, 1989."

Tom opened a manila folder. His poker face was on. Not good. "Ryan, you have the right to have an attorney present. Do you wish to waive that right?"

"What's going on here?"

"Please answer the question."

"Yeah, I'll waive it. We're old friends, Tom."

Deputy Gonzalez wrote something down.

"Ryan, do you know Caitlin Marie Brooks?"

The air in the room changed. "Yes."

"Nature of your relationship?"

Ryan looked at the camera in the corner. The mirror that wasn't just a mirror. "We were involved. It ended days ago."

"Tell me about that."

"I went to her apartment. Ended things."

"Her reaction?"

"Upset. Angry. What you'd expect."

Tom pulled out a photograph. Pushed it across the scarred table. "Recognize this?"

Caitlin. Her face swollen. Bruises on her arms. Wrists marked red.

"Crazy. What happened to her?"

"That's what we're trying to determine." Tom's voice was flat. Professional. "Where were you this morning at 1:30 AM?"

"At my place. On the ranch. Asleep."

"Anyone verify that?"

Ryan's jaw tightened. "I live alone. Bri and I are separated."

"When did you go to bed?"

"Around 11:30. We had a family gathering. Everyone was there. My father, Esther, Ethan, Karl. Even Tawi, our cook."

"And after 11:30?"

"Went down to my house. Went to bed."

"So, no one can verify your whereabouts after 11:30?"

"No."

Deputy Gonzalez leaned forward. "Mr. Weinhardt, we received a call at 2:45 AM from Ms. Ferrante's sister, Maria. Caitlin had managed to leave her phone on. It was around 1 AM. She heard her sister being beaten, realized it was an emergency. She's head something earlier about meeting at the old packing house. When Caitlin didn't answer later calls, Maria got worried. Called us."

"The packing shed on Lovall Valley Road?" Ryan's throat was tight. "That's on our property."

"That's where we found her at 3 AM." Tom tapped the photo. "Beaten. Tied up. Left there."

"That's not... I didn't do this."

"She says you did."

"She's lying."

"Why would she lie?"

Ryan's mind raced. The Krueger deal. The merger he'd just turned down. Otto's threats. "I don't know."

"Mr. Weinhardt," Deputy Gonzalez said. "Ms. Ferrante says you wanted something from her. Pictures. Videos of the two of you together."

Silence filled the room like smoke.

"Did such materials exist?" Tom asked.

"I need to call my attorney."

Tom studied him. Twenty years they'd known each other.

"You sure of that?"

"I'm sure."

"Alright. Deputy Gonzalez, please note Mr. Weinhardt has invoked his right to counsel." He clicked off the recorder. Stood. "You're free to go, Ryan. On your own recognizance. But don't leave town. And get that lawyer. You're going to need one."

The family had gathered in the great room. The same room where last night Karl had told them about his great-grandfather's gambling debt. About old sins and new beginnings. Now they sat in a rough circle. Eden in his wheelchair by the fireplace. Esther beside him. Karl on the leather couch. Ethan pacing. Tawi standing near the kitchen door.

"Tell us again," Eden said. His voice steady despite everything.

Ryan stood by the window. The fog was rolling in early. "Caitlin's accusing me of kidnapping her. Beating her. The sheriff says they found her at the old packing shed on Lovall Valley at 3 AM this morning."

"Beating her. What time did this supposedly happen?" Ethan asked.

"Around 1:30 A.M. Her sister was listening on Caitlin's phone. Heard her being beaten."

"You were here," Esther said. "We all saw you. The family dinner went until after eleven."

"That's what I told them. But after that..." Ryan paused. "I went down to my house. Alone."

Karl's eyes narrowed. "No alibi."

"No."

"This is the Kruegers," Ethan said. "Has to be. You turned down their merger. Now this."

"A woman's been hurt," Eden said quietly. "Badly hurt, from what you're saying."

"I didn't do it."

"I know that." His father's eyes were clear. Trusting. "We all know that. But someone did."

"Our lawyer will handle it," Karl said. "Sam Morrison. Best defense attorney in the county."

"We'll stand with you," Esther said. "All of us."

Karl nodded. "Family stands together."

Tawi slipped out the kitchen door. Silent as fog.

Caitlin's apartment was dark except for the television. She sat on the couch, holding a bag of frozen peas to her face. Every movement hurt.

The knock was soft. Almost didn't hear it.

She looked through the peephole. Tawi stood in the hallway, his weathered face calm. He held a worn leather pouch.

"How did you..."

"Ryan told me. May I come in?"

She opened the door wider. He entered, taking in the small space. The broken life.

"You're hurt bad," he said simply.

"I'm fine."

"No. You're not." He set the pouch on the coffee table and sat across from her. Patient. Waiting.

The frozen peas were melting. Water dripped on her shirt.

"Where's Madison?"

"At my sister's."

"How's she taking it?"

Caitlin's voice caught. "She hasn't seen me yet. Like this. My sister's with her."

Tawi nodded. He opened the pouch and pulled out small bundles wrapped in cloth. Dried leaves. A paste in a tiny jar. The smell was earthy, sharp. Ancient.

"This will help with the swelling. Old recipe. My grandmother's grandmother." He gestured toward her face. "May I?"

She hesitated, then lowered the frozen peas.

His touch was gentle. The paste was cool, then warm. It tingled against her bruised skin. He worked in silence, his hands steady, careful around the worst of the bruising. He applied more paste to her split lip. Dabbed something cool beneath her swollen eye.

"Rest your head back."

She did. He placed a damp cloth across her forehead. It smelled of lavender and something else. Something older.

"Let it sit. Let it do its work."

For a long moment, neither of them spoke. Just the low murmur of the television.

"Caitlin." His voice was soft. "I've known you since you were a child. Watched you grow up in this valley. You know me. You know I wouldn't lie to you."

She opened her eyes. Met his.

"I've known Ryan since he was a child too. Watched him grow up. Chase lizards in the vineyard. Help Karl with the vines." He paused. "He has his father's temper. His father's pride. But not this. Never this."

Caitlin said nothing.

"You knew him too. Before all this. The real Ryan."

A tear slipped down her swollen cheek, mixing with the paste.

"Was he ever violent with you? Ever raise a hand?"

She shook her head slowly.

"Even when angry? Even when you fought?"

"No." Her voice was barely there. "Never."

"Then this..." Tawi gestured gently at her face. "This doesn't sound like the Ryan we both know."

"I can't..."

"You're scared. I can see that. Someone's threatened you."

Caitlin's hands trembled. She looked at Madison's door.

"They know where we live," she whispered.

"Who?"

"I can't say."

"The Kruegers?"

Her silence was answer enough.

"Eric?" Tawi's voice stayed gentle. Steady. "Did Eric Krueger do this to you?"

The dam broke. "He said they'd take Madison. Said they knew people. Salvadorans who... who traffic..." She couldn't finish.

"And if you blamed Ryan?"

"They'd help us. Money. Protection. Get us away from here."

"But if you didn't?"

She touched her face. Fresh tears on old bruises.

"I know what men like that can do," Tawi said. "My people have survived them for generations."

"There's no way out."

"There's always a way. My people, the tribal council. We have services. Safe places for mothers and children who've been hurt. Threatened."

"They'll find us."

"Not on the reservation. Not under tribal protection." He leaned forward. "But first, we need to go see Tom Hendricks."

"The sheriff? I can't. Eric said..."

"Tom's an old friend. A good man. He'll listen. He'll protect you."

"You don't understand. The Kruegers control a lot of politicians."

"They own some of them. Not all. Not the parts that matter." Tawi stood. "Pack light. Only what you need."

"Now?"

"Now. Before they know I was here."

"And then?"

"Then you tell the truth. All of it. Let Tom do his job. And we keep you and Madison safe."

She stood slowly. Everything hurt. "Why are you doing this?"

Tawi moved to the door. "Because some sins need to stop. Some circles need to be broken. And Ryan's a good man who doesn't deserve this. Neither do you."

Caitlin to pack her and Madison's life into two small bags. To trust this stranger who offered hope in the darkness.

Outside, the fog had swallowed the world whole.

CHAPTER THIRTY-FOUR

KRUEGER ESTATE

SONOMA COUNTY

"Wine discovers judgment."
Herodotus, Histories

A week had passed since Eric took Caitlin. Seven days of confidence. The plan was working. Ryan and his family, the mighty Weinhardts, were about to go down. Eric hadn't been worried about his interview with the Sheriff. Why would he be? Routine, the officer had said. Caitlin would never risk her daughter's future. She'd take their offer. Madison's future secured by Krueger promises. A small price for her silence.

Three Sheriff's SUVs crunched up the gravel drive. No sirens. No lights. Just the weight of what was coming.

Hans Krueger met them at the door. Old money posture. Forced smile. "Tom. This is unexpected."

Sheriff Hendricks didn't smile back. "Hans. We need to speak with Eric. And the family."

"Of course. Come in."

The great room smelled of leather and old wine. Otto stood by the fireplace. Eric lounged on the couch like he owned the world. Cheri sat perfectly still in a wingback chair. Watching.

"Eric Krueger," Tom said. "You're under arrest for the kidnapping and assault of Caitlin Brooks."

Eric laughed. Actually laughed. "That's ridiculous."

"Stand up, son. Don't make this harder."

"You have nothing."

Tom pulled out a warrant. "We have your DNA. Got it from the cup you drank from. Matches what we found in Ms. Brooks's wounds. Where you hit her."

The room went cold.

Cheri turned to Hans. Her voice low. Venomous. "The men in this family are really stupid. He should never have gone in for that interview without our lawyer, no matter how confident he was in Vega's claim that he had everyone paid off. What was he thinking, you never allow your DNA to be taken like that."

"Shut up," Hans said. But his hands were shaking.

Eric stood slowly. Still playing tough. "This is a setup. The Weinhardts..."

"Save it for your lawyer." Tom nodded to his deputies. "Cuff him."

Otto backed against the fireplace. "I don't know anything about this. Whatever Eric did..."

"We'll be talking to you too, Otto. Don't leave town."

They led Eric out. He kept his chin up. Swagger intact. But his eyes were scared.

Hans sank into a chair. The patriarch suddenly looked ancient.

Cheri watched it all. Face like stone.

Cheri stood on the terrace; phone pressed to her ear. Two hours since they'd taken Eric away in handcuffs. The view stretched across the valley. All those vines. All that money. All that power shifting like sand.

"Lucien's been on the phone with me," Vega's voice was smooth. Confident. "It's time for the Kruegers to fade away. They've not been the best of pawns."

"The chess board is changing."

"Exactly. Lucien wants us to move in. Hans is fleeing to the east coast tonight."

"Running scared."

"He's given ownership to Lucien. Traded it for a way out. The cartel has judges in their pocket back east. They won't be able to extradite him easily."

Cheri smiled. A real smile. "So, we're the stewards of the Krueger estate."

"If we handle this right, Lucien promises us part ownership. Just what we've been hoping for."

"And with Eric in prison..."

"Grounds for divorce. Finally."

She could hear him breathing. Picture him in his office. That expensive suit. Those hands.

"No more Airbnb," she said softly.

"No more sneaking around."

"When?"

"Tonight. Hans will be gone by midnight. The house will be empty. Yours."

"Ours."

"Yes. Ours."

The line hummed with everything they weren't saying. Everything they'd been planning in those rented rooms. Those stolen afternoons.

"I'll wait for you," she said.

"Two hours. I have papers to file first. Make it look legitimate."

"I know how to wait."

She hung up. Stood there watching the sun sink behind the hills. Inside, she could hear Hans on the phone. Frantic. Booking flights. Calling lawyers.

The mighty Krueger empire. Falling apart in one afternoon.

She went inside. Poured herself wine from a bottle worth more than most people's cars. Sat in Hans's chair.

The house already felt different. Like it knew.

By morning, everything would be changed. New locks. New names on the accounts. New power flowing through old channels.

Cheri raised her glass to the empty room.

"To stupid men," she said. And drank deep.

CHAPTER THIRTY-FIVE

WEINHARDT'S RANCH

SONOMA COUNTY

"Good wine finishes the feast."
Italian Proverb

The drone lifted from the eastern meadow and swept west, deftly controlled by one of the photographers there to document the wedding. One year to the day since the fire in the cellar. Below, the Weinhardt ranch spread across the valley like a living map. Row after row of vines, their leaves turning gold and crimson three weeks after harvest. The cattle grazing in the far pastures. The hills rising to the west with the Pacific Ocean a silver line beyond.

An unusual fall afternoon. No fog this morning. Just clear October light painting everything golden.

The drone banked over the great house. A century of California weather in its bones. Practical. Majestic. Built to last.

On the lawn in front of the welcome center, a white tent billowed in the breeze. Tables set with crystal and silver. A band playing. And there, in the center of it all, Lauren and Ethan Weinhardt turning slowly in their first dance.

She was splendid in cream silk. He couldn't stop smiling. The whole valley seemed to hold its breath watching them.

Ryan stood at the edge of the dance floor, Bri beside him. Their son still proudly wearing his ring bearer suit. Their daughter twirling in her flower girl dress, pink petals still in her hair.

"They look happy," Bri said softly.

"They are."

The song ended. Applause rippled across the lawn. Time for the meal. Time for the wine.

Jake Fisher, the ranch foreman, helped bring in the barrel. Special vintage. Been aging since the fire. Esther took the wine thief, drew out samples for the gathering of sommeliers. The best in the county had come. Even François Dubois from Burgundy, back for the annual festivals.

They swirled. Sniffed. Tasted.

"Mon Dieu," François murmured. "The smoke. But underneath... fruit, earth, promise. Like your 1906 after the earthquake fire, no?"

"Better," said Maria Santos from Sebastopol. "More complex. Like the family itself."

Esther smiled. Filled more glasses. Passed them around.

Now at a corner table, Jake, the ranch foreman chatted with Jim Rouke from the Press Democrat between courses.

"Read your article about the Kruegers," Jake said. "Eric got ten years to life?"

"For the kidnapping. Otto's being prosecuted for arson. Word is Cheri turned state's evidence."

"Against her own family?"

"Ex-family. She divorced Eric soon as the cuffs went on. Married that Vega fellow. Investor from Mexico."

"And old Hans?"

"Still hiding back east. Feds can't seem to find him."

Jake took another sip on his wine. "What about the estate?"

"New ownership. Cheri and Vega supposedly. But there's rumors about silent partners. Someone from Chile. They're trying to muscle into the wine business here."

"Chile?"

"Big money. Cartel money, maybe. My editor's sending me down there. Investigative piece."

"Be careful."

"Always am. By the way, what's this I hear about a restaurant opening here on the property?"

"Yes, a major possibility. The brothers are working out the details. It will feature our best wine and a menu based on Tawi's recipes."

"From what I tasted here today that place will be a hit."

The band struck up again. Eden wheeled her chair to Lauren, took her hands. Mother and new daughter-in-law began to sway to the music. Karl and Tawi stood together near the bar, watching it all unfold. The old German and the Native elder, taking in the moment they had both hoped for.

Tawi's cell phone buzzed in his pocket. He glanced at the screen, then touched Karl's elbow. "Excuse me a moment."

He stepped a few feet away, reading the text from Caitlin: *Madison's dental work went well. We got settled in the new apartment the tribe provided on the Rez. We feel safe. By the way, I know it's a secret, but please tell Mr. Weinhardt thanks for paying Madison's school fees this year. He's a saint. Love, Caitlin.*

Tawi smiled, tucking the phone back in his pocket. He returned to Karl's side, watching the celebration continue. After a moment, he leaned closer. "That was Caitlin. They're doing well. Safe in their new place." He paused, then added quietly, "She wanted me to thank you for Madison's school fees. You're a good man, Karl Weinhardt."

The Weinhardt's learned that long ago. You pay your debts."

The two friends stood watching the vineyards catch the last of the evening light.

"Two blessings in one year," Karl said, stepping up beside him. "I'm not sure what I did to deserve it."

Tawi smiled. "The wedding or the letters from Washington?"

"Both." Karl took a slow breath. "Five generations, Tawi. My great-great-grandfather planted the first vines on this hill. And now they're finally telling us what we already knew."

"The AVA."

"American Viticultural Area." Karl let the words sit in the air for a moment.

The designation meant the federal government had studied the soil, the climate, the way the fog rolled in off the coast and settled in this valley and nowhere else quite the same way. They had drawn a line on a map and declared this place distinct. A place that made wine that couldn't be made anywhere else.

"Took them long enough to figure out what we've known for a hundred years," Karl said.

Tawi nodded. "Like a birth certificate for the land."

"Something like that. From now on, when we put Sonoma Coast on the label, it means something. It's protected. Nobody in Texas or New Jersey can stick those words on a bottle and pretend they're us." Karl swirled the wine in his glass. "My grandfather used to say the dirt remembers. Every vine we've ever planted, every harvest we've ever brought in. The dirt holds all of it."

"And now you have the paper to prove it."

Karl watched his son spin his new bride across the dance floor, both of them laughing at something only they understood.

"I used to think the recognition was for me. For my father and his father before him. But standing here tonight, I think maybe it was always for them." He lifted his chin toward the young couple. "For what comes next. We're just the ones who kept the vines alive long enough for the world to notice."

Tawi raised his glass. "To the dirt that remembers."

Karl touched his glass to his friend's. "And to the children who will tend it."

Ryan pulled Bri onto the dance floor. Their children ran between the couples, laughing. Ethan spun Lauren, her dress floating like morning mist.

The photographer called out. "Family photo! All Weinhardts!"

They gathered on the lawn. The newlyweds at the center with Eden and Karl on the right side Ryan and Bri with their children on the other.

Esther and her boyfriend from Davis on the end. Tawi, on the other side smiling with an arm around Ryan.

Behind them, the vines stretched to the horizon. The house their great-grandfather built stood witness. The fog bank waited offshore, but not today. Today was all light.

The shutter clicked.

One moment. One family. One piece of earth they'd fought to keep.

The band played on. The wine flowed. Stories were told and retold. The sun slanted toward the western hills, painting everything the color of the wine in their glasses. Golden. Complex. Worth saving.

Ryan's Vido Noir vines stood bare in the October light. Low crop this year. They'd pruned them hard, way back. Next year would be different. Confident now the bitterness would be gone. The promise of a sweeter harvest ahead.

The Weinhardt legacy. Roots deep. Branches high. Still growing after all these years.